REMEMBER US

REMEMBER US

A NOVEL BY

LINDSAY BLAKE
& LAYNE JAMES

NEW YORK

LONDON • NASHVILLE • MELBOURNE • VANCOUVER

REMEMBER US

Published in New York, New York, by Morgan James Publishing. Morgan James is a trademark of Morgan James, LLC. www.MorganJamesPublishing.com

Publisher's Note: This novel is a work of fiction. Names, characters, places, and incidents are either products of the author's imagination or used fictitiously. All characters are fictional, and any similarity to people living or dead is purely coincidental.

ISBN 9781642790849 paperback
ISBN 9781642790856 case laminate
ISBN 9781642790863 eBook
Library of Congress Control Number: 2018943612

Cover Design by:
Kevin Grimes
Design511

Interior Design by:
Chris Treccani
www.3dogcreative.net

Editing by:
Bryony Sutherland

Morgan James is a proud partner of Habitat for Humanity Peninsula and Greater Williamsburg. Partners in building since 2006.

Get involved today! Visit
MorganJamesPublishing.com/giving-back

For Carsen
You are my favorite.
My greatest gift.

Dream big.
Work hard.
Take risks.

All with your eyes focused on the Son.
If you fail, you are not a failure.
You are courageous for getting up and trying again.

I've got your back.
I love you big.
Always and forever.

LINDSAY

For my family: my aunts and uncles whom I adore, my mom and dad who gave me many good things, and my grandmothers who were strong and beautiful.

LAYNE

PART I

1
May

Reese

"Hi, sugar," she whispered, and I blacked out, standing straight up as her pinked mouth moved and the wind raged and my heart crimped along its edges. I should have slammed the door in her face, yelled profanities at the closed structure afterwards, but instead I stood frozen, arm suspended above the handle.

I hate her.

"I took a taxi, well, a plane first. I came to help, you know." Her hair lay in drenched strands plastered around her face; black lines streaked down each of her cheeks. She was backlit by the porch, by the rain. My head tingled along the top, and I shuddered.

It was 10 p.m. exactly—I remembered seeing the green numbers on the microwave as I'd scooted, confused, through the kitchen to answer the insistent doorbell less than a minute before.

"Can I," her voice squeaked, "can I come in?" Still I stared, the seconds taut between us, all ability to form syllables lost along the thirteen years since we'd last been in this place together.

There was movement at her side and a furry, barking head poked itself from her fuchsia purse and into the porch-lit night. She tugged the Chihuahua out with ringed fingers and shoved the offensive creature toward my face.

"This is Rocky. He can help too."

As I opened my mouth, finally finding my words, there was a pressure at my elbow where Ben had presented himself.

"You need to get out of the rain." He reached for two of her three large suitcases as he glanced at me. We shot each other telepathic messages until he shrugged and widened the door, inviting her inside with a wave.

As they disappeared into the house behind me, I walked out into the rain and sat on the wet porch as if I could float away on the sea of the storm.

I'd spent the entire eight-hour plane ride back to Omaha drinking mimosas, one after the other like it was a cheap game, wondering how I could fix the chaos that was my life. I'd been back now for a few days, but hadn't yet found the answers I so desperately needed.

"Tell me again how you found out Dad was sick?" It was easiest to direct my anger at my twenty-five-year-old twin.

The oppressive green walls of our childhood kitchen had not faded with time, and I sat at the scratched oak table with Ben, pestering him for information once again. This had become a ritual since I barreled into town the previous week, but his explanations never seemed to satisfy.

"Reese, we've been over this. I found a dozen pill bottles in his medicine cabinet. It didn't take a rocket scientist to figure out something was up." My brother leaned back in his chair and exhaled. His espresso-colored hair stuck up at divergent angles, a sea of exclamation marks.

"But why were you going through his medicine cabinet in the first place?"

He tapped out a beat on the table in front of him and smiled. "Would you rather me tell you I needed a Band-Aid or are you okay with the fact I always go through people's cabinets when I visit?"

"You count moving back in with Dad for two whole months as a visit?"

"Don't nitpick my terminology, sister. Your twenty questions are almost up. And then it's my turn, I have some questions for you about Charlie." Behind black frames, his dark eyes were infuriatingly calm.

We'd looked at each other like this so many times through the years, his eyes as familiar to me as my own, our prolonged stare full of unspoken questions and an overarching understanding, the mountain of unsaid things between us prodigious and daunting. I sighed and shook my head.

"Ben, don't be lame. This is serious."

"Okay, actually, I'll save us both time. Let's re-cap for the umpteenth time. My company is starting a branch here in Omaha. You do remember I work for a Big Deal marketing firm?"

"I will not deign to answer such ridiculous queries." I punched his arm.

"Right, well, said Big Deal marketing firm sent me over to little ole Omaha to be the project manager for our latest plant, since I'm a native and 'know the vibe.' Maya came with me for the first week, because we hadn't been up to see Dad since Christmas, and we like to come a couple of times a year anyway. You know, like kids do."

"Don't. Just don't."

"So here we were. Here, also, were the pills and a little thing called cancer that Dad had hidden from all of us. I called you right away. Anyway, he's only supposed to have a couple more rounds of treatments. I knew even though—"

A determined click of heels and the scent of wisteria presented themselves behind me.

It had been two days since Bernice, formerly known as Mom, showed up like an apparition—*more like a nightmare*—in the night. The last two days had witnessed a dance of avoidance between us. The day before, she'd waited outside the bathroom for me, and even at seven in the morning, her slightly chubby five-feet, two-inch frame was bejeweled from head to toe. Her blonde bob was coiffed into big curls, tightly sprayed. She gave me a hesitant glance, and I tripped down the hallway in my hurry to escape.

"I only want to help." Her hopeful yells chased me to my room in surround sound.

Her version of being useful was to give us each worried looks in turn and spend hours in the kitchen concocting a variety of casseroles, soups, and hams. She was from Mississippi and her love language was of the greasy variety.

"Why is she here?" I mouthed to Ben. It was the first time she'd come back since she'd walked out without a goodbye, all those years ago.

He shrugged. We didn't invite Bernice, didn't expect to see her, but I wasn't accounting for her strength of personality, her need to be at the center of any drama. *Lord knows, she loves to be needed.*

As she ran toward Ben with a weepy look and open arms, I left. I ignored Dad's prone figure on the couch and headed outdoors.

The air was warm, dense, and replete with the sounds of insects chattering. I plopped onto the porch swing and gave myself a push. Vines grew along the western side of the porch, sprawling, darkened in the golden hues of the late afternoon light. Dad, the ever-eager architect, had made many changes to our house over the years, but my favorite would always be the pillars and planks that comprised the front porch. It had been my favored escape for as long as I could remember. When things were tense between my parents or when everyone had been in the house looking through rather than at each other, I'd abscond being a Hamilton and search for serenity outside our walls. Late at night I'd breathe in the air of the stars and dream about a new family and life far away from Omaha.

My first kiss was with Carsen Finkle after a swim meet in the fifth grade, right outside the pool where I'd just won my heat. But in subsequent years, I'd had my share of kisses on this porch. The summer of my eighth grade year, after Bernice left, I made out with the entire track and field team on this porch. Ben finally put a stop to it, storming out and ordering Philip Dyer to go home and tell his friends none of them were welcome to come back.

After our parents split, Ben grew more present, more protective, even as I melted into a perpetual state of numbness. Dad worked later and later at the office each night, so it was Ben who cooked our dinners and biked the packages of hotdogs and macaroni and cheese home from the grocery store. When Dad finally returned home, long after Ben and

I headed upstairs to our separate rooms, separate lives, he ate his leftover dinner cold. I knew this because I once went back downstairs after I heard the door close firmly upon his entrance, a bolded period at the end of a sentence.

I descended the steps covertly and paused in the kitchen doorway. The tiles were cold beneath my toes, the only part of me brave enough to enter the room. There was my father, head bowed, prodding the congealed dinner we'd left him hours earlier, his tater tots and pizza an offensive shade of yellow against the ruby-tinted circle before him. The plates were my mother's doing, of course. She'd bought us a set of bright red dishes around the time we were five, which she said gave our family a bit of class and energy all at once.

He held the edges of the cheery plate, and it wasn't until I moved closer that I saw the tears at the edges of his eyes, vivid and insistent. I turned on my heels and left without a word. He noticed neither my presence nor my absence. In adulthood, Ben and I dubbed our teenage years "Dad's Black Hole" because even before she left, he'd grown absent, cool, distant.

A week later, when I couldn't be at school another second, I instructed Ben and Charlie to tell the teachers I was sick if they asked and biked home in a fury without bothering to excuse myself at the principal's office. Dad's truck was parked in the driveway and I raced inside, cheerful at the thought of a whole afternoon with my father. He stood in the kitchen, his back to me, packing up the red plates. One after the other, he settled them into a large brown box. When he got to the last plate, he held it for so long I thought he'd fallen asleep, but without warning, he turned and threw it at the far wall, shoulders heaving, sobs leaving his body in stuttered cadence.

The crash of it hitting the corner resounded through the afternoon quiet of our kitchen. I jumped. He propped himself against the counter, as if the granite would give him the strength he needed for a lifetime alone. I moved forward, reached to pat his back and convey that I, too, felt weak, let loose.

"Dad?"

After a pause, he turned and offered a forced smile. "Hey kiddo." With that he shuffled over to pick up the box and, for the first time, I noticed gray at his temples.

"Wait!" I raced to where he'd halted in the doorway.

"I want two of them." I placed one of the plates on the kitchen table and aimed the other one at the facing wall. "This sucks." I launched the red plate, watched it fracture into its new configuration.

"Reese, honey," he said, and I whipped around to face him. We watched each other over the expanse of the kitchen. Finally he nodded. "I'll sweep it up later. Be careful for now; don't walk on that side of the room in your socks." He didn't ask me about school or where Ben was.

As he escorted off our remaining dishware, I took the second red plate up to my room and placed it reverentially beneath my second pillow, the serene pink roses on my pillowcase reassuring any viewers all was ordinary.

I'd been back in Omaha for a week and had created a routine. Dad still went to work most days, Ben too, so I divided my time between checking on Dad the days he stayed home, avoiding Bernice, responding to work emails, and editing photos. By mid-afternoon on Thursday, I drifted through the silent house to the kitchen. The sun slanted sideways through the windows, creating a friendly pool of light on the counter where Ben had meticulously lined a row of full shot glasses across the length of the granite.

"Drinking again, brother?"

"Please darling, I never stopped." He patted my hand, and I rolled my eyes at his bow tie and the two empty shot glasses off to the side.

He motioned for me to sit down and before I could refuse, he pulled a package out from under the counter.

"What's that?"

"It's for you, and here's how this will work. I'm going to ask you a question and you will tell me an answer. For the sake of your conscience and liver, I recommend the truth because I am Sherlock Holmes. We will drink if I think you're lying."

"Um, *I'm* Sherlock. You're Watson, and I'm not playing." I scrunched up my nose.

"As I was *saying*, when all the shots are gone and the whole truth is out, you may have your precious package."

"Bennjjjjiiiii, your game doesn't even make sense, you weirdo. And why aren't you at work?"

He took a slow sip of the water and ignored my eye rolls. "I took off early. This is Scotch, rum, bourbon, some of Dad's fancy *Irish* whiskey, vodka, gin, and tequila. As you can see, I've arranged them from lightest to darkest, but we may proceed in any order you'd like. This one here is water; you're welcome." He drummed his fingers along the counter and paused for effect. "For example, how is Charlie? I only hear from him on occasion, and you were with him up until you returned. What's happening with my brother? Don't be pithy."

"He's not your brother, you nob."

"Oh, but he is. As our lifetime neighbor and subsequent best friend, he is better than any brother Carl and Bernice could have given me."

"Charlie is, you know, Charlie. He's getting jobs left and right. He's full of charm and natural talent. Everyone loves him. Everyone wants him. He has enough ideas for the next five years and is always on the lookout for something new. He only launched the media company three years ago, but he's ready to add a video component to our team and a product line and, and, *and*. He's great. May I have my package now?" I forced a polite smile.

"I need a recap. You two graduated photo school four years ago and got an internship or two together. Then you each set out to freelance on your own, but you signed up to work with him six months later. Am I missing anything?"

"Ben, you make it sound like I didn't try. Six months is a long time and you don't know everything that happened. You're not always as smart as you think you are. Working with Charlie was the wise choice." I rested my arms on the counter.

"You mean the safe choice."

"I mean the choice that made sense."

"And now? You're content, working with him still? Are you considered partners or is he your boss? Actually, hold those answers. Which shot are we doing first?"

"Hey, that's not fair—I answered your dumb question."

"Aha, you did."

"Ben! It's three in the afternoon."

"Reese, Reese, calm down. Alcohol should be consumed with joy, not angst. I'm thinking you're thinking gin, so here you go."

"You're impossible."

He successfully blocked my lunge toward the package and shook his head, nodding toward the drink. "Bottoms up, babycakes."

I knew the only way he'd be placated was to play his game, so I drank the shot. "Charlie is great, ecstatic actually. He loves that we work together, tells everyone we make the best team. And we do. He loves the fashion side of photography, so he's in his element. By the time he's thirty, you can officially say your best friend will be a big deal. He's well on his way. Just remember you heard it here first."

"You're still pulling the best friend card, are you?"

"What's that supposed to mean?"

"I mean it's an easy cop-out. After all these years you're still trying to fly under the radar of the whole best friend notion. I thought you were better than such small-mindedness."

"Now you're making me angry. You don't know anything about it."

"Okay, fine. Are you happy?" He sounded somber.

"I'm happy. Of course. I mean, I'm a photographer traveling the world with my best friend. People would kill for my job. I am the poster child for a happy life." I batted my eyelashes and grabbed a full shot glass, which I threw back without his nudging. "I guess I always thought I would go a bit more in the documentary direction, be more gritty with my work, but that can come later. These photo shoots and experiences are invaluable and a once-in-a-lifetime opportunity. I mean, I met and photographed Taylor Swift. I'm living anyone's wildest dreams."

"Wait, what?"

I took Ben's brief interruption as an opportunity to snag another shot, and as I slammed the glass on the table, my cheeks flushed. "Well, you know Charlie's parents know everybody. So we got in as assistants on the shoot. It was small. But still. I held a reflector from ten feet away."

"Did you actually talk to Taylor? How have you never told me this before now?"

"I mean, no, but she said 'Hi' to Charlie right before the shoot. Of course, who could resist his handsome face? She probably wanted to date him."

"And then write a song about him."

"She probably kissed him!"

"And then wrote a song about said kiss." Ben slid a shot glass of rum in my direction and plowed forward. "Sister dear, you're looking a bit green, and we are getting off track. Speaking of dating, are you and Charlie snogging?"

"What, are you Harry Potter now? And is this rum?" My nose touched the glass. "You know I hate rum."

"Then drink it fast. One, two, three, go."

"No, I'm not dating or snogging Charlie! No. Not then. Not now. Wow, I'm feeling the gin."

"Are you sure it's not the rum?"

"He's adorable. Brilliant. Hilarious. Too much to handle. My best friend. Gorgeous. Have you ever noticed his lips? Of course you haven't. Well I have, and Charlie Beck has great lips. Not that I've ever touched them. But they sure do look nice on his face. Only it's not like that."

"Then what is it like? I'm not an idiot. I know there's always been a little something between you two. You've loved him forever; I knew it after that Halloween party when the three of us dressed as the Three Amigos and sang 'My Little Buttercup.' I was Chevy Chase playing the piano and you two were Martin Short and Steve Martin singing. I saw you fall in love with him that night."

"Sure, Dr. Phil. Sure."

"Reese, mine eyes have seen the glory."

"Maybe I have thought about settling down in a cottage built for two with him. So what! But Charlie will never, and I mean *never* like me like that. We are Snoopy and Charlie. Period."

"Wait, are you Snoopy or are you Charlie?"

"I'm leaving."

"Okay, okay, Snoopy, I didn't mean to ruffle your fur. But speaking of drinking…"

"I said nothing about drinking."

"Here's your Scotch. Drink it like a good girl."

"He's too busy becoming famous to think about love anyway. At least that's what he tells me."

"But you love him."

"I mean, whatever. We're best friends. You're best friends with him too—does that mean you're going to marry him? So you *have* noticed his lips. I'll need another Scotch when I break the news to Maya; make it an entire bottle."

"Your belligerence has earned you your fifth shot. Dealer's choice. There's a lot more where this came from. Ah, the Irish whiskey, an excellent choice. Speaking of the Irish, how are things in Ireland these days?"

"Oh, ya know. Green and magical, as always."

"So. Did you make any friends while you were over there? Anyone to *write* home about? Anyone *special*?"

"You are spectacularly annoying."

"The fact that you enunciated 'spectacularly' correctly lets me know it's time for our next shot. Let's go for the bourbon and save the vodka for a clean finish. So what's up with Irish men sending you packages?"

"Oh wait, that's from…He's this guy I met when I was there three years ago. It's not a big deal."

"Sister, Irish Santa Claus beamed you a package from halfway around the globe. That's not nothing."

"Is it going to sound bad if I say we met at a pub?"

"Only if you had six shots with him. Keep going."

"Well, he's nice. And gentlemanly. Our age. He studied his undergrad at one of those proper schools, Oxford or Cambridge or something."

"Oh, you mean Hogwarts?"

"He's getting his Master's in writing at some fancy university, and he lives on a sheep farm with his grandpa and dad."

"You're making this up. A sheep-farming writer? Yeah, right. Take a shot. Take two for that matter."

"Whatever, Ben. He's a really, really nice guy. A good guy."

"He sounds boring."

"Right? Only he's hot. I mean not." I blushed. "He's smart, but he never talks down to me. He's quirky and witty in an understated way. We hung out every day for two weeks straight when Charlie and I were there assisting for that shoot three years ago."

"I'm sure Charlie loved him."

"Well, they never met. Charlie doesn't know about him. It never came up. He was busy during the trip, so I was busy. Blake and I only got to hang out a couple of times on this past trek to Ireland before you called me back to the home front. Thanks for that, by the way."

"You've been dating an Irish guy for three years, and you've never once mentioned him to me *or* Charlie? Drink this vodka, and tell me exactly how hot he is."

I took the glass and threw it back. "Ugh, no, we're not dating. We're letter writing. We're friends. We're nothing."

"You're *letter writing*?"

"Like I said, he's clever and wants to write for a living. You know how much I hate social media, so when we met three years ago, he asked if we could write letters, and I agreed. He said, 'I find handwritten epistles of this variation modish in a manner little else in this frenetic world is.' I didn't understand half of it, but it sounded like fun."

"Really, it did?"

"It is fun. Remember having pen-pals from South Africa in third grade? Blake and I have never even exchanged numbers; we thought it would be more real this way. And Blake is one of the nicest things in my life right now. It's simple. He's simple."

"Can you use the word *simple* one more time? And there's no love there? Reese, people don't just write letters. Tell me you've kissed."

"Well, don't you ask a lot of questions?"

"So that's a yes."

I avoided eye contact, only smiled.

"How did this Blake get our Omaha address? That's creepy, Reese. Creepy Irishman who refuses to be on the grid knows where you live. I'm imagining a hobbit looming over me in my sleep tonight."

"Hobbits are from New Zealand and leprechauns are from Ireland."

"Well, technically—"

"Shut up. Sending him my specific geographical location is a habit now. You know I travel a lot, so I have a stack of postcards in my purse. I send him one as soon as I land any place I'll be for more than two weeks. I think I even mailed it on my way to the airport when I left Ireland. Like I said, it's uncomplicated. He's probably been the most stable part of my last three years. Hey, what's that?"

By the time Ben turned around, my package and I shoved past Bernice, who stood like a fixture in the kitchen doorway.

"Don't forget to hydrate," Ben called after me.

I closed the door to my room with epic force, the noise reminding me of the headache that was slowly making its entrance. I settled into the middle of my sagging mattress and opened the package with more anticipation than I'd known in ages. A beloved black box sat inside.

As I held my camera close, I allowed myself to rest in the peace of something familiar; an old friend had come to visit. It wasn't until I grew aware of the wet on my hands, saw it on the back of my camera, that I realized I was crying.

After a few moments, an hour, maybe two, I noticed the protruding corner of something else in the bottom of the box. I pulled out a book and ran my fingers over the front cover, taking note of the bumps and worn edges. It was Hemingway; I'd never seen Blake without it. I opened the cover and skimmed the pages. It looked tired, its pages yellowed with age. It smelled musty and keeping it flat was a chore, as its permanent place seemed to be his back pocket.

The inscription on the title page stopped me short:

To my dear, darling son,

Blake, you bring me great joy. I love you everywhere and back. A billion times forever. Never forget.

Love, Mom

P.S. Remember as Tolkien said:

Not all those who wander are lost.

All we have to decide is what to do with the time that is given to us.

…

Courage is found in unlikely places.

Still round the corner there may wait

A new road or a secret gate.

And deeper in the box still, I saw a note, folded. I held my breath as I opened it. The crinkle of the paper unfolding sounded loudly into my room. Scrawled in dear, familiar writing, it simply said,

Reese,

I found your camera after you left the house in a hurry. Sorry it took so long to find its way back home. Know that I am here if you need me and when you're ready.

With hugs,

B

It was enough.

I lay back on my pillow, closed my eyes, and let my thoughts carry me to sleep.

2

Reese

When I woke up three hours later, I forgot for a moment that I was back in Omaha, that Bernice was in town, that life as I knew it was on a decided pause. For sixty seconds squished in a blissful row I was content, relishing the feeling of a lazy day and toasty covers.

And when I remembered, when it came back to me piece by painful piece, I went to find my brother.

"Want to go outside?"

We sat in our tree house until after sundown, poking sticks along the crevices of the wood. The two of us had built those four walls one summer: all hammers, nails, and heart. Charlie was away at acting camp and when he came home, we blindfolded him and marched him promptly to our new resort. It was our feeble attempt to imitate the Swiss Family Robinson, and I loved it more than I loved most people. We'd dragged an old rug out there; pieces of cloth had been hammered to the windows. I'd hung a shelf and snuck out a few of Dad's books to brighten the space. The boys mocked my domesticity, but I spruced up our mini home with every treasure I could find. With Dad's guidance we'd waterproofed the tree house and even after all these years, the interior was snug and dry. Now the decorations looked tired, put out, but they still added a wistful ambiance to our hideaway.

It was an hour before either of us spoke.

"Remember that time you had a sleepover up here with Sarah and Natalia, and you wouldn't let me come?" Ben said. "So I snuck up after you were asleep and stayed to prove myself to you?"

And so it began.

"Remember that time Uncle Paul brought us a birthday cake to the family reunion, only he'd forgotten to add sugar?" We stopped going to family functions around the age of eleven. First, because Mom was too busy to make it happen and Dad didn't even notice. Then, of course, because Mom left.

"He was always so strange. I always thought you looked like him."

"Stop! Remember that time Bernice was so angry she threw both her shoes at the kitchen wall?"

"They were her red heels. She always had a thing for loud colors. I think the marks are still there."

"Oh yeah, right by the hutch. Remember that time we smoked a cigar with Anne in the field before prom?" There were no parents around to take photos, but we'd learned self-sufficiency, and shot through an entire roll of film with Charlie and his tripod. That year Charlie and I attended prom together; he'd broken up with his girlfriend the week before. For the whole of the night, I hung on his arm, ignoring the glares of his ex and her friends.

"Oh, sweet Anne." Ben sighed. "The one who got away."

We simultaneously hushed and stared out at the stars. The luminous fireballs held our united gaze, stalwart and true. Even when the world was crumbling, falling into a thousand minuscule bits at my feet, those Midwestern stars symbolized peace. They were home. And tonight, they were exactly what we needed.

Ben coughed. "I remember our parents laughing together late at night after we'd gone to bed. I remember movies and pizzas on Friday nights. I remember Dad filling the kitchen with Mom's favorite flowers on their anniversary every single year and taking the day off work every year for her birthday." He ended in a whisper.

"Ben, don't."

"Why won't you remember the happy moments from our family?"

"Because she left us, Ben," I squinted at him, unable to move, "and never returned. Why aren't you as mad as I am?"

Ben looked down at his hands. "I don't understand why Mom left us, but I refuse to accept that our lives have been all bad, as if we are the victims of some poorly written novel. I remember us as a family. There were some happy times, even with Mom and Dad."

"Maybe we were, once upon a time. But now?" I held his gaze.

He shook his head and lay on his back.

When we went back inside, Bernice was roosting atop a stool in the kitchen, Rocky dozing at her feet, and the sight of her looking so settled sent a spike of anger through my gut.

"When are you leaving?"

Startled, Bernice put down her pen. "Well, sugar, I only want to be helpful. So as long as your dad is sick, I can be here to cook or run errands or take him to the doctors or whatever."

"Ben's here. He can do all those things." My arms were statues across my chest.

"Uh, well, technically speaking *maybe*, but also I'm working so I can't do everything." From his place at the fridge, Ben ignored the daggers I shot in his direction, grabbed a spoon, and dug into his cottage cheese.

"Sweetie?"

"Don't call me that."

"It makes sense for me to be here. You both need to work. I can work from here. It's no bother for me, really."

As Ben inched his way closer to my side, my nostrils expanded three sizes. "It made sense for you to be here before too, but where were you then?"

"Reese, sugar, I did try, but—" her lips trembled.

"No, you clearly didn't." I left the kitchen before either of them could respond.

And just like that, we were transported back to square one.

As the silence grew, so did the tension. I realized the weight of why we were together in every inch between us. I stood beside Ben in the unfriendly hallway outside Dad's hospital room, praying I wouldn't need to ask him.

Ben held my gaze for what seemed like hours, trying to find the words.

"How bad is it?"

"We're still waiting on the test results. But Dad's a fighter. He'll bounce back." Ben was forever positive, overly optimistic. My throat throbbed from the stream of questions I couldn't ask.

While I'd spent the morning at a coffee shop looking up tickets to fly back to Charlie, Dad passed out and fell down the stairs. And with my phone on blissful silence, it took them hours to reach me.

We weren't yet sure if it was a full-blown relapse or something minor.

"Dad's not invincible, Ben."

"The Superman T-shirt he's wearing under his gown tells me otherwise. He's going to be okay, Reese." Ben thought Dad looked like Superman—he did look like Clark Kent—so Superman was forever his superhero of choice and he'd even bought him the shirt. He hugged me again, but I didn't hug him back.

I hated placation.

The air was stale and the insistent beeping of the machines annoyed me at every turn; the bustle of nurses and fellow patients up and down the hallway providing a constant hum of activity. Hours turned into days, and while Bernice and Ben went back to the house each night, I refused what felt like solace and the cowardly way out. I hadn't left the hospital since I arrived and hovered in a timeless state of exhaustion and worry. Ben brought me my camera and some fresh clothes, and I arranged myself into the blue chair by the head of Dad's bed as the sun set each evening. Sometimes I entered some version of sleep, other times I studied my sleeping father and asked myself how we'd gotten there.

Dad looked tiny in his hospital bed, pale and fragile, the wires across his body a neutralizer between us and our demons. The long hospital hours were easily the most time we'd shared in the last decade.

Late one night, Dad stirred. I was the only one in the room, and he rolled over and stared at me. He reached across the bed and grabbed my hand.

"I need a notebook."

"Why?"

"I need to write down a few thoughts." He coughed and rubbed the stubble across his face.

"Fine, I'll ask Ben to grab one on his way here after work tomorrow."

"Fine." He closed his eyes again.

The one time Dad visited me in Atlanta, he, Charlie, and I spent the entire weekend talking about the Braves. Baseball ran thicker than blood in our family, so we went and saw a game which was the solitary highlight of my adult life with my father.

"That was nice." Afterwards, Charlie stood with me on the street as we waved goodbye to Dad.

"Uh, were you in the same universe as me? That was ridiculous. He didn't even ask one thing about my life or job here in Atlanta." I crossed my arms and didn't look at Charlie.

"Reese, I think he was trying."

After spending all those years with my family, I was shocked at his ignorance. It was easier to talk about baseball, easier to keep the conversation light than to deal with the accretion of resentments heaped in disarray between us.

And I don't think Dad even noticed the difference, knew there was a *Before*, an *After*.

It was as if, somewhere along the way, he'd completely disconnected the father veins inside his brain. He could have been the mailman I saw in passing every day. It was as if he'd forgotten what happened between us and was struck with selective amnesia, as if he didn't remember how to be a dad.

When Charlie, Ben, and I were little, we played superheroes for hours on end. We made our cousin, Andrew, sit by the maple tree for hours, ropes flung all around, while we fought off the dark villains. That's what I thought about on those days as we sat on either side of Dad's bed, taking turns fetching the paper or helping him walk down the hall. He didn't need both of us to help, but it made us feel better, made me feel better.

"We need an army of stormtroopers to rescue Dad." Ben inclined his head to the man who slept between us under a blue blanket. My eyes hurt and there was a crick in the confines of my neck, which I massaged at intervals.

"Well, strictly speaking, I don't think we'd want stormtroopers." I offered him a superior expression and shook my head.

"Um, I am not turning away any help." He waved his hand over Dad's insensate form.

"Stormtroopers are part of the evil Empire, Ben."

"Wait, what? I thought they were good." His eyes widened.

"Stormtroopers were only 'good' when they were clones in the first two-and-a-half prequel trilogy movies."

"Well, what happened in the second half of III?" He kicked off his shoes and placed his patterned socks on the end of the bed.

"Order 66 happened. They turned on the Jedi halfway through III."

"So they were bad halfway through III until forever?"

"Yes. Do you not pay attention when you watch these movies every year?"

"Who says I watch them every year?"

"You know, May the 4th be with you? Revenge of the 5th?" He pushed his glasses toward his face. "Never mind. They were clones in I, II, and III. The clones were then replaced with recruits and conscripts of the Empire in the original trilogy. But in *The Force Awakens* an undisclosed number of stormtroopers are abducted as young children by the First Order."

"Who?"

"The stormtroopers. Do you really not know this stuff?"

Ben put his hands on his head. "Use the Force, Reese," he held my gaze, "because that's what Dad really needs." He rolled up his plaid sleeves, a giveaway he was getting serious.

"Ben, I don't care. I'm suddenly exhausted." Ben liked to show off his smarts on any given subject and now that I knew he'd been kidding, this wasn't a hornet's nest I wanted to disturb.

"Important it is, my young Padawan learner."

"No, it's not."

"I'm just saying if we're going to make a galaxy-wide plan for Dad, we're going with mine."

"Your what?"

"Come on, Reese. Stay with me. The Force. Dad needs The Force."

"Hmm." I rotated my neck back and forth.

"Yoda? Luke Skywalker? Obi Wan? The Force is a metaphysical and ubiquitous power."

"Luke's a twin."

"Yeah, with Leia."

"Luke and Leia Skywalker."

"Not really."

"Not really what?"

"Technically, Leia's last name is Organa. And she is a princess."

"Okay, I knew that. All hail Carrie Fisher."

"RIP." Ben doffed a pretend hat. "Leia is indomitable and later she becomes a general."

"I can be indomitable."

"She lost everything and was never once tempted by the Dark Side."

"I can be indomitable."

"Reese." He leaned forward and patted me on the head. "You already are."

We went to church when we were growing up; a fuzzy memory holding little beyond the story of Noah and his ark. But what I vividly recalled was Dad helping us get ready on Sunday mornings, until we grew tired of his assistance.

While Mom declared a coup on the parameters of their bedroom and bathroom on church mornings, Dad was in charge of making sure we wouldn't be visiting God with dirty ears. So Dad made a game with us about getting ready and picking out clothes. He'd pick an item, then we'd pick an item until we had the entire ensemble in order, ready to march straight to heaven's gate.

"Well, aren't you three just pleased as punch," Mom would say with a shake of her head and pink-lipsticked smile. She pursed her lips at our plaids and patterns, our bright colors and accessories, but she never intervened.

She always wore heels to church, a flowered dress, an extraneous squirt of hairspray to fortify her curls on high. She smelled differently on Sundays, and I melted into the sturdy comfort of Chanel N°5, week after week. The only other times she brought out the golden bottle was on special occasions, like holidays or in February on Ronald Reagan's birthday.

Even after all these years, I would catch a poignant whiff of Chanel from a stranger on the street or at a restaurant and float back twenty years to a sense of love, security, and home.

While Mom was getting ready, I'd sit on the edge of her bed for an hour straight as she curled her hair with precision, adjusted her shoulder pads, applied her eye shadow in studied strokes. She didn't talk to me, but I didn't mind. I was mesmerized at how beautiful she was—art breathing, fragile and flawless.

Then I would be called back to my father, to start or to finish my preparations. Namely my thick brown hair, which fell in waves down my small back. On Sundays, it was up to Dad to tame the beast. Dad and I consulted on my hairstyle as well. I went one entire year demanding braids and he'd sit me down for a laborious half hour, swearing and sweating above my head as he commanded his hands to weave the sections of hair into something resembling a braid. The results were generally dismal, but by the time the verdict rolled in, it was too late to remedy the situation and Dad would quickly add another bow or three as Bernice shooed us out the door.

"Carl, we can't let her go out in public like that," she would whisper, but I'd hear her, shimmering above me.

"Bernice, it's fine. She's five. We can pay for her to go to counseling later, but for now, we can't keep God waiting."

"Well, fine then, maybe I can do something in the car."

She spent the entire ride swatting at my hair with saliva-licked fingers. My mom always had soft hands with clean, manicured nails.

I pranced into church between Dad, Mom, and Ben, feeling loved, feeling pretty.

Through the years, I often wondered when those feelings of security dissipated. Was it one second at a time over the span of decades, or was it all at once in one moment of anger?

As I watched the lines of Dad's heart machine, I told myself I may never know.

So I waited in the white and blue hospital room, holding his hand, saying little and wondering where this road would lead, praying the minutes we had left to fix us would be infinite, that they would guide us home.

I picked up Dad's notebook and hesitated before opening it. He'd been writing in it every moment he was awake. I read his neat, boxed writing with the covers half closed, in case he woke up.

Some thoughts before it's all too late—I find myself wanting to write, to immortalize this life I feel no control over keeping. A testament? A goodbye? Maybe I'll figure it out as I go along.

When Robertson told me I had cancer, I didn't believe him. I walked around for an entire week thinking I was in a dream or in a scene from someone else's movie.

It was the first time in years I'd missed my midweek badminton and squash games. I didn't want to talk to anyone or their mother, so I ordered take-out for days on end and sat on my couch with the curtains closed.

I didn't tell the kids.

I'd always been fit. I was the star point guard on my basketball team in high school for Pete's sake. I know my desk job as an architect has slowed me down over the years, but not this much. I knew I'd lost weight, had been more worn out over the last months, that when I gazed into the mirror, my eyes stared back at me pellucid and uninspired. I told myself I was getting old, that was it. But my yearly check-up confirmed what I hadn't dared envision.

A week after the news, I showed up at Dr. Robertson's office without an appointment and paced in his waiting room until he called me back to his office. He gave me five minutes.

I had to make a plan, had to know my options. I needed to know if I was going to die.

Dad's handwriting became slanted, as if he'd fallen asleep while writing. Then it perked up again.

When my boy flew down the stairs, leaping past them two at a time with his hands full of pill bottles, I considered denial. I listened to his torrent of questions and finally patted the couch beside me.

"You weren't going to tell me, tell any of us, were you?"

I didn't meet his look.

"Dad, why didn't you reach out? I'm your family. Your son. You don't have to do this alone."

"So I should probably tell you I have cancer. I was diagnosed in June. I kept working, first full-time, then part-time as my chemo treatments intensified. My boss says I can return to full-time when I'm ready, and not a day before."

He was silent for so long I thought the conversation was done. "Last June. Okay, we've got a long ways to go. But I saw you in November and then in December. How did you not tell me?"

"You have a busy life. I thought you might propose to Maya at Christmas; I didn't want to get in the way."

"You're unbelievable, Dad. What are they saying, how many rounds of chemo do you have left? Let's talk about our options."

Our options. As if he were the one with the broken body, heaving through the night, taking a taxi to and from the hospital because he was too weak to drive himself.

"I'm actually on the uphill swing. I've gone through most of my treatments, and I'll be dancing in no time."

Ben could never leave well enough alone. Since he found out the news, we had four days together before Reese showed up and then another four before Bernice arrived behind her. I was surprised by the former, utterly unprepared for the latter.

It's been ridiculous having them all here, which is why I didn't tell any of them in the first place. The whole lot of them annoy me, stomping around, making noises, hovering about day and night. I have a variety of glares reserved for each of them in turn.

We are all grownups and know it doesn't take three adults to nurse one man back to health. Yet here we are. My kids are Hamiltons through and through—we don't do stuff in half measures. It's all or nothing.

Except my sickness. I am only half sick.

I don't know how long they plan to stay, but they seem single-minded for the first time in ages, united in their desire to nurse dear old Dad. It would be touching except this group gathering is the first of its kind in over a decade. The upside is that it has been years since someone cooked for me regularly, so I pretend they are my servants.

I am furious with Bernice, and while I wait for her daily attendance I imagine sitting her down and shouting through her long list of transgressions. The anger fuels me, gives me strength. Then I remember my own list.

But when she enters the room, my rage exits, or maybe it is my courage that leaves me without a trace. I wait for the inevitable moment when she will leave me again. She beams at me, pushing back her shoulders as if her charm and smile will mend the thousand misunderstandings between us. She is the optimist, living in a dream world of her own making. I am the realist, looking at the cruel, callous facts.

She left me once; she'll leave

There was a page of doodling. I scrubbed wet out of the corner of my eyes and turned until I found a page with words.

The first time she left, I'd come home late from work. I'd finished up the drawings for one last building before I turned off my computer and drove home fast through the cold and windy spring night.

The house had been dark when I arrived, and I found Reese and Ben in their rooms, wrapped up in their teenage worlds, inattentive to the muted kitchen and the desolate rooms about them. I asked Reese and Ben if they'd seen her, but they shrugged in turn, oblivious to the panic escalating inside me.

Bernice never worked late without letting me know, and I got the answering machine when I called her office. I ordered pizza and told myself she'd be home with a collection of shopping bags and a laugh to explain her delayed arrival. I nursed a beer as I watched the clock and the door and listened to the sounds of my children far above me. As the minute hand crept soundlessly along the parameters of the clock, her non-appearance grew louder. Right when I was about to call the police, the Marines, spend the night scouring the streets, I found her note, scrawled in cursive across a pink card. It was on her half of our bed, as if her words could replace her very being.

"Carl, I've tried, but I can't live like this. I need a night away by myself to think. Maybe three nights. I don't know. I feel isolated, overwhelmed, desperate. I can't do this right now."

It was unsigned, as if the conversation was still open for discussion, as if it was an acceptable way to shred my heart into infinite fragments.

Only it wasn't.

She looks at me now, as if we are in the middle of something. Something intimate. Like we made love this morning, had breakfast in bed, were hours into a cozy weekend morning in our home of domestic bliss.

Only we aren't.

"What are you doing?" Dad rustled the sheets and looked at my hunched form suspiciously.

"Nothing." I moved one hand to his head and slammed the notebook shut with my other.

"I'm tired," he croaked.

"I know, Dad. I know." *Me too.*

3

Bernice

As soon as Benjamin called to tell me Carl had cancer, I commenced making plans. A week later, Benjamin was showing me into the guest room of my old house. He said goodnight and I made Rocky a makeshift bed on one of the pillows, then waited until the quietude settled to tiptoe up to Carl's room. I stood at the foot of Carl's bed for a minute, or maybe a hundred. It was late, but I was awake as I'd ever been. He stirred and opened his eyes to give me a kind look. I shifted to hold his hand.

"I haven't dreamed about you in so long. You look divine." He smiled as I moved my thumb over the back of his hand. I couldn't speak. "I prayed you'd come." He sighed. "There are so many things I need to tell you."

"Did you? I was terrified you'd throw me out on the street." A stream of salty grief raced down my cheeks. It was cold, it was warm, it was a river.

"No, no, not you. Not ever." A single rivulet glided down his face.

"Carl, I—"

"Bernice, it's been so exhausting without you. I didn't know how to go on. But then I had to anyway. I loved you, you know. Once upon a time you were my whole world, and now I don't know where in the world you are. And it's hard. It used to be devastating."

"I loved you too, Carl."

He turned over, went back to sleep. Maybe he'd been asleep the entire time. I brushed at my damp face and headed back downstairs to the guest room.

Wide awake for hours, I burned into the edges of my memory the interaction with Carl. When I woke the next morning, I kept my eyes closed for a long time. When I opened them, it was still early, but I heard Benjamin in Carl's room so I shuffled up the stairs and stood outside in the hallway.

For long moments, I basked in the comforting sounds of their murmurs. Then, "I have a surprise for you Dad, it came last night. Let me go get it." Benjamin rounded the corner and found me, waiting. When he motioned me into the room, I walked forward hesitantly, trembling, and blinking too fast.

"Hi, Carl. I popped in to see how you are."

"*Popped in.* Why are you here?" He closed his eyes.

"This is quite a scare you've given," I gulped, "the kids."

"I need to take a nap."

"That's fine, Carl, I can wait to talk when you're ready to wake up."

"We don't need to talk."

"I think we do."

He cleared his throat hard and fast. "Ben! Come here, come now. I need you, Ben."

"Carl, I didn't mean to upset you. I want to help. To make less work for you, to let you know…" I stayed at the end of his bed, twisting my hands.

"I'm fine. Thanks."

"I'll be downstairs if you need me."

Carl ignored me, wrapped the fleece blanket around his shaking body, and I raced out of the room as if there was a band of horses chasing me.

I was the only one in the hospital room when Carl roused. He glanced over at me. "The offspring are fluttering around as if I'm going to expire and leave them $10 million apiece. Okay, kiddos, have you seen my bank account?"

"It's okay, Carl, it's okay." I patted his hand, but he pulled it away.

"I'm not old, not that sick, only a bit tired. If you all would give me some space, let me get some actual rest into these bones, I'd probably start to get better. Reese acts like I'm dying." He plucked at his hospital gown, his tone growing stern. "And you, you're acting as if there wasn't an explosion the size of Mount Pinatubo between us thirteen years ago, and we'll go back to feeding each other bonbons in the nude at any second."

"Carl." I swallowed hard.

"The doctors act like I'm a medical mystery, inspecting me as if I'm a fossilized specimen, not a living, breathing human."

We eyed each other. Since my arrival, we'd made no attempts to talk about my previous departure or my current presence: Carl's sickness an easy excuse to let everything else stay under the rug for the time being.

"Carl." I shifted in my seat and leaned forward, placing my face within inches of his.

"No."

"Carl, we need to have this conversation."

"Not here. Not now." He turned his face to the ceiling.

"You know, you weren't a saint either…" I couldn't hold in a sniffle. "And what if—"

"What if what?" He rolled over and snapped his eyes shut. "Good grief."

I fell asleep in the chair beside him and woke to Benjamin bustling about in the corner. I guessed he was on the phone with Maya from the way he said over and over, "Dad loved them. He was ecstatic, I promise," as he assembled the pieces in front of him.

I peeked at Carl, who was glowering. It turned out Maya had sent him half a dozen essential oils and a contraption to diffuse their scent.

"Why the heck would I need oil? I've got a barrel of Canola in the kitchen, and a frying pan to go with it. This is the most ridiculous—"

Benjamin hushed him and tucked his blankets in tight so he couldn't fight. Carl snorted so loudly, I hoped Maya couldn't hear it through the phone lines. When he glared back at me, I closed my eyes once more.

I don't know how many girlfriends Benjamin had through the years, but I adored Maya, knew she was a keeper. Why it had taken Benjamin so many years to move toward something more permanent with her was beyond me. I stopped asking him after the first year because he got ornery about it.

If there was anything I'd learned about my offspring it was that they had minds of their own, and it simultaneously stupefied me and made me proud.

"Yeah, I'm working on it now, love you babe. Talk soon." From my squinted vantage point I watched Benjamin shove his phone into his pocket and move toward Carl with the gadget. I always thought Maya was a little goofy with her "snake oils," but they smelled comforting. Lord knows nothing else in this dismal place smelled even halfway as decent.

As Benjamin lectured Carl on being open-minded, telling him the oils would support his body systems, I held in a grin. Carl looked as if he was gearing up for a fight, but before he made his vexing public, Benjamin spilled an entire bottle of Frankincense over them both.

"Is it because you forgot the gold and myrrh?" Carl glared at our son.

"Dad jokes," Ben muttered as he grabbed a purple bottle, placed ten drops of an oil he called "Forgiveness" into the gizmo and turned it on.

"I don't like the smell." I hadn't thought it was possible for Carl's frown to deepen, but there it was.

"That means you need it."

"Says who?"

"Maya."

"Oh, okay then, that changes everything." Carl made little attempt to mask the oozing sarcasm.

"Dad, give it a rest already."

"Humph." Carl closed his eyes and let the Forgiveness wash over him. *If only it was that easy.*

Carl opened one eye and scowled. "Of course, I'll be a free Carl in this second chance at life. I'll be open-minded and wild, grow out my graying locks, maybe get a tattoo. But there is no need to talk about it, no need to squash my soul with a lavish speech."

And with that, he turned his back on us both.

"Lord have mercy, son, I'm elegance personified. I haven't had a T-shirt on this body since 1979, and I don't plan to start now." I felt the lightness of my silk shirt under my folded arms as I offered what I imagined was a superior expression to my son. Benjamin, who'd bought the three of us Superman T-shirts "so we could match Dad," stood across the kitchen counter from me.

"There's no need to lob it at my face, Mom. And this is for Dad, you know, the man you flew from another country to see." He brandished the offending offering in my direction.

"Benjamin, unanimity begins in the heart, not displayed across this body in tawdry form for all the world to see." I pulled out a bowl and spoon, measuring cups and a knife.

"I'll keep it for a few days in case you change your mind." He grabbed his laptop from the kitchen table and shoved it into his satchel.

"There's really no need." I cubed the butter. "*But,* I will purchase a nice Superman brooch off the Amazon which should keep the peace and keep it classy." I watched his strong shoulders disappear down the hallway as he departed without comment. It mystified me that he and Reese were once small enough to live inside my body and now they were so full-grown; so full of opinions.

I would wear the brooch proudly, especially since I'd never seen Carl look worse, not even when he had pneumonia on our second anniversary, not even when he had his annual man cold. He was clammy and green about the edges. I was shocked when I arrived and saw the state of things. Shocked. Carl looked plumb awful, all gray and wispy. They were barely feeding him.

I snuck casserole after casserole into the hospital room, but those nurses must have been born with a sixth sense. I got into more than one wrestling match with them, just trying to feed my man. Every time I came back, the hospital staff handed me another list of preferred foods they'd compiled for him. It started with kale and ended with carrots.

"Dullards." So I was back in the kitchen, starting from scratch.

Benjamin reentered and moved to the table, pulling out a stack of papers.

"This mama's got a family to feed and Lord knows no one else has their head screwed on straight enough to throw together a decent meal in this place. It's fully up to me and Loretta Lynn." Having Carl in the hospital gave me a renewed sense of purpose for coming. Day after day, I turned up my Loretta and marched back to the stove.

Benjamin offered me a thumbs-up. "I'm going to get a bit of work done, if you don't mind me sitting here, Mom. My room is too depressing."

"Go ahead, sugar, you know I'll keep to myself." I eyed with dismay the ingredients lined out before me. "Good gravy."

"Hmm?" Benjamin didn't look up.

Thankfully, I had mad talents in the kitchen and I concocted a carrot, coconut, and kale casserole I knew would be world famous. I added extra cheese, extra love. I threw some butter and crackers on top. Carl would drool. He'd always loved my cooking. If there was any way to lessen his hatred of me, it started with butter, ended with cheese, and would be assembled in this kitchen.

"When I have time to myself again, after nursing Carl back to life, I really should consider writing a recipe book." I slid the casserole into the pre-heated oven and watched Benjamin look between his computer and the stack of papers.

"Uh huh."

"This morning I purchased a colossal sequin purse to sequester today's casserole, and I applied a bit more blush and a pretty purple hat to distract the guards."

Benjamin sighed loudly and typed something on his computer. I slipped surreptitiously through the doors. I had time to apply some fragrance before the food would be ready for transportation.

Baby, I'm coming.

When I arrived, Reese stood at the foot of her sleeping father's hospital bed like a sentry, and I excused myself yet again. Benjamin was my only ally. And Rocky too. Reese hadn't spoken twenty words in a single sentence to me since I arrived, and I needed to minimize her opportunities to flaunt rejection.

Laws, she was pretty as a peach. I was surprised at the difference between the photos Benjamin had shared through the years and her youth and beauty up close.

It had been years since I last saw my Reese. One thousand, four hundred and twenty-eight days to be exact. I did the math on my plane ride south. I saw her at my father's funeral and right after that Benjamin had us "run into each other" at his place in Knoxville without giving either of us a heads-up, as if multiple sightings in a row might make a difference. She'd insisted on sitting at the exact opposite end of the table from me that night, was marginally cordial, nothing more. But I would have known my baby girl in a crowd any day of the week. That mattered little, as she didn't want to see me.

Over the past thirteen years, I'd seen her a total five times, and after she led with, "Hey," she categorically refused to go deeper.

"Well, I'm fine, thanks for asking." But she walked away even as the words left my lips. She didn't wait to hear whether this was true or only a lie I told myself and others.

I knew deep down my babies needed me, so I came. Sure, I had other things to do, but I've always been one for taking care of my kids. Okay, some would insert the obvious here, that I left them in their formative years, which wasn't quite the same as taking care of them. But I didn't leave them, I left Carl. They happened to live in the same house, and it got complicated.

I had a psychiatrist once tell me the twins probably thought I abandoned them too, but I'll tell you what I told him: I don't want to talk about it.

I had my life all set up in Canada, but I left the maple syrup and the igloos in a hurry to come be with my people. When I made my plans to travel back to Omaha, my friends fluttered about me and asked what it would be like to see Carl, to go back home after all this time, but I didn't tell them my secrets.

I told them it would be horribly painful, which was true.

I didn't let them see how much it hurt.

I said it would be surreal, seeing Carl and my kids all together again.

I didn't tell them the thought of that ripped my heart clean in two.

I said it was needed.

I didn't say it was thirteen years overdue.

When I left all those years ago, I moved to New York, to make my big city dreams come true. My parents said I was being childish, they begged me to go home to Carl, then told me sternly. I stopped talking to them. Carl's parents wouldn't take my calls. My best friend, Bryony, listened for hours, told me she understood, then told me to go home, that I should talk to Carl, say to him all that I said to her. I stopped talking to her too. I couldn't bring myself to call Neil and Leah, hear the accusation in their voices, so I didn't bother picking up the phone to ring Charlie's parents.

Nowhere, nothing made sense. And just like that, New York was suddenly too dingy, too overcrowded, too close to Omaha and all I'd left behind. But where to go from there? The world, which had once seemed so full of life and possibilities, a vibrant map of the unexplored, grew stifling, stale.

When I was young, maybe seven or eight, my great-uncle Henri moved in with us. He told me story after story of his childhood in Canada. He told me he had a cottage and made shoes and sang. He was happy. He painted his stories with colors so glossy I was in the meadows with him, and I was happy too.

I decided to move to Canada.

I wanted to be happy again.

So after three weeks, when New York was too confining, I bought a one-way ticket for the only other place in the world I'd ever craved, a place I'd never been but knew I would grow to love.

When I flew to Canada, thirteen years previously, I was squished in a row with a family of five. The children were all younger than the twins, but it didn't check the nostalgia. Reese used to wear her hair in pigtails like their youngest's. The last time I'd seen Benjamin, less than two months before—but still more than a lifetime—he'd been wearing a red plaid shirt like their eldest's.

The three squirmed and complained beside me, and their mother gave me a squinty-eyed glare when I watched them. I wanted to say, "No, it's fine, I have kids of my own. I'm not annoyed. I'm not a creep. I'm just a mother." But my voice had left me, and I looked away as she hugged her daughter close. I cried the entirety of the three-hour flight from JFK to Toronto, the heartbreak issuing forth in salty tears I tasted for days.

When the flight attendant announced we would be landing soon, I gasped in great quantities of air, focusing it toward my wildly beating heart. My shoulders pressed hard against the airplane seat, and I closed my eyes. Canada would be my new home, my new life. My second chance to do it right.

My mom was a Canadian citizen so immigration was a breeze. When the forms asked me if I was married or single, I left the boxes blank, preferring deportation to admitting my new reality. There would never be a need to look backward. There was only here, only now. Until now became a moment that demanded my return.

4

Reese

After a week, Dad and Ben formed a united front to insist I leave the hospital for at least one night of sleep.

"Your odor is offensive and a shower is in immediate order." Ben was never good with subtle.

Three hours later, I sat opposite Ben's lanky frame on the porch swing, enfolded in the corners of Aunt Frances's homemade quilt, the detailed stitches lost in the darkness between us.

"I talked to Charlie today." I pulled my feet onto the swing and readjusted the towel around my wet hair.

"Cool."

"He's doing okay."

"Okay." Ben shifted and the swing moved with him.

"I asked him if I should stay longer or come back to work."

"Geez, Reese. You've been telling us all what to do since you were seven."

"Ben, he's technically my boss, plus he knows all the weird dynamics of life here." I missed Charlie, and some days I trusted his opinion more than my own, especially when it came to family stuff.

"Right, no one knows it better. So what did he say?"

"He said to come back."

"So what are you going to do?"

"I think I'll stay." The doctors weren't saying much and I'd become paralyzed, fixated on the reality of death. It was as if, for the first time, I'd allowed myself to acknowledge there truly was an end in this life. The knowledge had settled in my bones, seducing me with the notion of

staying here, caught in time, of family too, forever. "But being here…"
I couldn't finish.

"I know." Ben exhaled.

The night was alive with the sounds of crickets, the neighbor's
barking dog, the anticipation of a coming storm. So tonight I held the
blanket, I held the stars, I held all the pieces of the moment in the quiet
of my heart, and I let myself be. I rested my head on my twin's shoulder.

Everything about 5371 Florence Boulevard, from the furniture to
the smell, reminded me of That Day.

That day.

The second time my world crashed around me.

When everything changed between us.

The memory lived inside me so strongly I could have sworn it was
yesterday and not eight years ago.

"You're wasting your time with this photography." Dad's words
echoed in my ears for nearly a decade. "It's a nice hobby, but you'll never
make any money doing it."

"Dad, I don't care about money and not wanting your kid to be an
artist is so cliché."

"Asking art to pay the mortgage is a fool's errand." His nostrils
flared. "You need to care."

"I don't."

"You're just like her," he yelled and for a second, none of us moved.

"I hope I'm not like either one of you," I screamed back, heart
racing, blood pounding.

He threw the salt shaker toward me, narrowly missing my head.
"Pick a real career!" He slammed his fist on the table. "If you end up
going to that art school I won't support your decision or help you
financially." It was the most he'd spoken at dinner in years, the only time
my dad had ever yelled at me.

I saw red and fury mixed as his face blurred. My breathing slowed down until there was a hum between my ears.

Thank God for Ben. Out of nowhere, Ben stood up to our father.

"Reese is a brilliant photographer, Dad." He spoke with an authority your average seventeen-year-old wouldn't possess. "She can and she will make an excellent career with her work, and you will regret not backing her."

"Except I will not back her!"

I had never seen him stronger. Ben took my hand and we left the house, grabbed Charlie, and headed to Amsterdam Falafel & Kabob in Dundee. The vibrant colors and buzz of the shop stood in sharp contrast to my mood.

"It's probably because your dad is still sad about your mom," Charlie offered between bites. "Or because he grew up on food stamps and he's legit worried about the money." Charlie's parents were loaded and didn't care if he spent the rest of his life twiddling his thumbs.

"And remember, Mom loves all things artsy." Ben pointed his kabob at me. "So your foray into photography must've hit too close to home." Those crazy boys threw theory after theory at me, but I spent the next hour sobbing and shaking my head.

Afterwards, I didn't speak to Dad for the next six months. He didn't yell anymore, but he didn't speak to me either, his expanding taciturnity our new normal. There had been many low moments with my father, but I always counted that night as the worst.

Ben and I graduated, and right before I drove off to college, I gave Dad a quick hug. Nothing more. He kept his word too, not offering a dime toward my post-secondary education. Ben offered me half the checks he got from Dad, guiltily and generously, but I refused. I'd paid my own way since I was sixteen.

Dad was a practical man. He put up with my photography and entertained my camera obsession, but he never truly embraced my skill. It was Bernice who surprised me the Christmas before she left with our basement darkroom. She blindfolded me, and as we walked down the steps into the red-lit room, I could smell the chemicals. She had bought the enlarger at a yard sale and purchased the chemicals, trays, and paper from Rockbrook Camera. She told me she'd spent hours drilling the clerk on the proper supplies to buy, and she'd purchased double quantities of each.

"I imagine you will never run out of photos, so I didn't want you to run out of printing materials." She cradled my face between her soft hands and kissed me on the forehead.

Dad came down there once. I hadn't heard him call my name, and as I stood over the fixer he opened the door and barreled down. I showed him the image in the tray and he looked back at me without comment. He didn't get it.

After she left, it became my sanctuary. My escape.

In all the years since, I could never untangle the root of his aversion—was it a lack of understanding or something more? Was it a place to focus his frustrations or a version of concern? Whatever it was, it built a thick-bricked barrier between us, which widened by the season.

He didn't attend my senior exhibit, where I won the showcase. He didn't show up for my college graduation either. Over the years, I had been both impressed and disgusted by his stubbornness, pride, and short-sightedness. When I thought of our father, there was only a messy mix of confusion and sadness. Dad's Black Hole. In my adult life, I saw him once every couple of years. Being too busy to be bothered turned out to be easier than I thought, and Dad didn't push me if I said I couldn't make it home.

That day and my career had been the elephants in the room ever since. We'd called an unspoken détente since I'd been back under this roof, but I wondered if he sensed the hurt seeping through the walls like I did.

"Okay, so what's our plan?" Ben looked at me expectantly the next morning. From my perch atop the kitchen stool, I watched him pour the boiling water into the French press.

"Good morning to you too."

"For someone who slept in a bed for the first time in a week, you're awfully cranky."

"And you're Pee-wee Herman."

"I know you are but what am I, infinity!" Ben squinted at me, a childhood tic he'd never outgrown. He handed me a black coffee. "Drink this fast. You should probably consider going back to bed, sis. I won't tell anyone you're playing Rip Van Winkle for the day."

"You've always been so generous."

"Oh, I know. Speaking of which, I'm stopping by the bakery to buy Dad a treat on the way to the hospital today. Any requests?"

"Nope, sugar is poison for our bodies. But speaking of treats, since when does Dad, Mr. Folgers himself, own a French press?" I gulped back a scalding mouthful of the smooth caffeine.

"Maya gave it to him for Christmas. She spent an hour explaining to him the subtleties of why he needed it. I broke the seal on it this morning; she must never know. Anyway, we need to decide what we're going to do."

"I say we don't tell her."

"No, what we're going to do about *Dad*. He was supposed to be done with his treatments soon, but now…"

I didn't know how to enter this discussion. I took a weak sip of my coffee and bit my lip. "If I go there'll trouble, and if I stay it'll be double."

I knew Ben wouldn't be able to resist, and he let out a high "Weeee" before adding, "Let's at least pretend to have a real conversation about it."

"Or we could rock, paper, scissor it."

"Right."

"And you need to tell that lady with the big bangs that she needs to leave."

"Reese, she wants to help. Or to make amends with Dad before…" Ben cleared his throat. "Anyway. She wants to help."

"She's a psycho."

"Just let it rest. You're busy with your editing, and I am here to open a 'preeminent think tank that produces compelling results for future minds,' so I'm a little busy at the moment. It doesn't hurt to have someone here strictly for Dad."

"Ben, I don't need your marketing pitch. You're going to be in Omaha for *six more weeks*. And Dad is recovering. He'll be fine." I told myself this every day on repeat, to make myself believe it was true. "I just decided—I should probably leave soon too."

"You told me last night you were staying, Reese. Make up your mind."

"Ouch. You don't have to be so mean." I felt small.

"You're right, though. If you hate being around our parents so much, then you should go back to Charlie and your exotic life."

Unbelievable. I marched away from him to hide the sudden effusion of tears building behind my eyes.

I couldn't tell him that the day he called and told me Dad had cancer, my entire world had swirled to a slow-motion stop and that my ears hadn't stopped ringing in the days since. I couldn't tell him that the realization of how close we'd come to losing Dad kept me up for hours each night and that when Death came knocking, he brought an offering of perspective I wasn't yet ready to face. I didn't want Ben to know that some small part of me was glad Bernice was here, her semi-familiar presence more comforting than I'd ever anticipated. I didn't want to admit, even to myself, that I was glad for this excuse to escape from my life with Charlie, that I'd been unhappy on many fronts, but had been oh-so-unsure of how to fix it. I could tell my brother anything, and I needed him to know, but I wanted him to read it out of me. I knew he would, he always did. It was only a matter of time.

When I showed up at the hospital hours later, Dad and Ben were each three cupcakes in, high on sugar and laughs.

Ben dangled one with purple sprinkles in front of my nose.

"Ben, you know I'm trying to avoid sugar!" I planted my hands on my hips.

But when he went to eat it, I snatched it away and settled back as he danced to "Cotton Eye Joe" with Dad's night nurse.

"This is a sight for sore eyes. I left for one afternoon and you went crazy. It's not as if I was gallivanting around the town for the fun of it." I looked up from using Dad's bed as a bongo set to see Bernice standing in the doorway, all five-feet, two-inches of her sparkly and outraged.

I smiled as she stomped into the room in a sea of wisteria, hair lofty and proud, somehow preferring this fiery version of my mother to the docile one who'd been hovering about since her arrival. The clomp of her heels matched the beat pouring from Ben's phone.

"After my nail and hair appointments, I went grocery shopping, for Pete's sake. Those muffins don't bake themselves." She launched a basket of muffins into the window sill as her exclamation point.

"Welcome to the fun room, Mrs. Hamilton." The nurse giggled as she passed Bernice to leave.

"She's not—" I jolted upright. Ben and I made eye contact as Dad closed his eyes.

"And I turned up at the hospital to find you all giggling to beat a banshee, getting Carl all riled up. On second thought, a banshee would be calmer." As she threw herself into the chair, her bracelets clinked. "You two need to get back to the house, no buts about it." She pointed her ringed finger between me and Ben and didn't wait for a response before turning her attention to Dad.

"Sure." I was in no mood to stick around with Bernice. "Hey lumberjack in the see-through gown, do you need me to bring anything when I come to the hospital tomorrow? Maybe a razor?" His facial hair was scraggly, and decidedly taking over his face.

"No, I'm growing out my beard." He glared at Bernice.

"Carl, are you sure? You know it looks terrible."

"I know—" His face shaded red.

"Shh, Carl, *shh*." She patted his head in a calming cadence. "Slumber calleth thee." Dad offered her one quick look of resentment before closing his eyes. She looked up to find me unmoving. "Go, go." Her hands twinkled us goodbye. "And don't you dare take those treats. I saw three cupcakes of glory still poking up out of the box, and I'll be darned if I let you get away with eating every single crumb of that goodness without saving any for mother dearest. I don't mind the calories. You know what I say: Live today, no regrets tomorrow."

By the time we'd gathered our stuff, she was unaware of our presence, her energy fully focused on Dad. I could have sworn her expression was almost tender, a surrender to something I didn't understand.

"I think someone escaped from the psychiatric ward," I told the first three nurses I saw, pointing them toward Dad's room, and took the stairs two at a time down to the main floor.

A week later, we brought Dad home at night. Before we left, the doctor reminded us that Dad would be in a lot of pain. He talked of morphine pills, dizziness, and exhaustion.

"Carl, you're getting better, should be back to full speed in a month, maybe two. But, you cannot drive until I say so." The doctor looked at Dad.

"Humph." Dad crossed his arms and looked away.

"That's an order."

Dad's clothes hung loosely off his body, but he marched out of the hospital with all the pride of someone who knew what he wanted. He didn't even blink as he neared the car, which Ben had covered in streamers and silly string, and headed to the driver's seat.

"You wish, Dad." Ben opened the passenger door for him and waited expectantly.

The following morning was rainy, and I was glad because it matched my mood. In the light of early dawn, while the birds chirped beyond the window, the tones inside were smooth and even. I sat at the foot of Dad's bed and before I could change my mind, slipped my bare feet cautiously onto the cold, wooden floor and tiptoed to my room. I grabbed my Leica and glided back down the hallway. I focused on Dad's sleeping form and recomposed before I pressed the shutter. *Click.* Life should be lived; hope should be documented. It was the last frame; I rewound the film slowly. Though I doubted he'd stir for hours, before heading downstairs I made sure Dad's slippers were on, his blanket wrapped tightly about him, and a glass of water waited beside his bed.

In the dim basement, I turned on the radio and pulled out the chemicals. They were under a mound of unlabeled boxes, and I spent half an hour organizing and mixing my supplies. Methodically, I lined the trays in a row, neighbors once more.

For the first time in as long as I could remember, I felt an anticipation to see my photos. The smells of the developer and fixer pulled me back a thousand miles until I saw my life in one seamless mixing of what had been, what could be. For long moments, I stood still, doing nothing, letting the cool of the basement envelop me, settle me.

It had been years since I knew a desperation to hold my camera so heedfully, but I'd been carrying it with me everywhere. The sharp click of the shutter echoed as I documented Bernice in the kitchen, Dad reading, Ben talking to Maya.

Nothing else in my life seemed concrete, nothing but working with my hands again, in a way that was organic. I'd gotten into a routine of writing again too, every night for an hour before I went to sleep. It was my sweet therapy.

Charlie was the only person I'd told what I was doing, and he didn't understand, but told me I should keep documenting if it made me happy.

"It doesn't make me happy." I listened to the rhythm of his breath through the phone and smiled.

"Okay, then, what does it make you?"

"Sane. It keeps me grounded. It's hard to explain." I shrugged although he couldn't see me. It was hard to articulate, almost too sacred to expound upon.

"It seems like it's enough?" His voice was kind, soft about the edges.

"It is." I wasn't sure what I hoped to accomplish, only that it was vital.

It had been at least two years since I'd hand-developed my film and it felt good. Agitate, bang, wait. Agitate, wait, slam, bang.

This was peace.

This was happiness.

This was my small piece of stability in the disarray around me.

The only thing that made sense was my camera, letting the tiny row of negatives slowly but surely bridge the gap between my father and me, between me and some sort of greater understanding of my life.

"You've got mail." Her voice echoed down the stairs a few hours later, and the fact she held an envelope up to the light when I entered the kitchen did little to lighten my mood.

"Thanks, Bernice," I muttered as I grabbed the missives addressed to me and snuck away to a quiet corner.

It was a postcard from Charlie, with a photo of an ice cream cone and a skunk on the front. On the back he'd scribbled simply,

Sometimes life stinks, sometimes it's sweet. Hang in there.

Love,

C.

I texted him a quick *thanks*. He'd know what I meant.

The last time I saw Charlie, back at the hotel room all in a rush, had been confusing.

"My Dad has cancer, Charlie," I yelled through tears. "And you want to know where I've spent my time after work?" We'd been in Europe two weeks, Ireland one. We were three days into the shoot when Ben called me.

"Reese, I know," his voice was full of compassion, "but I've barely seen you this trip. You freaked out yesterday when I tried to tell you about…And, well, I had this idea. About a cliff and the sea and us."

"Wait, what? That makes no sense." I looked up from my green duffel bag, knowing my last words came out harsh. Charlie looked away. The only sound was our breathing, intense in rhythmic staccato.

"I know." His expression remained unreadable. "I care about you, and there are things I want to say. We haven't talked in ages."

Were we really having this conversation—whatever this conversation was—when my Dad was dying?

After a belabored interim, Charlie spoke. "Reese, I feel like I'm losing you." He moved a step toward me, his tall physique hesitant. I smelled his soap, his piney aftershave, sharp and comforting.

I left my Leica in the guest room at Blake's farm. And Blake; I'd departed his house in a frenzy that morning without explanation while he'd been out on an errand.

Seeing the look of hurt in Charlie's eyes made me wonder if I was thinking out loud. "Charlie, you aren't losing me. That's dumb."

"This was supposed to be our trip, a big break for us together." His blue eyes watched me with a hundred questions.

"I know, but we both know it was actually just yours all along. I only helped you look good." I had to break eye contact with him. I'd never known such distance from Charlie—the first man I loved, the person who knew me inside and out—but something was changing between us.

"Reese."

I placed my luggage on the floor and walked over to him, throwing my arms around his smooth neck and kissing his cheek lightly.

"I'm sorry. I'm awful sometimes." I held him tighter, burying myself into the safety between his arms. *But you know it's true.* I choked down the words and truth between us and held him for a moment longer.

I missed Charlie. Since we moved away after high school, he was the piece of home that had stayed with me through the miles. He was the calm to the storm of my life. We attended the same college and since we had the same major, we took most of our classes together. We shared two internships and were hired together for various jobs post-graduation. He was often the last person I saw at night, the first person I saw each morning.

I tapped his postcard against my hands and wondered if he missed me too.

My heart did a rebellious flippity flop before I set aside his card and turned to the other offering, a letter from Blake.

Reese, Reese,

You disappeared less than a month ago, but it has already been too long. Even the sheep are growing unruly on the roadways without your charm.

Da asks about you every night at the dinner table. Yes, every night. I wasn't lying when I said you were the most exciting thing to happen to the Kelly men in ages. When they are out at the pub, they still tell the stories about you traipsing about our sheep farm in too-big wellies and Gramps's old shirt as if you'd been born to farm. And about the time you were attacked by a goose, of course, and tried to fight it off with your camera. Wars should be resolved with diplomacy but there was no convincing either you or the goose of this wisdom.

For unbelieving men, I do think they took the ewe giving birth to twins the first night you came out all those years ago, as sign of a sure friendship. They'd never say this in so many words, of course. Da complains every day that he only saw you once last month before you left. He assures me you are sad about this too.

I know you were just here, but I'm already planning your next trip out! (You know I loathe any sort of overt and unnecessary usage of exclamation marks in life or writing, but I find nothing else will do. Actually, it's more like this—!!!!!)

I think of our next visit! (exclamation mark and all!) as I'm driving down the lane, walking around the farm, sitting in our corner of the pub with a pint of Gat.

We can re-visit our old haunts and find some new ones too. I will wet the tea and you can bore me with stories of your new friends and all your fabulous travels. I will be your most attentive listener, promise.

I've written down three new book ideas in the idea journal you made for me. What dreams are you writing in your own book?

I will be thinking of you from my little corner of the world and sending you hugs in the interim. They are warm and smell like cherries.

Yours, etc.

Blake

P.S. I thought of you yesterday when I read this (yes, I've been delving

*into Dumas of late): "There is neither happiness nor misery in the world;
there is only the comparison of one state with another, nothing more. He
who has felt the deepest grief is best able to experience supreme happiness. We
must have felt what it is to die… that we may appreciate the enjoyments of
life. Live, then, and be happy, beloved children of my heart, and never forget
that until the day God will deign to reveal the future to man, all human
wisdom is contained in these two words: 'Wait and Hope.'"*

What do you think?

"I think I'm so confused right now." I peered at the collection of
dishes Bernice had spent the whole day cooking. I'd avoided the kitchen
and was ravenous, but from my vantage point at the foot of the table,
the assemblage of food was baffling.

"Well," Bernice stood at the head of the table, unsure, "since it was
our first family dinner in a while, and your father's first day home from
the hospital…" She twisted her apron between ringed hands.

"This isn't a family dinner."

"I made everyone's favorite." She clicked back to the kitchen, red
apron swishing over a coral dress. I caught whiffs of wisteria between the
savory smells as she spun in circles, bringing more dishes to the table.

Chicken and rice for Dad. Spaghetti and meatballs for Ben.
Macaroni and cheese for me. Rolls and a green bean casserole for her.
Something unclassifiable for Rocky. The smell of garlic and butter hung
low in the air. I plopped into my seat.

As stress seeped tangibly through the dining room, I shoveled food
into my face between the sounds of scraping forks and growing silence.
I was two minutes from escaping when Ben spoke.

"High and low?" He winked at my glare. When we were in
elementary school, before our parents imploded, exploded, we ate
family dinners religiously at six o'clock. Charlie joined us most nights as
his parents were too important for a regular schedule, and every evening,
Dad asked us the high and low of our day. I hadn't missed the nightly

counseling sessions.

"Pass." Bernice had fancied the table, and the stiffness of the red tablecloth brushed my thighs as I reached for my glass of water.

"Pass the sass, don't be an ass." Ben's overt attempt at cuteness was annoying but of course our parents laughed.

"Story of my life," I muttered.

"Sorry, I didn't quite catch that sister, dear."

"Whatever, Ben. What about you, Dad. High? Low? Did you get high? Do you want to get high? I'm sure Ben can hook you up."

"Actually, not a bad idea," Ben pointed his fork, "medically speaking and all. Dad, we'll talk."

"As a matter of fact, I had a splendid day. It has been high. Did you know you can order anything off the internet? It really is the most handy thing. Over the winter I found this website for tracksuits that are the perfect polyester cotton blend. I've been ordering one a week, and now I have some nice colors. You can borrow them while you're here, son." The facial hair on Dad's face could not hide his smile. I'd never seen him so cheery.

"You should probably save some of that love for Reese at Christmas, Dad," Ben said.

"Oh yes. Good idea. I don't think they make them in a girl's cut, but don't worry. The velour is flattering for any body shape." Dad nodded at me.

"As long as you get a matching one for brother dearest."

"Reese, honey, you have been mumbling all night. Your father and I aren't spring chickens anymore. Can you repeat that?" Bernice leaned forward expectantly.

"Never mind."

"Reese, have you filled in the parentals on you getting your pilot's license? You're pretty close now, right?" Ben grinned at me because he knew I didn't tell our parents anything, ever. I'd only had three lessons, my last Christmas gift to myself, but I nodded.

"I'd fly in a plane with you any day of the week." Bernice beamed, earrings waving.

"What a sweet idea. I'll see if I can set up a little date for the two of you before we all leave Omaha," Ben said, and I pinched him under the table.

"Well, since you asked, I had a good day. In case you were wondering it's been quite the challenge to keep my business afloat while I've been here, but I've been doing what I can. I started getting up two hours early to get my orders finished for the afternoon shipping."

"If it's a problem, you could go back to Canada," I said.

"Mom, I don't think Reese or Dad know anything about this business. Why don't I go clean up while you regale them with tales of your business acumen?"

"No, sugar, I want you to stay. You know you are such an inspiration for me."

I burned disapproval into the side of Ben's head and stabbed a piece of chicken, biting through the layers of buttery garlic in a fury.

"My business is called Bernice's Masterpieces. I was only one glass of wine in when I came up with that."

"Mom, it's genius."

"Darling, that's exactly the word I used. Genius."

"No more law?" Dad said, a look of interest flashing across his face so fast I almost missed it.

"Well, no. It's a sewing business. I sew articles for the classy, the sassy women of America. And Canada of course." She tittered.

"Are there a lot of those out there, floating about?"

"I make napkins. I make aprons for cooking or just for wearing, if you know what I mean. Do you want lace or *extra* lace? Okay, ma'am. Wink, wink, wink."

"Ben, why are you winking too, can't you see that's Bernice's job?"

"I spend hours shopping for fabric online and in stores buying the cloth with tractors on it for all the farmers' wives out there, whole bolts of cloth with little chickens and kittens on them too. It doesn't get any cuter. I buy miles of pinks and purples, of bow patterns and of little sunshines and sparkles."

"Watch out, Ralph Lauren. Mom, I'm proud of you; I didn't know

51

it was this big."

"Let's just say I know how to speak to the myriad of cultures across the nations. I connect with my ladies. Okay, Benjamin, let's do the dishes. This afternoon, I used the interweb and downloaded Queen B's 'Run The World' track for us to practice."

"Who runs the world?" Ben pointed at her.

"GIRLS, we run this motha!"

"Yeah!" Ben high-fived Bernice as he stood.

I sat immobile at the table while they started the dishes. I wasn't sure why we stayed put, in this counterfeit reality of family. I only knew this space was sacred, like the smallest prick of a pin might break it, so we all tiptoed softly.

5

Bernice

I'd perfected my craft for the past few years, working away toward a little nest egg. I wanted to show my daughter, future granddaughters, what it meant to be a high-power woman in today's society. I wanted them to see what it meant to have drive and pizzazz, to be respected and treated with difference.

I would lead by example.

Once upon a time, long ago in Omaha, I was a lawyer. I was promoted to partner around the time the kids were ten. It was unseemly in those days; the other mothers shoved their superior looks in my direction the limited occasions I could make it to a school function during the day.

Back then, I was proud of myself, of my accomplishments. But when I moved to Canada, I couldn't practice law even if I wanted. As it turned out, I no longer desired the profession that reminded me so much of the life I'd deserted.

Strangely, I took up sewing. Sewing had been my mother's job, and her mother's before her. When I was young, I saw how hard they worked, tired to the bone, and I vowed to go an entirely different route. Law school was a challenge, mostly because no one understood why I was going in the first place. Even Carl looked embarrassed when our friends, whose wives stayed at home, asked us how it was going. I finished as I was nearing the end of my pregnancy and took a couple of years off to stay at home with the dirty diapers and days full of crying babies before fully throwing myself forward into my chosen profession.

It got complicated when my career soared while his floundered.

In the end, it didn't matter anyway. So inch by inch, I stitched together my empire and basked in the glory of being a different kind of power woman. I let the rhythm of my sewing cool me down on long summer nights. Sewing had become my sweet therapy, my escape when I didn't want to wander the million miles of *what ifs*. It was my happy place and paid enough to keep a roof over my head.

Since being back in Omaha, I'd wrestled my mother's old sewing machine down from the attic and started on a little project for Reese, just a cute gift I'd been dying to make for her. I had to wait until she was asleep to sneak into her room and grab the few items I needed, but no problem. I was aiming for her birthday, but at this rate, I'd be lucky to have it done by the end of the summer. I stayed up late most days of the week to work on my undertaking, where Reese wouldn't find out.

The medications had Carl sleeping most of the day, but he was up half the night too. It was often only the two of us wandering about in the dark hours. Night after night, I tiptoed to the edge of the living room where Carl sat with one of his Louis L'Amour books. Some things never changed. One night after he'd been back from the hospital for a few days, I dropped my pile of supplies on the couch opposite, thinking we could form some sort of truce. He glanced up and held my gaze for long enough to let me know I was unwelcome, then went back to reading.

I shuffled back to the kitchen and poured a glass of wine. The kitchen table would have to do.

The next night I waited until Carl had gone to bed and waited another hour before slipping into his room and settling into the rocking chair we'd had since the twins were babies. I'd moved it up from the basement while he was in the hospital. He was sleeping now, so I grabbed his hand.

"I don't know what happened to us." It was easier to bring up the hard stuff when he was comatose.

"I do, you left." Carl kept his eyes closed.

"Carl."

"I don't want to talk about it." His lips pressed together. I studied the new lines on his face, the unfamiliar gray in his hair.

"Carl, you did a good job with the kids. They're incredible. They're both so beautiful." I wiped my eyes with my apron. "Thank you for that."

He opened one eye and watched me through the shadows. "I wouldn't say it was all me." He cleared his throat. "In fact, I'd say they turned out this well in spite of me. And they had a good mother. You were a good mother when you were here, Bee." He hadn't called me that in so long I thought my heart would plumb fall onto the floor.

He closed his eyes, and I squeezed his hand.

"Carl, I—" I blinked back the tears.

"I said I don't want to talk about it." He commenced snoring, and I let myself out.

I woke up the next morning knowing it would be a hard day for me. I threw on a pot of coffee and was already drinking a hot mugful in the living room when Benjamin shuffled in behind Carl looking like a younger version of his father. My heart squeezed. My handsome son threw in a cheery "Happy Mother's Day!" and ruffled my head on his way to the couch. Reese gave me a half nod, which was on the nicer side of how she'd treated me since I arrived, but to tell you the truth, it still hurt my feelings.

"Let me tell you people, pregnancy was for the birds. Two toddlers were for the birds. Two middle-schoolers were definitely for the birds. Getting my body back to this state of bliss was nothing short of purgatory." I slammed my mug on the side table and went to make more coffee. I didn't hear a peep as I exited and good riddance.

Reese wandered into the kitchen, holding out her empty coffee cup. I shook my head. "Having kids was your father's idea in the first place. Carl originally wanted to have more children, like seven. Seven! But after I did it once, and two came out, but no way was I going to put this body through that sort of trauma again."

"I need my tiny violin." Reese looked annoyed.

"I told him he could carry the rest of the babies himself and that shut him right up." I wiped my hands on my apron, feeling my blood pressure rising. "I gained double the weight with you two. Seventy pounds, people. My feet were so swollen, I'm surprised they didn't fall off my body. They were each the size of Noah's ark. I had to wear Carl's shoes." And how you each came out weighing a mere five pounds, I will never understand. Where did the rest of that weight go?

We needed to buy double the gifts at birthdays, buy double the food. Double the toddler meltdowns, the laundry, the stains on the couch.

Double trouble.

Double disaster.

I thought I'd get double gifts from them as they got older, but let's be honest, that never happened.

"Uh, I'll come get my coffee later." Reese turned on her heels and practically ran out of the room, like she couldn't stand more than a few minutes in my presence. I leaned against the kitchen counter as if it could hold in the rising tide of emotions.

I avoided them as best I could for the rest of the morning, and not knowing what else to do, I decided to start on the night's dinner early. The busier I made myself appear, the less likely anyone was to make a fuss about me still being there. I liked being around my kids, under the same roof again, and I wanted to stretch it out as long as possible. I came to make my peace with Carl, but got distracted with my offspring instead.

I was halfway through my preparations when Benjamin entered and set up his work station at the kitchen table.

"You shouldn't work so much, son. It's not good for the body or soul."

"Hmm."

"Take a lesson from your sister, she's got the relaxation piece down pat." I shoved two dirty bowls into a sink full of sudsy hot water. "But I'll tell you one thing: I wish she'd stop taking all those photos of me." Benjamin was out working through the week, so it was nice when I saw him in the evenings, the weekends. He was as low-maintenance as me, his presence a nice break.

But my sweet pea Reese was another story. There was definitely something going on with that little lady. When she was home, she spent more time with her camera and mooning over that fool journal of hers, like she was Shakespeare, than with her own family. She'd started writing in a journal when she was ten, and I used to read it, long after she fell asleep, to make sure she was okay. It's a parent's right, you know.

Since I couldn't find her current journal, I decided on a different plan. If anyone could help me figure out the labyrinth of my daughter, it was my son. I looked at him expectantly.

"It's her thing, Mom." Benjamin settled his papers around the kitchen table, and I added salt to the green bean casserole I was whipping together.

I'm worried about her. "Of course, I want photos of myself, but she takes them on days when I'm only wearing my robe and my face isn't on. Yesterday, I fussed at her and chased her down the hall, but she did it again today." I waved my spatula at him, but he didn't look up.

"Uh huh."

She's struggling. "I worry that camera will give me a double chin. Or weird shadows that look like growths. Or a mean expression on my face." I wiped my hands on my apron and made a note to buy more butter. To tell the truth, I was a little pleased too: every time she turned her camera on me, it proved I wasn't as invisible to her as I felt.

"I hear ya." He typed furiously.

"You can't have any more cookies until further notice." I silently dared him to make eye contact with me. I'd been making cookies every few days, filling the house with delectable smells, and even more reasons for me to stay put.

"Uh huh." He reshuffled his paper stack and sent a text. I rolled my eyes at his bowed head because he was the main cookie monster between these walls.

"I tried to tackle her yesterday to see the images, but she ran to lock herself in the basement with all those chemicals which I know can't be good for her."

"Right." He leaned back in his chair and didn't take his eyes off his work.

"'It's film, it's film, it's film,' she yelled through the basement door, and I just shook my head. The chemicals have already started eating her brain." I'd moved to stand in front of Benjamin and placed my hands on my hips.

"Yeah, that sounds terrible." He looked up in time for me to bop him over the head.

Reese

When I got up at six, I dressed quickly and headed to the porch to watch the sunrise. The morning was chilly, slow, and the gentle lines of the sun rose one by one and warmed my face. I waved at the father and son walking by with their dog and reveled in the calming stillness of dawn. When I re-entered the house, Ben was alone in the kitchen, holding an empty cup at the counter.

"You do realize it's six-thirty in the morning?" He looked confused.

"Even before coffee you're annoying. Noted." I smoothed the bun atop my head.

"Why are you so gussied up? Hillary left a message. She wants her pantsuit back, the uniform that claims to care more about substance than style." Ben made an A-OK sign before he pushed down the French press.

"I found it in the back of the hall closet." I turned a full circle for inspection.

"So it's either Mom's or it belonged to one of Dad's lovers. You know that, right?" Ben gave an exaggerated slurp of his coffee and settled onto a stool.

"Disgusting. I know nothing except I have a shortage of clothes here, and I'm desperate." I ran my hands over the gray fabric.

"Clearly. Just don't get caught up in Cleavage Gate. We don't need that scandal hanging over our family."

"Whatever, Ben."

"Does Charlie let you dress like that when you work for him?"

"Charlie doesn't *let* me do anything. I make my own rules." I poured my coffee.

"What rules would those be?"

"I don't have time for this. People are waiting for me."

"Do tell." He saluted me with his mug.

"At Dad's office. Dad's boss said I could come in and help. You know, like the good old days when we both worked there during high school. Or I can come work with you?"

"Have you ever heard of Cain and Abel? Sometimes the whole twins going out to the field thing just doesn't work out. For anyone."

"First of all, Cain and Abel weren't twins. Keep up. I think you meant Cal and Aron? There are a plethora of clever options waiting to be chosen. Second of all, I can't spend another day here with our parents. Yesterday, Bernice sang full-blast through the entire *Love is the Foundation* album. There's only so much I can handle."

"Viola and Sebastian!"

"Whatever, Ben. I'll go hang out at Dad's office since you obviously don't appreciate my talents."

"Why don't you go back to your real job?"

I watched him, contemplating. "Um, because Dad is sick. Besides, she *has* to go back home soon; I don't know why she's still here. I can't talk to her—you need to."

"Reese, I think she's trying to make things—make something—right. She's trying to help." He gave me a searching look. "Sister, are you sure you're okay?"

"Things have been weird with Charlie and work." *And on every level.* "I don't know if I belong there anymore, or what to do if I don't."

"What do you mean?"

"Never mind. It's complicated. I'm here until Dad is better. I'd feel strange being anywhere else." Dad's health was an easy excuse to put my own life and looming decisions on the back burner.

"Alright, no need to get your power suit puckered. Meet me on the porch in two minutes, and I'll drop you off on my way into work. The world needs to see you shine, and I'm pretty sure you shouldn't walk in those heels, let alone drive."

I smiled at him wordlessly because the lump in my throat wouldn't permit me to do anything else.

When I came home from work, I walked into a Norman Rockwell-esque picture of Ben and Bernice cackling around the kitchen table.

Like a couple of high school girls. I scowled at their bowed heads. Ben had always been a Mama's boy, had sold out by her second batch of cookies. I snorted and slammed the door behind me. Did they even remember Dad was sick?

"Reese, I made you a cookie with an R on it!" Bernice called.

"Uh, it's okay, I'm gonna check some work emails." I scooted into the living room. The truth was, Ben always got along with both of our parents better than I did. But at the end of the day, I knew Ben and I were each other's number one. After Mom's unforeseen departure and Dad's Black Hole, it was Ben and me against them, against the world.

"I'm an artist too, you know." Bernice appeared in the living room and set a plate with the R cookie beside me. She settled high on the arm of the worn couch, absently petting Rocky, who jumped up onto her lap.

"Is that what we're calling you these days?" I typed furiously, not looking up. I'd always found the clicking of the keys reassuring. It made me feel strong, like I was making a plan, had a destination. She pulled lipstick out of her pocket and applied it with broad strokes.

"I'd say you got most of your artistic talents from moi, as a matter of fact." She smacked her lips loudly.

"Is that so." I gathered my laptop, book, and pens and stood.

"Well, just because your father's an architect doesn't mean he's actually artistically talented. He's better at the numbers and lines. And at a few other things too, trust me on that." Bernice set Rocky down, rose and ran her hands over her hips as she sashayed toward me.

"Ah, okay."

"I've been thinking about your photo business, and I have a few ideas. I'd love to give you some business coaching sessions."

"I don't have a photo business; I work with Charlie's photo business."

"Exactly my point." She pursed her sticky lips, and wafts of spearmint filled the space between us. "You've been following him since elementary school. You know I love that boy, but he's your weak link."

"I haven't been following anyone. I'm fine where I am and happy. I'm doing what I want."

"Reese Mae. You have more talent in your pinky finger than that boy has in the whole of his arm." She held up her left pinky and her right arm to illustrate her point.

"That's not true. You haven't even seen his work, or my work, but thanks for the pep talk."

"I follow him on the Facebook, so I see his photos all the time. I see your stuff too. I still don't know why you won't respond to my friend request." Her eyes looked shiny.

"Really, you don't know?" What I meant was, *Why did you leave me?* It was the question always at the back of my throat, like a rock at the bottom of my heart.

She set her shoulders. "You listen to me. The life of an artist is one of peaks and valleys, of accolades and deserts. I've been there, baby girl, I've done that. If you need to borrow a little money to go out on your own, I'd love to finance your company." She pulled a bottle out of her bag and sprayed herself with wisteria. "I can design you some shirts to give out to your masses, and you can wear them on your shoots. I'll sew your name on the front pocket."

"Thanks, that's generous, but I'm fine." When she pointed the perfume bottle in my direction, I ducked behind the door frame.

"Baby girl, we Hamilton women don't do fine. I mean, we do *fine*, but what we do even better is *extraordinary*. You are extraordinary, sugar, and I want the world to see it. We'll talk about this again later."

She yelled the last to my back as I took the stairs in twos. I didn't look back at her. Even with my bedroom door closed, I could still hear Ben's and Bernice's cheerful voices in all the corners of my room, so I turned on music.

She'd never even apologized.

It had been thirteen years, almost to the day. It was in the spring when she threw up her hands and left us while we were out and about, so we didn't discover her absence for hours, when we were all back from school and the office and found the kitchen, the living room, the sunroom, everything uninhabited. Ben and I didn't even register anything was amiss until the following morning when we found Dad at the kitchen table with his head in his hands. Perhaps that space and time between the leaving and the knowing said so much about her lack of presence in our everyday lives at that time. She never once came back to say goodbye.

I'd seen her precious little in the past decade, her appearances efficient, abrupt, and uninvited. And here she was once more, settled in neatly between us, as if she'd simply visited the bathroom during the intermission of a play.

For years I'd had this image of what having my mom around would be like, and now that she was here, she was both everything and nothing like what I wanted her to be. She read to Dad for whole segments of the day, fluffed his pillows, and talked to us incessantly. I knew in the end she'd insist on taking all the credit for his recovery, negating us, the doctors, medicine, and everything in-between.

I was journaling when Ben knocked on my door an hour later.

"Reese, what's wrong?" He seemed genuinely befuddled, and I gave him a tight-lipped smile.

"Nothing." Nothing at all.

I absently stared at the pearly margins of a pristine piece of paper and as the warmth of the mug spread between my fingers, the heaviness of the steam met my cheeks. I picked up my pen.

Blake, dear friend.

Thanks for your kind words these last weeks (and always).

Thank you from my heart's depths.

I have so much to say, yet so little.

To recap on why I left your house in such a whirlwind: my Dad was sick and though he's fully stabilized, all my words and emotions have converged into one giant vat of pudding, one unending road through a forest with wolves all about, one ceaseless sentence of pain and hurt, rage and hope.

There, was that dramatic enough? I feel dramatic these days. Not dramatic in an "I'm being dramatic" kind of way. More in an "I feel so much, every single day" kind of way.

And most of all I am aware
this
hurts
like
a
mother.

(Do I need to note my cleverness just there?) Anyway, as I was saying, Dad is finally on the mend, doing better by the day. We haven't talked much about the last eight years, but we get on well enough in a generic sort of way.

Why then is my heart so raw, like it's been slaughtered by a splintery 2 x 4? For that matter, like I've been run over by a herd of elephants or ganged up on by a pack of hyenas. Oh, oh! Or like I've been the brunt of a kindergarten room full of jokes.

My mom is back, did I tell you? I haven't seen her in almost four years and now I'm ready for another four-year break. She showed up, uninvited of course, at 10 p.m. in the middle of a storm (very telling) with three suitcases, her pet Chihuahua Rocky sitting high in her fuchsia purse, and mascara running down both cheeks.

She drives me crazy, but some insane part of me is glad she came. It's hard to explain. I somehow always and never miss her. And when I see her, I get this giant ache inside, something yelling at me that it's nice to have a mom. Then she opens her mouth, and I lose it. Ben says we are just alike to annoy me. It works.

If you get even two more letters like this, please have me committed. You can keep this letter as hard proof.

This is a bit all over the place, like a Dali, but I think you get the gist.

Thanks for being my friend, for being you.

R

That night after dinner, Ben and I uncovered our bikes in the furthest corner of the garage, tucked behind the Christmas tree, the lawn mower, and the stack of watering cans. The path at the end of the street took us straight to our elementary and high schools through two miles of hills and parks. Charlie had waited for us at the edge of his driveway every day for ten straight years for our commute to class.

The night was surprisingly cool, and I was twelve again, flying along the winding path, allowing the weight to lift off my shoulders with each pump of my legs.

"Do you want to head downtown, get some ice cream?" Ben yelled over his shoulder.

"Nah, too much sugar." I sped ahead of him. "You need to see the documentary I watched about sugar. It will cure your sweet tooth for good."

"Except you just stuffed your face full of carbs," he called to my back.

"Shut up."

We rode in silence; there is an exhaustion far deeper than the physical. When he said "Race you!" I pretended for a few minutes I actually wanted to win before I slowed enough for him to leave me, unseen, by the hill.

I pulled over to The Tree which housed The Hollow where Charlie and I had spent years leaving messages and treasures and a pirate's cove of secrets. It was a quarter mile from our houses, in a dilapidated playground. We'd kept it undisclosed from Ben all these years, a victory in itself.

The opening was smaller than I recalled, and I stuck my hand inside, hoping beyond hope I'd find a collection of long-lost booty. The tired cigar box was still there, despite it all, but it was empty inside, and I couldn't remember what we'd last left in there anyway. I dug into my pockets but came up empty. I slipped my watch off my wrist, nestled it in the box, and carefully placed the package back where I'd found it.

If only capturing time were as straightforward because the tricky reality of life is, inevitably, you never know when something will be your last.

6

June

Bernice

"Should we add a few of Reese's photos to your online dating account?" Benjamin suggested as he diced the peppers beside me in the kitchen.

About two years ago, Maya and Benjamin visited me for a long weekend and, after a couple glasses of wine, Benjamin took out my computer and signed me up on some online dating site. I told him I wasn't interested, but he didn't listen. Wouldn't listen. He pestered me with questions.

1. What are you looking for in a relationship?
2. Who has been the biggest influence in your life?
3. What is your favorite way to spend a Saturday?
4. What is your favorite vacation spot?

The questions, now they had been fun. Maya and Benjamin made a game of answering them for each other as they helped me find my own replies. We started at nine and didn't hit Save until midnight. Within three minutes I had two messages in my inbox. I didn't look at them for three days.

"Why, Benjamin?" I wasn't in the mood.

"Here's the thing most people don't know about me: I'm a romantic. Maya says my 'hero spirit' is what she loves about me most of all. I don't remember if that was her phrase or mine."

"I told you, I'm worried Reese's photos won't do justice to my good looks."

"Well, there's only one way to find out." He grabbed a mushroom off my cutting board and threw it in his mouth. "I love coming home after a day at the office and cooking." He smiled, denting my heart.

"I don't know, Benjamin." I stuck my head in the fridge. When I re-emerged, he was studying my hair.

"What?" I patted it self-consciously. It did seem bigger than usual.

"Nothing. How many dates have you been on in the last two years since we signed you up?"

"I don't know."

"Mom, you are one hot commodity. You know that, right?" Benjamin emptied his peppers into the sizzling pan.

"Yep." My lips sealed tight on their own accord.

"How many men on average message you a day? Two, ten?" He moved the vegetables around with precision, wafting the pop of their tangy juices between us.

"I don't know, maybe one." Tears formed in my eyes, and I stabbed the onion.

"Ah, Mom, you're onion crying." He patted my back. "Come on, it's definitely more men than that."

"I don't know."

"Guess."

"I said, I don't know. I don't *know*, Benjamin. Why don't you go wash up, and I'll finish this supper. You go now." I was frazzled, and Benjamin backed out of the kitchen with a nod. I was left alone with my onions and my tears.

They said Carl was getting better by the day, but I had to be prepared for the worst. Sometimes, in my daydreams about Carl dying, I fast-forwarded six months. I imagined that's how long I could keep the frisky young men at bay. I grabbed another onion and sliced it with force.

One of the men from Benjamin's dating site claimed to be a nurse, a widower himself. He also claimed to like puppies and long walks on the beach. I told myself "What the heck" and sent him a wink the very next day.

It spiraled or accelerated from there—whichever way you'd like to think about it. He messaged me every day. He sent me roses one Friday and gaudy balloons the next.

I put off meeting him for as long as possible, but people find me magnetic. Besides, he was the perfect distraction, even if I wasn't quite ready for a full-blown affair. After I hemmed, hawed, and placated him for weeks on end, I could tell he was getting anxious, so I suggested Saturday evening at Oscars.

Reese hung up on me when I told her over the phone. She was off in New York City, figuring out how to be an adult, and I didn't add preamble to the announcement. So our conversation totaled precisely forty-seven seconds, and I figured it would be approximately forty-seven days until she'd pick up one of my calls again.

Benjamin, however, paused then said "Okay," the way he does when he's unhappy but resigned to an idea. Besides, he was finally engaged to Maya, something that should have happened years ago. They were busy planning for their big day, and I made a mental note to send her a list of suggestions.

I wore my red dress for the date, breaking my vow of wearing only black for the year. It had long been my sassiest attire. To go with it, I shaved my legs, got a pedicure, and paid an exorbitant sum at the beauty salon. It wasn't that I wanted to put in so much effort for Mr. Met Him Online, but rather that I didn't have the energy to do any sort of maintenance myself.

If I needed a makeup artist to paint some joy on my face, so be it.

I couldn't be bothered being on time for my date, but he was there waiting and much sexier than his online profile suggested.

It turned out he was fifteen years younger than me, but didn't mind the age difference. He could also carry a conversation and had a Southern drawl that put mine to shame. He matched my dazzle on every level, but I snuck out over dessert when he went to the bathroom.

Maybe I was scared; maybe commitment had never been my forte. Maybe I knew I didn't deserve someone so great. Or maybe no one could ever compare to Carl.

I sighed and shook my head; I would need to work on my dating game. If I put my heart into it, getting back on that horse would come easy, but the biggest trouble was, Carl was the love of my life. Through all the years and all the miles between us, I'd never stopped loving him, knew I could live a hundred more lifetimes and marry ten times over, and I'd never find a love like we'd had again.

Once upon a time we respected each other, were each other's biggest cheerleaders.

But these days, Carl hated me. I saw it in his eyes, in the shortness of his scrutiny upon me. He never used to be able to tear his gaze away from me, but he did it now, again and again. I couldn't leave him in this state, but his lack of interest in me, in reigniting our story or finding some sort of closure, kicked me where the sun don't shine. Even after all these years he could hurt me the most.

So I pretended it didn't matter. I cooked their dinners, let Benjamin imagine new husbands for me, and hoped they wouldn't notice my smile was plastic.

Reese

Charlie sent me three copies of the magazine. One for me, one for my Dad, one for Bernice, I suppose, but I decided to frame it instead. She didn't need any pieces of Charlie. He was mine.

I texted him a selfie of me and the magazine. He responded with a thumbs up and a fruit emoji. *Weirdo.* I shook my head with a smile.

Charlie and I shared our first camera, a pristine Leica, which we found at a garage sale when we were twelve. We'd spent the next five weeks researching and practicing how to use it, photographing each other and any other willing model, which was mostly Ben and our parents. They soon became unwilling models, but still we pressed onwards.

Even as novices, Charlie was a natural artist with an uncanny eye for beauty. What took him a few tries took me hours, if not days, to figure out. But that didn't stop me. I loved taking photos, working extra hard. For me, photography spoke what I could not say.

I think it was the same for Charlie.

Although Charlie and I both received scholarships to Savannah College of Art and Design, Charlie was the star and I shadowed behind him. My favorite teacher, Dr. Stephens, kept me after class one day to tell me I should never trail after a man, any man. I thanked him and left. It was Charlie; it didn't count.

We stayed in Georgia after graduating, determined to make our way in the world. It was a three-hour drive from where Ben settled in Knoxville, and ideal on every front. Charlie got the work calls first, but he included me on each and every adventure. We had photographed the world over, side by side.

Until now.

The spread covered four pages and looked stunning. I imagined how I would have shot it differently as I critiqued the angles and juxtaposition of the subjects one after the other. But it was perfect, by far Charlie's best work. I was proud of him and concurrently frustrated I'd missed this hour in the sun with him. We'd both assumed I'd be back by his side at the end of a month at home, and though each day multiplied the distance between us, it wasn't time for me to go back. I couldn't explain it if I tried, but I knew I wasn't done in Omaha.

The note he'd scratched out a week before simply read,

Leaving for Paris tomorrow; I think I have an in with Vogue. *I'll be charming. Fingers crossed.*

All my love,

Charlie

Over the years, Charlie had dated a few girls, the high-power types—lawyers, models, doctors. At first I hated their perfect hair and gym-sculpted bodies, but most of them were so nice, they won me over despite myself. But when he got serious with one of them, I faded into the background, keeping myself scarce in his social life and making up for it during working hours.

He almost kissed me last spring, a week after Cambria broke up with him, while we were at the Porter Beer Bar, celebrating our latest booking. He got this look in his eyes and the hum of the bar muted as I watched him angle toward me in slow motion, his blue eyes pools of familiarity. His blond hair looked thick and soft and for one nanosecond, I could actually experience the pointed ends beneath my fingertips, little pricks of happiness. Before I knew what was happening, I was already jetting away from him.

"I need to pee!"

By the time I got back to our seats, Charlie had paid and waited by the door. We hadn't talked about it then or since. I didn't regret not kissing him; I knew it was the right thing to do.

"He was so obviously on the rebound." When I got around to telling Ben about it a month later, he wanted to know all the details.

"You don't know that."

"Oh, but I do. I was there, and it would have ultimately made things worse." But whenever I recalled that night, I still blushed.

When I was little, I used to sit in the attic for hours, going through old boxes, reading letters. I'd try on my mom's wedding dress and prance around in front of the old mirror, dreaming of my Prince Charming.

After she left, I moved her wedding dress down to my closet. No longer because I dreamed of a Prince Charming, but rather because I needed some tangible bit of her nearby. I waited months and then years for her to come back the way she left, silently and without explanation. I'd sit on the edge of my bed late into the night and study the driveway, imagining every beam of passing headlights was hers, coming to say she was sorry, that she loved me, that everything would be okay.

But eventually I got used to my new life. I got used to Dad being alone, to confiding only in Ben. I got used to Bernice being a distant idea of something that Once Was. I accepted the limitations of my existence.

I kept Bernice in her Bernice box, Dad in his Dad box, and Ben in a box the size of the whole world over. I grew accustomed to the separations between us; it was easier that way.

Seeing my parents love each other had made me believe love could exist. But when even they couldn't fix themselves, I let myself grow cold at the idea of love, stale about the heart as if it wasn't a tangible commodity to be grasped. Sometimes I looked at Charlie and grew confused about the issue, as if love might be something real, but the moment always passed, lost between the wind and things unspoken.

It seemed Blake was a man of consistency; unless there was a holiday, what letters he sent arrived on a Thursday.

Faithful Blake.

We'd grown close in our years of letter writing, and I knew we both anticipated what the time in Ireland would have uncovered. On my first trip out there, all those years ago, Blake and I had spent as much time with his dad and grandpa as we had alone. They were warm and boisterous, ready to show off for the only female who'd ventured out to their farm in years. We'd shared numerous dinners, chats around their fireplace, and treks through the rainy fields. And then Blake and I started finding more and more excuses to go off on our own.

Of course I'd kissed him. Once upon a time, a hundred or a thousand days ago, in a cunning Irish town.

It was on my second trip to his home country, a week before I'd flown back to Omaha. We'd met up at the same pub from that very first trip, all those years ago, unplanned but seemingly by design.

It was inevitable.

I was two beers in and the quirky acoustic band had been playing for over an hour. When he tilted close, all I could hear was his throaty chuckle and taste the bitterness of his beer-laden breath. As I breathed in the scent of him—sun, sky, wind—I imagined lacing my fingers through his hair and—

He didn't even ask, except maybe with his eyes, only moved his lips over mine. A promise, a prayer. I imagined the light and breadth of that first kiss married only with the romance of a sunset and an ocean, but there it was in the middle of a raucous pub, and it was just the sweetest thing.

It took me by surprise.

It took my words away.

It took me to places unimagined and there I remained for the rest of the night as we danced and swayed, drank beer, and nuzzled close. We stayed in our cocoon despite dozens of curious onlookers.

There lingered an understanding as his hand remained on the small of my back, and I danced against the nearness of him. We held each other until the bar closed, and he brought me back to his house. I was a breath from fainting under the persuasion of his soft, insistent kisses between the nape of my neck and the light of the half moon. We settled inside by the fireplace, talking and kissing until sunrise.

But those days were cut short and now, holding his letter in my hand, I didn't know how to ask myself what it all meant. I only knew it mattered.

Bernice

I sat on the porch swing with Rocky, ignoring the three full loads of laundry waiting for me, exhausted from working on Reese's project late the night before. When we'd been married all those years, Carl did the family laundry—it was a promise I'd extracted from him at the very beginning of our courtship. But far be it from me to ask that of him now. He gave me fewer glares than when I first arrived, but we weren't exactly sharing secrets either. I found myself drifting down the *what if* train when the door banged open.

Reese didn't notice me as she flew out of the house and plopped on the steps with her journal. I didn't even know she was back from Carl's office.

"Reese, dear, have you thought about going dairy free?"

"What?" I only could see half of her face from behind the porch post.

"Well, all you've been doing is sitting around with your letters and how many calories does that burn?" Reese looked a bit soft around the edges, and not the good kind of soft. I honestly thought it was the cheese—my baby had always loved her dairy—and we all sat on our derrieres over here, doting on Carl, not taking enough care of ourselves. "After all, self-care is essential to a healthy life."

"What are you talking about?" Reese was breathtaking, this baby girl of mine, but when she was angry, her whole face looked as if it had been painted pink, and it wasn't becoming. I'd tell her about the dangers of those brow furrows later, show her a mirror and hand her some cream, but that needed to wait.

"Dairy free. I reduced my dairy intake five years ago. My muffin top has decreased significantly." I patted my hips and then pointed to her bum.

Her death stare told me I should switch directions.

"Maybe you and Benjamin could start running together in the mornings. Get the lungs working, those legs moving, and burn some calories."

"Right." She jumped up.

"Look at Mama; I know what I'm preaching. Mama doesn't get this figure by dreaming about it all the livelong day." I gave her a pointed look.

Reese threw up her hands in response and zoomed away. It was the fastest I'd seen her move since I'd arrived. I'm just saying a little momentum would do her a pile of good. I threw up my hands too and headed to my kitchen. It was beneath me, but maybe I would use the low-fat cream in tonight's sauce. We were all in this together and as much as I hated it, I would play my part.

"Bernice, where's my stuff?" Carl glowered from the kitchen doorway.

"Carl, I organized it. I spent the whole morning sorting and cleaning, and you're welcome."

"You—you had no right to touch it!" Carl hit the wooden frame beside him, making Rocky yelp in surprise.

"I don't think this house has been cleaned in months." I ignored Carl's shaking body and turned on the oven. "It was disgusting."

"I like it that way," Carl roared before slamming the door behind him and sending Rocky scuttling for cover.

I enjoyed two whole minutes of peace before Reese cornered me in the pantry.

"Has anyone ever told you that you are manipulative? And selfish. And *narcissistic*."

I sighed and grabbed another can of cream of chicken soup. Can't a Mama just put some food on the table for her babies?

"Really, when you want to talk it's all fine and dandy, but when I have something to say, you're suddenly short on hearing?" Her hands were on her hips and her nostrils were flared up to her pretty eyeballs. She was on her high horse, riding around like she owned the place. *Neigh, neigh, neigh* for all the world to hear.

I make a point to keep only pleasant things in my life, so I hummed to tune her out while she shouted, and waved her bad energy away with my free hand. "Sugar, can we do this another time? I'm on a tight schedule to get this on the table."

"And I was on a tight schedule to grow up, but were you thinking about time then?"

She was red-faced and crazy-eyed, waving her hands and demanding answers. I started to explain myself, until I realized she didn't actually want my answers. She wanted to hear herself yell, plowing through her grown-up vocabulary of fighting words like it was her job.

Big fancy words for my big fancy girl.

Did you see me telling her what to wear, how to think, who to be? No, ma'am, I did not. Though I did have some fashion tips I'd like to casually pass along. I'd consider it part of her inheritance. How a daughter of mine dressed like that was beyond my understanding.

"Well, sugar, I have a few things to tell you too." I stretched into the full height of my frame.

"Oh, I can't wait to hear this." Reese cocked her head with a snarl.

"Okay, we'll start with this." I flourished my finger into her sweet, blotchy face. "Step down, baby girl. *Step down.*"

Reese

"Bernice is on a rampage." I found Ben working in his room after my nuclear meltdown with our mother. "Correction: Bernice is a rampage." With every passing day I'd grown more accepting—or maybe was it resigned—to her presence. But every other day she did her best to help me remember why I didn't want to be in the same country as her, let alone the same city.

"Oh Reese, give it a rest." He pushed his chair back from his desk.

"Ben, I'm not kidding. I don't know how much longer I can handle this. I was on my way to Dad's office yesterday, packing up some snacks, and your mother came in with a tirade about eating more green leafy substances, how *I* should eat less sugar. How I should exercise more. I swear, she talked for an hour straight. Here's the kicker—she handed me a leftover container of green bean casserole to take with me. 'Like I said, more greens.' And then she *smiled*."

"I can see where that smile would be your undoing."

"I had a zit, *one*, and she said I was pretty, but the zit was distracting. As if I'd missed it. Then she printed out twelve pages of acne solutions and left them taped to my bathroom mirror."

"Do Fred and Wilma even know how to use the printer?"

"Are you telling me it was you?"

"If this is the Spanish Inquisition, I confess nothing. I'm simply saying it would make your life, my life, easier if you let some of this go. You know, take a breath now and then. Go for a walk. Smoke a cigar. Roll your eyes. Healthy coping mechanisms. Don't let Mom get to you so much."

"Or we can send her packing."

"I think that ship has sailed."

"I caught her on my email yesterday, though she claimed she was only dusting my desk."

"Okay, now you sound like a crazy person."

"This morning she told me to give up dairy, as if I could ever part with my Gouda."

"Reese, she tells me the same stuff. I think it's part of the Code of Motherhood or something."

"Uh, she's not allowed to use any Code of Motherhood." My snort was louder than I intended.

"Okay, would you prefer Mom's caring or Dad's indifference? I've personally found they balance each other out, at least on some levels."

"I printed out twenty pages on motherhood and taped them in her pantry, on Rocky, on her mirror, in her underwear drawer. She can't miss that."

"Wow, I'm officially banning you from human interaction today. And that includes me. You need some Reese time and I'm going to give it to you, starting now. Remember what I said, Grasshopper, and this too shall become a thing of the past. Okay, see, there you go. Those are the eye rolls I'm talking about. Get it girl, get it."

I shoved his shoulder and exited.

Since I needed a break from the rest of the Hamiltons, I holed myself up in the basement for the rest of the day. Rocky insisted on following me down the stairs. He barked and barked when I shut him out, so I gave up and let him into the basement with me. He followed close to my heels as I moved between the trays. Freaking annoying dog.

I balanced myself against the sink and watched the images appear in the tray before me. Though I usually listened to music while I printed, today I worked in silence. Above me, I could hear faint and intermittent sounds of the family walking around. For hours I printed some of my favorite snaps from the last few weeks. I wasn't sure what to do with these photos; it wasn't as if I'd ever want the one of Dad lying sick in the hospital bed hanging in my living room.

But maybe this one—shot from behind with Bernice and Dad sitting on the edge of the porch. Her head was angled toward him and she was laughing, though you couldn't see her face at all. It was there, a bit in the motion of her shoulder, blurred with movement. They both wore hats, and the photo looked as if it could have been taken twenty years before. Back before she walked out of our lives, before Dad was, well, before everything.

I made a face at another frame of my mother sitting at the table, shoulders slumped, looking defeated. Even when I was little, Bernice and I knew how to push each other to the very brink and then beyond.

I don't remember this, but I'd heard the story a dozen times: when I was two, I got into Bernice's sewing basket and hid the various occupants of the kit around the living room while she was in the kitchen. She spent two hours finding it all and only at the end realized I still clutched half a dozen buttons in my hands. She demanded their return, but I only glared back at her. I'm not going to say it was Bernice's finest hour of parenting, but I'm told the stare-down lasted an hour.

"Give me the buttons, Reese." Again and again for those sixty minutes all gathered on end, but nothing could convince me to let them go. And Bernice wouldn't try any other tactic but demanding and standing.

I can't remember how it ended, only that Dad always said he had a vague memory of seeing a button in the toilet a few days later.

"I need Rocky." Her voice floated from the basement doorway. "We're going to run some errands."

We all fended for ourselves for dinner, ate in our separate corners of the house, and I was on the porch when Bernice arrived home late.

"I'm going to slip on in, is anyone awake?" Her lip trembled, and I shrugged as she tiptoed into the house.

"Bernice." The kitchen window was open, and I could hear every inch of Dad's frustration.

"Carl, I was just going to drink a little wine."

"Bernice, you had no right. You moved my stuff. You need...you need to go."

"Carl."

"I said go."

"Carl, can we at least talk about it?"

"No."

"You know what, yes. Yes, we can talk about it. This is what you did before. You shut down. You wouldn't talk or listen. We *are* going to talk about this." I could visualize her hands waving, her face resolute in her self-righteous anger.

Dad remained silent.

"Maybe I would have done it differently, Carl. Maybe I didn't do it the best way. Maybe..." Her words tremored, shuddered to a stop.

There was the slam of his hand of the table. "What, Bernice, what, exactly, would you have done differently?"

There was a long pause, and I almost missed her whispered reply. "Everything." I slid off the porch and walked into the night.

It was three days before Bernice and I talked again.

We called a truce to work on a surprise in honor of Dad's resilience against the cancer, and I headed to the car first. She got into the passenger seat and when she tried to grab my hand, I ignored her, shifting into third without a word. I cranked up the radio and concentrated on the road spanned wide in front of me.

When we were little, but old enough, Ben and I took turns riding shotgun. And, inevitably, Mom would switch to driving with her left hand so she could hold ours with her right. For miles, years, and all those errands, we rode around holding tight to that love and comfort. Her hands were soft and strong, her fingers covered in rings. We never talked about those car moments; words didn't fit inside the perfect perimeters of that gesture. But here we were, some fifteen years later, and I wasn't about to let her back into such a hallowed space. Not now. Not ever.

It took us two hours and four stops to find everything we needed and another hour at home to set it all up. We worked in silence and eye rolls. When we were done, we gave each other one appreciative nod before heading into the kitchen to roll out the pizza.

"I never wanted to be a mother, you know." Her back was to me and I froze, rolling pin suspended mid-air.

"What?"

"I didn't want kids; it was your father who decided it was time to start a family."

"Awesome, thanks for giving me one more reason to...you know, whatever." I took out my vexations with ruthless smacks and deep kneads of the garlicky, warm dough.

She cleared her throat, "My own mother was, well..." She turned and put her hand on my arm. I shrugged her off. She'd told me many stories through the years of her cold, distant, overworked mother.

"Whatever."

"Reese, I wanted you when I met you. You were gorgeous, perfection. I wanted you. I just..." Her lower lip quivered, and I almost felt sorry for her. "I didn't know how. I tried, but I didn't know *how* to be a mother. I always felt like a phony, and your father—"

"I don't want to talk about it." I turned my back on her.

"Everything changed the minute I had you. I swear. I couldn't imagine any world except one with you in it. I could never imagine *this*," she whispered and waved her hand at me.

I pretended I hadn't heard.

When we ushered Ben and Dad into the garden an hour later, dusk was falling, showcasing the glow of our twinkle lights. Our movie screen, one of Grandma's cream bed sheets, hung between two trees, and we'd carried the venerable green couch out from the sunroom. I'd placed large pillar candles around the patio and they flickered in the half light. The night smelled like freshly-cut grass and garlic. Rocky barked and danced between our feet, like Bernice always insisting on an extra measure of the room's attention.

It took the men a minute to take it all in. Ben said, "Cool," grabbed a slice of pizza, and dropped onto the couch. Bernice started to cry. And Dad, he didn't say a word, but smiled and smiled until the first movie came to an end two hours later.

For years, Friday nights had been a "stay in" night for us to watch movies and eat pizza as a family. They stopped altogether after she left.

So the four of us ate pizza and watched movies on a Friday night once more. Ben and I picked *Close Encounters* for our movie choice, and we let the parentals pick the second, knowing they'd go for something even older, like *Roman Holiday*, which is exactly what they did.

"Predictable," I muttered loud enough for only Ben to hear.

We drank two bottles of red wine and fell asleep under the stars and spring's warm blanket, right before the depressing part of the movie where Princess Ann and Joe Bradley decide they can't be together.

Because sometimes sleeping through reality is the only way to make it safely to the other side.

7

Reese

"Reese's Pieces, you know I love you." Dad and I sat together on the front porch swing before dinner.

"Dad, I know." He hadn't told me since I was ten.

"Reese, I want you to go back to your life. I'm practically healthy as a horse, or I will be by the time you fly to Atlanta and say 'Snickerdoodle.'" Above his ever-growing beard, his eyes read somber.

"Dad, I—"

"It's time for you to get on with your life, to go back and take some more of those photos of yours. The world is waiting, and I'm the only one with enough balls to say it."

It wasn't the most eloquent speech, nor was it an apology, but it was a start, and I made a mental note to tell Ben Dad said balls. "Dad, you know I'm staying, right?"

"I know, but I had to try." He pulled me into his chest.

"Dinner's ready," Bernice yelled out the kitchen window, breaking the moment in half.

We shoved food around our plates in silence until Dad farted, right in the middle of dinner, as I passed the peas and waited for the asparagus. It was loud and windy and for a moment I froze, staring hard at the table.

"You passed the peas; he passed the gas," Ben said under his breath.

We grew up in a house of strict decorum. Gentility was not dead in Mississippi and Bernice transported it all the way to Nebraska with her suitcases and her whole heart when she moved north in high school. So we didn't talk about farts; we called it "passing gas" if it ever had to be discussed. Nor did we indulge in discourse on sex, rock n' roll or the mediocrity of President Jimmy Carter. I called it The Code of the South but was never quite sure where my mother's mandates ended and where the actual Southern delicacies began. She used her Southern background at random, when it was convenient or she wanted to seem engaging.

So when he farted, I froze, obliged to ignore the rudeness and cover it with something distracting and generic. I cleared my throat and was preparing to dialogue in minute detail about the week's weather report, when Dad snickered.

Bernice looked conflicted; she'd always lectured Dad in these sorts of moments before, but when Dad let out another snicker, Ben was right behind him. *Boys and their farts. Let's be honest, what's so funny about that?*

On and on they continued until Bernice and I joined in, sides aching, a moment of sweet, happy relief we could not deny.

I grabbed my camera from under my chair, for what is better than capturing laughter and her lines? *Click.* In one millisecond, the moment was captured, a recording that proved for at least a moment we'd laughed simultaneously.

When we settled down, Bernice excused herself to dish up more food, and on the way back slipped, dropping the bowl of creamed, steaming spuds.

For a minute we couldn't tell if she was going to cry or curse and before we could live in the verdict, Ben, dear Ben, threw a dinner roll at her head.

It bounced off her well-sprayed curls. Rocky yipped in excitement and went chasing after it into the hallway.

Bernice's look of surprise didn't have time to grow old before Ben threw another and another and then one at me. And before I knew it, there were chairs turned sideways and a swirl of fatty Southern foods hurtling through the air while Rocky barked and danced between us all.

It was an absurdity—the shambles in the dining room, the parallel mess of our family. And then our hilarity shifted to tears, a steady river of grief, a prominence of words unvoiced between us as we huddled around Dad on those ancient wooden floors, laughing and sobbing intermittently.

As I watched my father cry for the first time in as long as I could remember, the earth shifted on its axis.

I didn't know then that we'd look a lot more broken before we laughed like that again. I didn't know some messes were meant to stay. I didn't know how complex it would be to sort the pieces of our family's story. I didn't know, so I remained in Omaha. When I looked back later, I would always wonder if that was the moment I should have walked away like Dad advised, wondered if it would have made any difference at all.

Bernice

On June 10, the anniversary of our first date, I wore my blue dress because Carl had always loved me in blue. I found myself dropping dishes, trailing off in the middle of sentences to Benjamin all morning.

It had been thirty-four years since we'd gone on our very first date to get ice cream. I'd worn a yellow dress and red shoes, and later Carl told me my pinked lips and blazing eyes had held him captivated as we sat at the park in the warm afternoon, thinking the sky was our limit, feeling as if we'd been there together forever. Even on the first date, I loved his laugh, silent and strong. I'd fallen for him in the space of one afternoon, two short hours. I put a finger on his shoulder, playfully shoving him, and fire flew through my body.

Through the decades, we'd always celebrated June 10. We both knew after that one date we'd found our matching half, and we felt it should be commemorated. Most people celebrated their wedding date, if they could actually get around to remembering it at all. But Carl and I, we honored both days—the one we fell in love and the one we committed to a lifetime together. Milestones matter.

For all our years together—except the last ones when he was too distracted to notice anything except the inches in front of his face—Carl had sent me bouquets of flowers on our anniversaries. Marigolds had always been my special flower, so he'd insist on extra of those, even the year there had been a bug infestation that ate most of the crop and they were selling for triple the price.

Even after I left, I'd celebrated our days annually. Every anniversary had been toasted with a full bottle of red wine and a call to Carl. I'd hang up as soon as he answered, of course, but hearing his "Hello," imagining the warmth of his breath through the phone, it was enough, almost enough, knowing he was alive in the world.

I wanted to ask when he had ceased to wake up with a catch in his heart on one of our special days and wondered if he'd call to mind the importance of the date this year. After all these years, I doubted he'd even remember. I was another girl; it was a different lifetime.

I craved his forgiveness, hoped beyond hope Carl would remember, would acknowledge all we'd had. If any remembrance could soften his heart, I knew our anniversary would be it. So by mid-morning, I'd convinced myself it was now or never. I went out and purchased a bouquet of marigolds, which I put on the coffee table in the living room. I slipped a note into the book he was reading. *Carl, would you please do me the honor of a coffee out today? I'd like to talk.*

I found a dozen excuses to walk by him for the next two hours, and when he finally nodded, I knew what he was saying.

"Great, let's head out before dinner." I turned on my heel, face afire, heart beating its way outside my chest. Carl had agreed to talk. To me.

We left before Benjamin and Reese got home from work, and I was so nervous during the drive, I didn't say one word. I paid for our coffees and we settled into a booth, studied each other like we were parlaying before a battle.

"Well?" Carl pushed his coffee aside.

"Carl." My heart dissolved into a puddle, some incoherent mess. "I want to know where we went wrong." I'd dissected it a million times since and always wished it could be narrowed down to one single decision, one irreversible moment setting the course of our future. But in my mind, it was more convoluted than that.

"You left."

"I did. I did." I took a deep breath. "But I think maybe you left me too. Before." He growled, and I tapped the table, a nervous habit which set my bracelets jingling. "I'm saying you stopped talking to me. You wouldn't go with me to counseling. I'm not saying this is your fault."

"Of course it's not my fault." He slurped coffee and slammed his mug back down. "I only agreed to talk to you today because I almost died. And that makes a man think. I've been doing a lot of thinking lately."

"That's good, Carl. I'm glad." He glared at me, and my insides sank. "Well, tell me where you think it started. Before."

"Do you want me to talk about the guy at your office—Adam, Ayron, whatever his name was—or your promotion first?"

"Carl, we've been over this. Nothing happened."

"Your definition of nothing is interesting."

"What about when Brett screwed you over with the investment property?" More than the money his friend up and took, there was the pain of a lost friendship, of loyalty smashed to pieces. Carl was laid off a month later and nobody was hiring in the recession, not even highly talented architects.

"It had nothing to do with it," Carl said, a second wave of sadness crossing his face.

"I think it didn't help." I forced out the words, even after all these years remembering the pain. I'd worked extra hours to carry us, much to his embarrassment. Months went by and then a year or two. I still saw no signs of my love in the listless man who came to the dinner table and my bed, night after night without a thank you, without a "How are you?" to break the silence. I tried to talk to him, to shake him, to reason with him in turn, but nothing worked. He was lost inside his misery and we became strangers.

"Well, maybe." Carl fiddled with his coffee cup.

"It was a hard time for us." I laid my hand on his and he didn't pull away. We'd been shadows, shells, existing but not living in our own story. We didn't talk, we didn't make decisions together. Biting words and disdain grew where there had been respect and listening. I don't know how it happened, only knew it was poison.

"Well," Carl said.

"Well," I replied. I was destroyed inside the nightmare. Every day I felt trapped, unseen, at the end of my rope. I thought I was going to burst, and no one understood when I told them what was happening behind our walls. They all said to give it time, to get ahold of myself. They acted like it was my fault. And then there was the baby—but of course he hadn't known about that.

"I didn't like how I never saw you. You weren't there for me." His look dared me to disagree.

"Someone had to—" I snapped before I stopped myself. "I did work a lot."

"You were never there." His glare stung.

On and on it went. Two decades of bottled hurt and anger simmered, boiled to the surface. He said this and I heard that. I remembered this, but he'd forgotten that. We ripped into each other, claws out, souls bared, and I wasn't the only one who found my eyes full of tears.

There was more yelling on the way home. He was still furious with me, but his anger helped me find a fury of my own.

We went out again the next day. And the day after that it was his idea to go out for lunch; he seemed a little fascinated, almost as if he was excited to spend time with me. The kids caught us getting out of the car mid-laugh and gave us strange looks but went back inside without a word. On the fourth afternoon, our coffee led to cocktails, which led to dinner, which led to more coffee, which led to staying up all night like we were sixteen again. We yelled over the first coffee, flirted through the drinks, settled down to ask questions and listen over the dinner hour, and couldn't keep our hands off each other during dessert. Hope grew inside of me like a fire, a train.

We continued our dialogue every day because there was a wasteland between us to be razed, but we were taking tentative steps through the chaos. He vacillated between anger, quiet, and desire. My own emotions were equally as complicated: frustration and love partnered at every turn. But in less than a week, Carl and I were on the upswing of friendly. It was the only miracle I'd ever witnessed firsthand, and I wasn't going to question it.

The morning after Carl and I sat in the living room kissing like teenagers until 2 a.m., Reese and I were alone in the kitchen. She wore a dated blazer and ill-fitting pants, and I hoped she hadn't noticed my grimace upon her entrance.

"Carl is as sexy as Cary Grant soaking wet," I proclaimed as she poured her coffee.

"Ew. No. Don't. I don't want to know what you're talking about." She shoved her face into the fridge as I took a dainty sip of my coffee.

"I'm just *saying*." We hadn't told the kids about our half-formed truce, but I couldn't keep the news entirely to myself either. "I get titillated thinking of the possibilities."

"Please never use the word 'titillated' again in my presence."

"Titillated? Titillated is a wonderful word. It speaks *volumes*." I arched my eyebrow at her. "*Titillated*."

She disappeared into the pantry.

"Speaking of which, my friend Ruth recently gave me a recipe for a hot chocolate bath and *my word*. Pass the whipped cream, sugar."

She reappeared, making a gagging noise. "I'm going into Dad's office for the morning."

"Are you taking your father with you?" He was certainly doing well enough to go back to work, but I for one didn't mind if he took another sick day.

"Nah, it sounds like you two have some catching up to do." She gave me the peace sign and left her fresh cup of coffee on the granite counter.

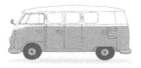

8

Reese

"Dad's turning fifty this month. What should we do?" I cornered Ben and Bernice in the kitchen while Dad showered.

"Let's have a partayyyy!" Bernice shimmied around the kitchen, hips wagging, braceleted arms waving wide.

"Uh, I was thinking more like a *party*, something simple." I looked at Ben.

"Ladies, this is Carl Clifford Hamilton we're talking about. Maybe we should look up something under the chill section of the menu."

In the end, we compromised on a picnic, a simple celebration to honor this father of ours. None of us dared to say out loud, "This could have been his last."

His birthday was June 21, stuck right in the middle of the calendar. We decided to widen the doors to celebrate his fiftieth and snuck his sister Naomi, the Fischers from across the street, his squash partner Earl, and his best friend Doug to our back garden without Dad suspecting a thing. Charlie's parents flew from Arizona to be there too.

The day was warm, not quite hot, and the clouds scattered low and puffy in the sky. The table lined with lemonade pitchers, desserts, and sandwiches took us all morning to assemble and the fence full of photos and notes even longer.

I don't know when I'd seen Dad as thunderstruck. The party commenced at three in the afternoon and at ten, most of us were still in the garden, tucked under the stars, sipping our Baileys and coffee.

"I'd like to propose a toast." Ben stood on a chair, the moon hanging precariously over his shoulder. He waited for everyone to quiet down.

"To my Dad. The one who taught me how to fish, how to love, how to keep going when all looked lost. I love ya, Dad." He raised his mug and there was a collective "Hear, hear," as people dabbed their eyes and took modest sips of their drinks.

"I'd like to say something too." Bernice appeared uncharacteristically nervous as she clambered up beside Ben. She looked at Dad, as if waiting for his permission, and his shrug was all she needed. "Carl, you almost died this last year, but you didn't. Thank goodness for second chances. Carl, you are a good man. A lot of people have misunderstood you through the years, thought you were hard-hearted or just plumb mean. But Carl, there is no one like you. I've travelled a bit you know, and I've never, ever—" She gasped in large quantities of air but couldn't get the crying under control. She'd definitely had her share of the wine tonight and Rocky's too.

While Ben comforted Bernice, I cleared my throat. "Well, not surprisingly, it seems I missed the Hamilton memo about giving speeches tonight."

The crickets sang into the still night as people chuckled politely.

"One of my favorite memories of Dad is back when I was seven, and we were out rafting on the river. *Someone* was being crazy and rocking the boat, ahem." I blew Ben a kiss and waited for the laughter to settle. "I thought I was going to fall overboard, but Dad reached out, grabbed my hand, and wouldn't let go. I don't know if I've felt so safe since. Thanks, Dad. Cheers." I was surprised at the story that rose so readily to the surface, and as echoes of "Cheers" filled the yard, I wondered once more if I would ever feel that safe again.

After seeing Charlie's parents at the party, I'd spent the next three afternoons in their kitchen. It was as if, with our collected love for Charlie in the same room, we could conjure up a veneer of him.

"Bernice said they'd get tired of me, but what does she know!" I'd found Ben in his room after dinner and sat on the edge of his bed. He nodded and strummed his guitar. "I mean, they were a second set of parents to me, you know, when the first set gave up." Ben grimaced and played louder. "She's probably jealous. She, Neil, Leah didn't exactly look chummy at the party." I dared him to engage in the conversation. I was restless, anxious, didn't know what to do with myself.

"They're fine, Reese."

"Have you washed these sheets in a while?" I pinched a corner of the white material.

"Reese, they're fine." My brother looked up from his guitar.

"I miss Charlie. He'd agree with me that your parents are being crazy." *Maybe it's finally time to go back.*

Ben stopped strumming. "You're the most decisive human I know. You can change a flat tire on your own. You don't *need* Charlie."

"Of course I don't need him, I—" I threw up my hands in surrender and departed. I'd spent hours thinking backwards, wondering how Charlie and I got here, to this indeterminate land between us. Sometimes I think it began with a phone call that I almost ignored, a forgotten passport, an adventure. Not all clichés are trite.

Sometimes I think it began long, long before that.

It had been almost three years since I got the call.

By the third ring, it seemed apparent the caller dialed my number intentionally. And so, with a loud lament for my audience of none, I threw myself over and squinted at the intrusive phone on the nightstand beside me.

5:43 a.m.

When the phone rang a fifth time, I fought my arms out of the blanket's tangle.

"Hi." My voice was thick with sleep and a glass too many of red wine the night before. I stretched my legs to the end of the bed and focused on my dream stealer.

"Reese, it's me." *Charlie.* I could pick out his voice in a crowd of thousands. "Pack your bags and meet me outside your apartment in an hour. David called and told me the photographer for that big shoot in Ireland got pulled away on a family emergency. David is shooting it now and he put in a good word for me to assist him. I wouldn't go without you, so I got you in on the deal. I got us on the 10:55 to Heathrow today. Then we'll jump on a little commuter flight to Dublin. We've got to haul dirt on the road this morning. Bring the Leica. And love? Don't forget your passport."

No longer tired, I sat up so fast my head spun, and jumped out of bed. When my jeans were halfway on, I toppled to the floor and dropped the phone. I was met with an image of wild hair; long, bare legs; and my engulfing cable knit sweater in the mirror across my small room. Head pounding, I leaned back against the scruffy rug.

"What was that?" Charlie asked with a laugh.

"Nothing." I grimaced at my reflection in the mirror opposite. "Come on, Charlie, fill me in." I didn't try to hide the annoyance edging my words. Charlie forever left out the details. He was always the first to be in the know, and he loved to make me ask the questions. Most days I didn't care but on occasions like today, I found it maddening.

"Reese, this is it—our big break!" I'd never heard him so giddy. I rolled my eyes at the phone. Again, no specifics.

Irritation faded as his words sank in. Plane. Ireland. Leica. I'd launched my freelancing career six months previously, and it had gone so badly I'd spent the day before filling out waitressing applications. I'd scrawled in form after form with my lucky ballpoint pen, until I had a dozen piled around me. After their completion, I hadn't had the willpower to take them around to the restaurants. I'd told myself I would do it today.

The applications watched me as I nodded. I still didn't have the full picture, but this was certainly better than serving Gong Bao Chicken. Besides, adventuring with Charlie was what I did best. So I followed him to Ireland and by the time we were back in Atlanta, it seemed I was his second shooter, or his sidekick; a state so natural neither of us noticed enough to comment on it.

The two months back in Omaha had left a hole where my best friend had always been. I needed to hear Charlie's voice, to have him tell me it was all going to be okay. After all those years of existing in the same space, thinking the same thoughts, I felt set adrift. So I called him straight away, not caring that it was 2 a.m. at the hostel where he always stayed in Paris.

As soon as I heard his smothered "Hello" on the other end, I stopped pacing and sank into the armchair with a thud.

"Charlie, it's me!" My turncoat whisper reeked of sentiment.

"Reese? Reese, is that you?" He sounded muffled, but my smile stretched to the edges of my face. I knew Charlie like I knew myself—his moods, his preferences, all his ways.

"Hi." And with that I had no more words, only a barrage of tears appearing so suddenly it was all I could do to keep them inside, red hot burning.

Slowly in, slowly out, don't lose it girl.

I hadn't counted on his voice cracking at the edges, splintering all the pieces of me into something unrecognizable. So I held the phone for long moments as he talked, and his tones soothed all the broken, bleeding pieces inside of me. He didn't tell me what I'd so desperately wanted him to, he didn't say anything right or tell me it was going to be okay. But hearing his voice, knowing he was so well in the world, gave me a renewed sense of hope.

I sat unmoving in the judicious chair long after we'd said goodbye. I didn't know it was possible for one little heart to hold so much love, so much ache, so much confusion all stirred together like it was concocting a stew.

I didn't know how it was possible—I only knew it was true.

Bernice

"That party. Those notes. This cancer. It's sobered me up." Carl peered at me from his place beside me on the couch. He'd barely spoken since the party, and now I knew why.

"Sugar." I tentatively reached for his hand and sighed when he accepted my offering.

"I'm not one for reflection, not one for the mushy stuff."

"You don't have to tell me twice."

"But it made me stop and think. And I can't stop thinking. It's as if my life has been unfolding in chapters in front of me. I've had a good life." His gaze was wistful.

"I'm glad." I'd never seen him so sentimental.

"I am grateful for the years. But there are also regrets."

"What regrets?" I breathed.

"Well, for one, my relationships with you and Reese resemble the aftermath of Hurricane Katrina." He looked at me shyly and my heart caught. "But things are slowly looking up with both of you."

"Things are looking up from where I'm sitting too." I wiped my eye with the back of my hand.

"I mean, sure, I haven't done any of those things I said I would when I was twenty. I haven't traveled, invented anything, gone sailing."

"You're young, Carl. You can still do so much."

He closed his eyes. When we were newly married, Carl and I wrote out a dream list. We'd been on a date for $4 burgers at the hamburger joint south of Main. It was raining that night, pouring by the time we were done eating, so we stayed at the restaurant late, writing our hopes in ink on the cheap paper napkin. We drank an entire bottle of wine, and I traced the warmth of his leg under the table as we envisioned ourselves on Highway 1, dancing in Monaco. We'd buy a VW van and take our trips in the summer. I shoved the list deep inside my layers and we raced, laughing through the downpour, back to our one-bedroom apartment. Carl undressed me layer by layer in the lamplight, kissing the pieces of bare wet skin as if discovering them for the first time.

I framed the napkin for our first anniversary, and it hung above the fireplace for more than a decade.

"Carl, can I ask you something?"

"Depends."

"What did you do with our dreams?"

He studied me. "After you left, I took them down, stuck them in a box." He shrugged.

"They were so lovely. Do you remember any of them?" I remembered every one.

"Well, let's see. I remember what I haven't done, which is pretty much all of them or anything we added after the kids came. I never took Ben to the Cubs game we'd talked about or you to the Greek Islands like you always hoped. But I'm putting that one on you." His smile was not unkind.

"Carl, we had our share of family vacations." I thought my heart would burst out of my body, leaving something sloppy and broken in its place.

"Sure, we started out with plans to go to New York or Boston, but when the time came, we camped at a nearby lake instead. Year after year. We never bought that VW, but we always had a set of wheels that got us from point A to point B."

"We did, Carl, we did." He was silent for so long, I thought we were done, but when I moved to leave, he sighed.

"Simple and perfect. Life hasn't been so effortless since." He wouldn't meet my gaze.

Over the next few days, I watched him spend his hours at the house poring over our family photo albums. There were hundreds of pictures Reese and I had insisted on taking despite our men's protests and groans.

When Carl went to sleep that night, I dragged out the albums for myself. I was glad for the documentation of our story, our history. They stared back at me, accusing me: baby photos of my kids, awkward teenage years, the years I missed too. Beautiful and terrible—a telling record of my mistakes. Carl was always by himself in the photos after I left, looking somber, unsure. I closed the albums with a snap. I couldn't bear to see them looking at me with the smiles and miles I'd missed.

For too many years, I thought every relationship sang like ours.

I wore it proudly, like his letter jacket, which I had with me in all seasons.

Sometimes Charlie and Reese reminded me of the two of us. His parents were our neighbors long before the twins were born. A single fence, with a cut-out section big enough to walk through, separated them for the entirety of their growing up. In the early years, Leah and I spent long hours in the backyard with our babies sprawled and crying on the blankets between us. While they screamed and pooped, we dreamed of a lengthy, happy life for them.

Through the years, we spent every holiday with the Becks, birthday parties too. Every year in early December, we'd parade over to their house to decorate and drink hot chocolate for hours as the kids raced around with yells. The next night they'd come to our house where I'd meet them at the door with a plate of cookies and mugs of Baileys. With most of Carl's relations scattered around the country, they became our surrogate family. I was an only child and relished embracing Leah as the sister I'd never had.

Charlie shared the best features of each of his parents. He had Leah's eyes and Neil's strong chin. He embodied their best characteristics too— Leah's kindness and Neil's humor. He was a charmer, too talented for his own good, and I loved him like a son. When I heard Reese talk about Charlie, saw her eyes shine with a shade of impossible bright, the pressure built, built somewhere between my heart and my throat. I once knew a love like that.

Sometimes people asked me why I left Carl; I saw that question in my children's eyes again and again. Here's the truth—there aren't enough words in the English language—in the known universe—to unravel the mess of that why. So somewhere along the way, I stopped trying.

9

Bernice

I'd fallen asleep at the kitchen counter late one night a week after the party, but woke when Carl said my name. He was in pajamas, bathed in the faint light from the hallway. My heart caught in my chest, and I knew I must be dreaming. His eyes were soft and sweet. We held each other's gaze, not speaking, as he haltingly made his way to me.

"Bernice." There it was again.

"Carl." I ached all over.

"I came down to get milk, but here you were, asleep, so beautiful. I…" He sighed, looked forlorn.

"I'll get you some milk."

Before I could stir, he reached out to stroke my cheek. "When you abandoned me, all those years ago, I went after you, you know. Ben blames me for not fighting for our marriage, but I did. I knocked on Leah and Neil's door and asked to borrow some butter. What I really wanted was my wife, but I could tell from their uninterested expressions you weren't there."

"Oh, Carl." My eyes filled with tears. Back then, I'd desperately wanted him to fight for me, for us. *But asking for butter is hardly a fight.* I shoved the thought back down.

"I drove to Bryony's next and saw your perfect silhouette in the living room window. I sat in my car, parked across the street and tried to figure out from your body language if you wanted me to stay or go."

"Carl, I wanted you. I was waiting for you." We were both so lost.

"The next night I brought you flowers and the night after that, too. I left them on the doorstep after you ladies had gone to bed. Bernice, you knew they were from me but when you didn't respond, I knew I'd lost you forever."

"There was no note. Carl, I—" I swallowed through the anguish. "I thought you were saying goodbye." For years, he'd escaped into himself, and I'd stopped understanding him, knowing him, and here was another proof of crossed wires, of misheard messages.

"I thought you wanted me to stay away."

"Never." We'd fallen apart, into some strange terrain where we weren't talking, couldn't talk to each other.

He seemed hesitant as I reached out for a hug, but he gave me a nod, and I fell into his arms.

"I'm still angry at you," he murmured.

"I know." I knew it wasn't over yet. I was angry at him too, at myself, at all the things I could never fix.

"Oh Bernice," he whispered into my hair over and over while my heart pulsed into his chest.

"Well, have you?" My tone climbed higher with each word, pounded right to the summit. We sat on the green sofa, no inches between us. After that night in the kitchen, things had shifted once more, and it looked as if our truce might be permanent.

We were dating, as if we were teenagers again.

We were untangling the miles of confusion, doubts, and hurts between us.

We were taking things bit by bit.

We still hadn't told the kids.

We waited until they were out and about to find our way to each other's arms.

"Bernice, don't worry about it. Didn't we say we would start afresh and sweep the last decade aside as if it never happened?"

"Yes, but it did happen, so let's talk about how many dates you went on." I was piqued and there was no way around this but straight on through.

"Hey, hey. I didn't go on any."

"None at all?"

"Definitely not. Not officially. No dates for me; I would have made St. Augustine proud. I was the monkiest monk that ever monked," Carl said, like he thought it was cute.

"Now you're just being silly, and what the Sam Hill does 'not officially' mean?"

"Well, you know Joe and Raemalee from church?"

"Of course I know them. We had dinner with them every Thursday for fifteen years. Do you think I'm an imbecile?"

"Darling, darling. If you would let me finish. We eventually rekindled the Thursday night dinners after you'd, ah, after you left. It was maybe six months later when we picked them back up. And occasionally they'd invite over a lady friend they thought might suit me. I had nothing to do with it, I swear!"

"Carl, stop swearing, it's unbecoming. Were any of them pretty?"

"Well."

"Carl, I swear."

"Bernice, you know you're the only woman for me. Every other female in the universe dims by comparison. Meryl Streep may be your second, but even she is light years behind."

"Well then." I snuggled in close, between his heart and his collarbone, where I fit best. I smelled spearmint and wisteria, cinnamon and tobacco mixed. He kissed the top of my head. "I still can't believe we're dating."

"As if we never stopped." He rubbed my cheek.

"We definitely stopped." I smiled into his chin.

"It's hard to date a person who lives in Canada," he said, his voice tinged with acrimony.

I sat up and held his face. "We're talking."

He nodded, and I lay back down, arms wrapped tightly around his frame, as if I could hold in all the good and keep out all the bad. "Talking—your favorite pastime." We could talk for the next century, and it wouldn't be enough.

Reese

I waited on the front porch swing for Ben's arrival. The early evening sun was warm on my skin; I drank in the smells of summer and the neighborhood's barbeques.

"Right on time, Hamilton," I called as he pulled up with his windows down.

"Hey." Ben looked disheveled, his plaid shirt wrinkled, his hair wind-blown from his drive home from the office. He slammed the car door behind him. "What's up with the welcoming committee?"

I handed him a beer. "Today I caught Bernice and Dad holding hands, and his burly beard is gone. They are acting like freaks, but aren't saying a word about it."

"You're right, they are kissing about it."

"Gross." I took a sip of my chilled beer, holding the bitter hops on my tongue.

"Mom and Dad sitting in a tree, k-i-s-s-i-n-g." Ben laughed at himself and tipped his bottle to his face.

"This is why I need Charlie; he can have an adult conversation."

"My theory is they are dating *or something*. Okay, maybe not *dating,* but Mom is wearing a lot of makeup, and she giggles at everything Dad says. He's no Jimmy Fallon, so something is definitely up."

"It makes me mad." I pushed off the porch with my foot.

"Yeah, I know." Ben took a long swig of his beer. The sun threw ribbons of orange and gold over the parameters of the porch.

"You're mad too?"

"Not really, I want them to be happy. They seem happy. I think this might be their golden ticket." He rolled up his shirt sleeve and leaned back into the swing.

"Yeah, but—"

"No buts, Mary-Kate. It's their thing, their life, their decision."

"Whatever, Ashley. It's irrational and immature, and you know it. The whole world knows it."

Ben shrugged and took another sip of his drink.

"And Bernice is going to leave again. How does he not see what's around the next bend?"

"You don't know that, and I think you should let it go. Que sera sera and all that." He tapped me on the nose and polished off his lager.

"You make a better Doris Day than I do, and we both know it."

"There is one way to solve that; I'll get us more beers."

I swung aimlessly in his absence and listened in the stillness for the elusive answers. When Ben returned, I accepted the beer offering without comment.

So many times I started to ask Dad about Bernice, about what happened, but getting those words past the edges of my teeth was like trying to fit an elephant through my mouth whole.

I was surprised then, when he brought it up the next day himself. We were driving to what we hoped was one of his last appointments when he broke the silence first.

"She's not a bad person." He drove fast, knew I couldn't escape.

"If you compare her to Cruella de Vil." I didn't want to talk about it; I wasn't ready.

He didn't respond, and I jumped out of the truck at a red light. It was worth the two-mile walk back to the house to get away from the unpleasant topic, but his words chased me all the way to our front door.

I sat on the front porch, thinking, staring at nothing. The mailman waved as he stuffed our mailbox with paper rectangles. Distracted, I wandered over to retrieve the mail. And there it was, looking weary from its journey. A letter, stuck between a flier and two bills. I moved to sit in the yard and opened it.

Hello Reese.

How are you?

In your depth, in your bones?

I stray away from asking you this often, because I imagine I know, but I don't want you to think you are neglected either.

I care how you are—all your thoughts, feelings, and the salmagundi betwixt. (Salmagundi—how do you like that?)

I so wish I was there to look at you, straight into those soulful sorrel eyes and ask you until you give me an authentic answer.

I've been dreaming up a little adventure, and I can't wait to run it by you. This is what we in the writing business deem "foreshadowing." Beyond that, not much is happening on this side of the globe—no revolutions or coups of which to speak.

More soon.

Know that someone from beyond the sea is remembering you.

My hug is waiting for your hug,

B

I leaned back into the grass, hugged by the earth and the light wind. The sun warmed my skin, and I let myself be. When Ben's hand slid into mine, I didn't open my eyes, but I had to smile. We lay there in the front lawn, two hearts undone, in the sun, until the dinner hour came.

PART II

10

July

Bernice

First things first. I'd gotten up early to make a pot of coffee, the nice hazelnut kind, and I'd bought a vanilla creamer especially for the occasion.

"Mom, it's eight in the morning, why do you have candles lit?" Benjamin wandered into the kitchen with his hair pointing in twenty directions, and I licked my palm to finesse the catastrophe atop his head.

"It's about the mood, son." His hair was not cooperating, and I focused my attention on Reese, who stomped into the kitchen after him as if she was leading an elephant parade. Her dark bun was lopsided and for once she wore her glasses. By Benjamin's side she reminded me so much of her seven-year-old self. They were beautiful, breathtaking. My heart hurt watching them.

"Happy birthday, babies!" I held my arms wide.

When they turned three, we hired some fancy photographer from Regency to document their cuteness. They cried through the whole hour and a half of the shoot, and I was livid. But now I loved the photos of their wailing faces, crimson red.

For their eighth birthday, we invited all the neighborhood kids and had a weekend-long sleepover in our backyard. Carl and I didn't sleep for seventy-two hours straight. We didn't know it at the time, but the twins and Charlie spent that year telling everyone they were triplets and all the other children showed up thinking it was Charlie's birthday too. The little scoundrel made out with a mound of presents of his own. All the photos showed their satisfied smiles smashed in a tight row.

I wiped my cheeks with the back of my hand, but they remained tenaciously damp. I had reached a disastrous plain of sentimentality.

"Why are you staring at us?" Reese didn't wait for my answer before heading to the coffee pot.

Carl was already seated with the paper and his coffee. He gave me a wink. For the first time in as long as I could remember, I knew what he was thinking—*we did one thing right.*

"I'll be right back, y'all." I ran upstairs and deposited my gifts on the kids' beds. When I re-entered, I gathered them around the table so I could regale them with the glorious tale of the day I became a mother. "We found out there were two of you at our first appointment. And did you know, your father passed out cold right there in the doctor's office when they told us?" Carl winked at me again, and I squeezed his arm.

Benjamin and Reese studied their coffees.

"He sure did, and the way those cute nurses fussed over him you'd have thought he was the one carrying two babies. I tried to help him up, but he sank into the care of that passel of nurses. I told him it was time to go, and still he avoided eye contact with my pretty blues. He let himself be *fawned over* for a good twenty minutes, as if he actually needed comfort. That man.

"Anyway, knowing there were two of you was enough surprise for one day and so we didn't find out if you were boys or girls. Besides, I knew you were boys. I knew it in my gut. I'm not sure what happened. We called y'all Twin A and Twin B. Twin B was always my favorite because he was calmer. Twin A was a wild-child like Aunt Naomi, and I knew we'd have our hands full with that one.

"Fast-forward to twenty-six years ago today. I was walking to the post office around ten in the morning because I hoped someone had mailed me a package, some thoughtful baby gift. There I was, looking like a whale in the pouring rain, when my water broke. At eight months pregnant, I'd given up all hope you were ever coming out. I'd embraced the idea of the three of us, with you in womb, growing old and dying together. A mother's sacrifices start so early on in the journey of life."

Reese glared at me and took a long swig of her coffee. I brushed away the forming tears with the back of my hand.

"As I was saying, my water broke on the corner of 60th and Grant when I was still six blocks from the post office. My raincoat only buttoned at the very top, and from the belly down, I was soaked right through. In every inch of my being I felt the pressure of your bodies fighting inside me, so I turned around and wobbled home.

"Now, these were the days before cell phones or pagers or anything, really. So we'd put Carl's office on high alert. Once I called, they were to hunt him down, no matter what meeting with what important person he was in. But I had to get home before I could call and figure it out.

"When I got to the house, there was a light on upstairs, so I grabbed the shovel from the entryway and I crept up to the baby room to see what crazy intruder thought he could steal all my babies' clothes. I was pretty scared, but I was also brave, so I shut my eyes and walked through the doorway, a'swinging that shovel like I was born to be a princess warrior. I was, you know."

"A real Xena." Ben smiled as he grabbed the coffee pot to pass between us all.

"A *princess warrior*, son. Anyhoo, your crazy father sat on the floor fiddling with something and don't you know, I knocked him out cold, with my eyes closed shut and everything. I guess he'd gone out and bought me this rocking chair I'd been hankering after to surprise me, and there he was dusting it when I thought he was at work.

"So I had to wake him up and then it was my job to drive us all the way to the hospital. In the pouring rain. When my contractions were only six minutes apart. But I was afraid I'd given your father a concussion—Carl, you know you were acting wacky when you woke up—and I wasn't going to risk him killing all four of us by letting him drive. I'm a better driver than him most days of the week anyway.

"Turns out he did have a concussion, but I didn't find that out until the next day because I spent the next five hours laboring like a farm hand. And after that, all hell broke loose. Twin B's foot got stuck under Twin A's head, making it impossible to deliver you two naturally. They rushed us in for an emergency C-section and the doctor grabbed the first foot he saw, and Twin A exited me first. After all those months of wondering, we had two tiny red screaming babies. A mini scarlet girl and a beautiful, perfect boy.

"Now, I wanted to name you Josephine Rose and Jasper Ray, but I fainted sometime shortly after your birth. And while I was passed out cold, your concussed father named you Reese Mae and Benjamin Maddox. He claimed he heard me say those names were pretty; it must have been while I was passed out.

"I'm sorry, Reese and Benjamin, he did and by the time I woke I was so tired, all I could do was feed you both and it wasn't until a week later that I fully realized what had happened. I thought it was all part of a dream, you see. But by then it was too late. Josephine and Jasper, you made me a mother, and it has been a wild ride, that's for sure.

"And here we are. The pancakes will be ready in about fifteen minutes. Drink some more coffee while you wait. Drink some water too, for that matter. It will help you all lose a few extra pounds and keep you hydrated. Oh, and babies, I left you each a gift on your bed. You have time to go open them before breakfast."

I was thrilled with the kids' gifts this year. I gave my Benjamin a small fortune, which I knew he'd love, but I was more pleased with Reese's gift. I wanted to watch her open it, but for the first time in my life, I was shy. I'd worked on her little project for weeks, it could have been years, and I was proud of it. It was the best I had in me, and I couldn't even bear to see the joy on her face when she saw it.

"Reese rhymes with Bernice. I thought it was cute," Carl muttered into his coffee cup.

I gave birth twenty-six years ago today, and today was going to be just fine. I shoved a napkin toward my face to hide the threatening tears.

Reese

I raced to my room after breakfast and crammed the large package from my mother into my closet. It looked homemade, and I'd deal with it later, when I had the emotional capacity, which was two miles past never. I sat on my bed to process the morning's events.

My mother had this thing about telling our birth story every year on our birthday. Even after she left, she attempted to reach out so we could remember her sacrifices. One year I had fifteen voice messages recounting her memory, which I promptly deleted without listening.

I was annoyed she force-fed us the story this year, but it had been more than a decade since I'd heard about our entrance into the world, and now it was so comforting I almost hugged Bernice. I shot a rubber band at Ben instead.

The last time I'd heard it was on our twelfth birthday. Mom woke me up with a mug of hot chocolate and my first tube of lipstick. I didn't think she'd noticed me watching her apply her makeup all those years, but maybe she had. I had been angry at her the night before, frustrated by something, but it was absolved between those cuddles and the solo re-telling of our birth story. She kept me back from school and we painted our nails a bright purple that lasted three weeks before it cracked and peeled off in mangled strips in one afternoon.

"Did you get a card?" Ben lounged in my bedroom doorway, holding an envelope.

After she left, Mom didn't call much, but she sent us cards every birthday and holiday. She even recognized holidays like Labor Day, which no one else cared about except for the fact they got a day off work. She was like that when we were growing up too—having a themed Memorial Day dinner or decking us out in red, white, and blue the entire month of July. She was all or nothing.

Ben and I refused to open the cards she mailed in her absence. We each took the box from our new Reeboks and made a big deal about indignantly adding card after card to the collection.

"No, I got some awkward-looking present. I put it in my closet."

"Reese."

"Ben, she can't waltz in here and act like nothing happened."

"Listen, I get it. Mom left us when we were young. It was a subpar thing to do and not one of her shining moments. She screwed up. But we all screw up."

"I think that's a kind way to put leaving your husband and two kids."

"Reese, come on. While her attempts at being a mother now border on the comical, she's trying. Think about how many cookies she's baked—she made you that R cookie."

"You and Bernice and those cookies."

"Reese, Dad wasn't here either. It's all screwed up, but it is what it is."

"Whatever."

He sat on my floor with an odd look. "I have to tell you something. The year we turned seventeen, I opened my birthday card from her, late at night when I was sure you were sound asleep." He picked at the rug. "I needed your REM cycle to block your twinly intuition, and I guess it worked." He shrugged.

"What? Why?"

"Dunno, I was tired of pushing her away, I guess."

I stared at him, mute.

"I stopped screening Mom's calls after that. If I was the only one home when she called, I'd talk to her for a few minutes. It hasn't been much through the years, but she's met Maya a handful of times and the three of us shared one Christmas two years back when your car broke down and you said you were too poor to buy a plane ticket. You know, the year Dad went golfing for the week in Florida."

"I *was* too poor." It sounded defensive.

"Some might think I don't take what she did seriously enough, but I think some people hold on to anger longer than it's needed. In all her outlandish extravagance, she cares. I know she does. Communicating it well just isn't her thing."

"Maybe she could learn." I crossed my arms, to show how upset I was at his betrayal, or maybe to hold my heart inside.

"We all have to start somewhere, Reese. Honestly, when Mom left, I was only half surprised." He lifted and dropped his shoulders.

Me too. I'd observed the tension growing between Mom and Dad for months, an inescapable tsunami. Ben went between them to repair the gaping holes each day brought forth, begged for clemency—a new, better understanding—but nothing worked. He was the fixer, the optimist; I was the realist and knew no intervention in the universe would make us better.

When Ben wandered off, I sat unmoving, wondering.

"Josephine, special delivery for you!" Bernice yelled up the stairs. Oh right, once she re-lived the splendor of our birth adventure, she insisted on calling us Josephine and Jasper for the entire day. Sometimes Dad joined in. Those two, they thought they were the funniest.

But no need to dissect the psychological wreck that was my mother, she said I had a *special delivery*. Charlie had done it again. He was particularly horrible at the bitsy details in a relationship, but he was so utterly fantastic at the grandiose, I absolved him for his next twelve shortcomings.

"One minute," I called around my grin.

"What is it?" Ben appeared in the doorway of my room, phone in hand. "Maya wants to know too." He waved his screen at me.

"Hi Maya. No clue, Jasper. But move aside Sauron, my birthday, my precious awaits."

My secret birthday dream was that Charlie himself would show up on my doorstep. The two months apart had been the longest separation in our lives, and he knew I loved surprises.

I took a final look in the mirror and scrunched my nose. I dabbed on mascara and a light layer of lip balm before I raced down the stairs, nearly tripping on the second to last step. Years later, and that death trap still wasn't fixed. I made a mental note to repair it within the week and looked around for my gift.

A familiar face rounded the corner, holding a red balloon. "Someone said special delivery?"

11

Reese

Blake looked endearingly rumpled and his dark hair crept out from under his baseball cap. The stubble was definitely working on him. Bernice danced circles around him, making a show of presenting him, as if he were my gift from both her and heaven, before fading into the kitchen behind me. Rocky, growling warily, trotted after her.

"What are you doing here?" My words came out guarded, stiff. We were both blushing by the time Blake reached for a hug.

"Happy birthday, Reese," Blake whispered into my ear. He smelled like cedar, spices, and morning. We held onto each other for a long moment and when we pulled away, ever so slightly, he offered the balloon.

"This is a rather extravagant birthday present."

"Yeah, I was fairly certain you were in need of a balloon. I could read between the lines." Blake winked.

"Yes. The balloon, definitely the balloon." I fiddled with its string.

I'd thought I wanted to see Charlie, and seeing Blake unleashed a multitudinous slew of emotions.

"So this is Omaha. Wait, I can't believe you're in Omaha! Are you on your way to New York or Dallas? Dallas, now that's a nice city. It's crazy hot most of the year, but they have Mexican food that would make you cry. How many days are you in Omaha? Just today? Tomorrow too? We can paint the town red. I'm up for anything. We can talk; we can walk. Hehe, that rhymed. I really don't know what I'm saying. I think Bernice must have spiked the morning coffee." I forced myself to stop and drew a ragged breath.

"Reese, come here." He reached for me, and I hoped he couldn't see I was blushing again. I melted into the cushioned periphery of his embrace.

"I'm sorry, Blake." I looked down at my feet and bit my lip. I had left his home abruptly that last morning, without an explanation, and I hadn't revealed much in the ensuing months.

He held my face with both hands. "Reese, you don't need to be sorry."

"Hey, get your meaty hands off my big sister!" We fell apart as Ben barreled down the stairs.

"Now Mr. Blake, who are you and where are you from? You were shaking so badly when I let you in I didn't dare ask, I thought you might faint." Bernice was back with a vengeance—sweet tea in one hand, a massive piece of coffee cake in the other. She never could leave well enough alone.

"Can't we let him sit down?"

My mother looked at me with raised eyebrows and the corner of her mouth turned up in her trademark smirk.

"Ben, Bernice, this is Blake from Ireland." I rolled my eyes with an excitement I wanted to show. "Blake this is Bernice, and this is my twin brother, Ben. But he prefers to be called Jasper, it's kind of his thing." I gave Ben a slight shove.

"Twin Jasper. Bernice—hullo." He kept one hand on the small of my back as he proffered his other palm.

"Why don't you have an accent? Why isn't your hair red?" Bernice looked suspiciously between me and Blake.

"Don't go all Miss Marple on him until he's sitting down," I said and communicated a lot more with my eyes.

She squinted at me and ignored his outstretched hand. "Well, nice to meet you, Blake. Have you had breakfast?"

"No, actually. I landed an hour ago, rented a car, and came straight here."

"Come into the kitchen, you can start with this." She shoved the sweets higher. "We have more pancakes and bacon." Bernice turned on her heels. "And if you're really hungry, I can whip up some eggs. I gave birth twenty-six years ago today, you know." She always knew how to command a room. Blake looked at me and smiled as we all followed Bernice into the kitchen.

"So how did you two meet?" Bernice waved the coffee pot around as if she were going into battle, and I ducked. Rocky whimpered and hid under the table.

"On a bus," Blake said at the same time I said, "At a bar." We both laughed. Having Blake in Dad's home felt like a roller coaster ride between two towns called Beautiful and Terrifying, but as I listened to him compliment Bernice about her cooking and discuss baseball with Ben, I found myself relaxing.

"But what if Bernice goes into one of her crazy cycles? Scratch that, what about *when* Bernice goes into one of her crazy cycles? Or her second one, or her third?" I moaned when Blake excused himself to use the bathroom and Bernice went to check on Dad. It was only Ben and me at the table, the vestiges of breakfast spread between us.

"Right, because she's the only one with insane tendencies here."

"Exactly. What's going to happen?" I exhaled and thumped my head into my hands. The upside was Blake was staying across town so there would be lots of excuses to send him over to his room when things in the Hamilton house got all stirred up. And they would most certainly get stirred up.

"Well, I guess it's going to be fun." Ben tugged my bun. "I have a few more questions for you, but I need to go into the office. I'll see you for dinner." He tapped out a beat across the table and pushed his chair back. "Oh, and sis, don't do anything I wouldn't do." Blake entered, and from the kitchen doorway, Ben pointed at him with a knowing nod and made a kissy face.

I remember the first time I saw him, well the second, but I count it as the first.

As the Irish say, he was fit. I noticed him as soon as I walked into the pub; he was incredibly handsome and his dark hair peeked from his Cubs hat, curled up at the ends. His five o'clock shadow was the perfect blend of rugged and masculine. I tried not to stare overtly, but he looked tall. Not weirdly tall, but normal, handsome tall.

He glanced up and my stomach went shaky. I turned and moved to a seat in the corner, tucked away but angled so I had a visual. I pulled out a book and attempted to read. I found myself reading the same sentence over and over as I covertly glanced between my book and Mr. Brooding Dark Eyes.

I'd been in Ireland three days, and it was time I drank a Guinness. Charlie and I had planned on celebrating our trip to Ireland and our first pint together, but in the end I grew tired of waiting for him. He was off schmoozing all the important people, and I needed to explore.

Mr. Brooding Dark Eyes sat with an older man. He held his beer loosely in one hand, and the two of them were playing cards. Poker, I suspected. He threw his head back when he laughed, and did I imagine his smile didn't quite reach his eyes? I pushed my black-rimmed glasses further up my nose and shook my head at the sure sign of his murky past or some complex tragedy. I knew he would tell me what haunted him on a star-filled night, under the moon. I could sense he wanted to tell me. *Come to me, rugged man; your secrets are safe with me.*

He looked over and our eyes locked. Crap. A smile flicked across his gorgeous face. He said something to his friend, slammed down his beer and hopped around the table, heading straight toward me. He was the perfect tall.

I'd been caught; how could I play this cool? The flush of my cheeks echoed in the warm fuzzies parading at varying angles between my stomach, heart, and head.

Don't panic.

"Do you always carry a book around?" His accent wasn't as thick as most.

I wasn't sure if he was mocking me and responded more defensively than I meant, with a curt "Yes."

"I do too." He held Zen. "I'm reading Hemingway at the moment." He proudly pulled a worn book from his back pocket as he sat across from me without an invitation. "I'm Blake." He reached out his hand. His hands looked rough and he smelled like cedar. A few wood chips were stuck to his neck.

"Reese." I held on to my book tighter, a lifeline.

"Nice seeing you again."

"Um, we haven't met."

He looked at me quizzically until I blushed. And then I remembered. *Of course.* I put my face in my hands. The bus. It was my first day in the city, and I had been standoffish. I was tired, flustered and completely out of sorts. Yet he had been so kind, gentleman-like really.

"I know it's reading hour over here, but would you like to come sit with me and my Gramps? If you're any good, you can play some poker."

And now he was here, in my kitchen, being drowned in a mountain of breakfast foods from the hands of Bernice.

"Death by breakfast, that's novel. But how will I break the news to Gramps?"

"Hmm?" Blake searched my face. I didn't realize I'd spoken aloud.

"Uh, nothing. Thanks for coming. I'm," I took a sip of coffee, "I'm glad."

"I told you there was an adventure afoot. For a little more foreshadowing: in the book writing business, we'd say the climax is just around the corner and a happy ever after too. Well, we can hope." He smiled until his eyes disappeared into the tops of his cheeks, and my stomach sang so much I had to look away.

Bernice

"As if I would let that young man drive across town each night to sleep. He is our guest, and I will not allow him to be shacked up in a dirty motel, with chigger sheets. Surely we can put up with a stranger for

116

under a week before he takes his bus over to Chicago?"

Benjamin and I huddled in the hallway beyond the kitchen and watched Reese and Blake angle toward one another. I smelled the morning's bacon on my son's breath.

"Right. To have another dude around the house will be legend. We need it. Another guy to help keep The Balance. He could be Voldemort for all I care."

"Your balance? No sirree. This traipsing off to a hotel is not how Mama hosts a guest." I racked my brain about how we could solve this.

"It's an Airbnb, Mom."

"Same difference."

"It's actually not."

"Is there a free corner of your room where we could set up a cot?"

"Mom!"

"I was thinking about how you and Charlie used to love your slumber parties."

"Yeah, but that was Charlie. This is some guy I hardly know. It's too weird. On the other hand, I don't want to say I have a man crush on Blake, but the dude is Irish, has a Cubs cap, and says he can shred the guitar. Evening jam sessions just got legit."

"You are plumb giddy, Jasper. The downstairs guest room will do fine." I'd unofficially moved back into my old room with Carl a week ago, but now I could make it official. "I don't have much time to throw together a welcome basket, but at least I cleaned the sheets and towels yesterday. I'll put the leftover grapes from breakfast onto a plate, stick it on his bed, and call it a day. Go grab his suitcase, will you? I need to stay here to see if he makes any moves on my Josephine."

"We should be so lucky."

"Feeding the babies, housing the babies, Southern Hospitality, you doth have a name, and your name is Bernice."

"Did you say something?" Benjamin turned back at the front door.

"Oh, nothing, sugar. I'll meet you back in the kitchen."

"I'm going to work."

"Well fine then. I'll take lots of notes and fill you in later tonight."

I barely caught his thumbs up before I swiveled my concentration back to my daughter.

"Why are you lying prone on your bed? Where's Blake? Did you open your present yet?" Hours later, I peered about the edges of Reese's room, but it was suspiciously barren of any traces of my gift.

"I told him I needed to powder my nose." She struggled to sit up.

"But you don't wear makeup."

"Right you are." She scratched the side of her messy hair and shrugged. She looked stunning, my baby girl.

"Baby, you are a hot mess today. I can do your makeup for you." I took three graceful steps to the side of my daughter and reached for her face. She scooted toward the center of her faded paisley comforter.

"That's okay."

"At least let me pluck a few eyebrows and do something with your hair. This is our day, Josephine." Since I brought life into this world twenty-six years ago today, I'd declared a protest against cooking dinner and booked a night out for all of us at The Grey Plume instead. Except Carl. He insisted tonight was a 7 p.m. bedtime, and I agreed. I wanted to soar tonight, and bless his heart, Carl had never quite been the soaring type.

"I'll throw myself out the window and be right down." She flung herself back into her pile of pillows.

"Josephine, let me help you."

Her only reply was a loud moan. I squeezed her hand but when I got nothing except more unintelligible sounds in response, I shook my head.

"I, for one, have some grooming to do." I spritzed her with wisteria and headed out. "Be downstairs in ten or we're leaving without you."

The Hamilton women needed a night on the town and Benjamin and Blake were our escorts. I looked regal in my red dress, curled hair, and six-inch stilettos. Mama still had game. I didn't wear my diamonds because this was Reese's night too, so I went with the pearls.

"Josephine, this is our night. We are worth celebrating, and I want the world to know it." I stood at the head of the table, wine glass extended high. By their glances, I could tell the world knew her mother was one hot lady.

"Uh guys? It's my birthday too?" Benjamin looked put out.

"Of course it is, sweetie." I patted his head. "No one's saying it's not."

"Well, it's *our* birthday, but to hear you two tell it, it's Reese's birthday and the day you gave birth, Mom." He brandished his champagne like a wild man.

"I did give birth, son." I winked at him.

"Contrary to the popular theory that babies get the most attention, it has always taken a lot of effort to get any acknowledgment around the Hamilton walls." He crossed his arms.

"Oh Ben, you're everyone's favorite, and you know it." Reese made a face at her twin.

"I see you found the tiara I arranged on your bed this morning, Reese." Benjamin looked over at Blake. "Although it should have been mine, she took the firstborn throne, and while I spent most of my childhood fighting it, I finally resigned myself to her bossy ways. I buy her a different crown each year."

"Thankfully Maya is a big believer in all that birth order gibberish, and she fell in love with your free-spirited, fun-loving, uncomplicated demeanor." Reese smirked back at him and my heart expanded three sizes. I was happy to sit back and listen to my kids.

"You know, Ryan Gosling is the youngest in his family, and I've had several people compare us, both in looks and personality."

"Riiight," Reese said.

"Technically I am the baby, and I consider myself to be the tender, more altruistic one. That Austrian, Alfred Adler, knew his stuff."

Right after I poured my second glass of wine and before we ordered our food, a wedding party walked through to their private room. I glanced around the table and raised my glass. "Tonight we wedding crash."

It was a challenge. I pushed my chair back and joined the crowd. The others followed like ducklings. I knew what my role was for the night—talk up my baby girl and entertain the masses with my wit and charm. Oh, and drink some champagne. Done and Done.

I grabbed a glass from the waiter's tray as he walked past and threw it back.

"Let's do this." I twirled myself into the party.

Reese

"Rise and shine, sunshine." Ben barged into my room at 6:27 with donuts and coffee the morning after our birthday.

"What the—"

"Good morning to you too, Bobbsey. I thought we should have some chats."

"Uh, no thanks."

"I have coffee. And donuts, the good kind."

I scratched my head before reaching toward Ben's offering. Once I had the donut and coffee grasped close, he pushed further.

"So, Blake."

I sipped my coffee. "Yes, Irish as promised."

"Reese, he flew halfway around the world to surprise you on my birthday. That's a big deal."

"Ugh, I knew you'd make this into something it isn't. It's decidedly not a big deal. He's headed to Chicago. By plane it's a short forty-five minute detour from his original destination. NBD."

"Okay, crazy person, I'm going to let you have that as you're clearly not in the mindset to be rational. But really, there's something there?"

"Something teeny, tiny. The teeniest of tiniest—"

"That's what she said."

"Don't you dare."

"You said you made out with him?" He waited as I polished off my second donut.

"Benji, stop staring at me. It's disconcerting. Besides, I said no such

120

thing."

"I'm waiting for the rest."

"What rest? That's all I have to say." Those donuts were good. I grabbed a third.

"Are you a Gilmore girl this morning? I bought the box for everyone to share. Actually, they're not for you at all—you don't believe in sugar."

"Unfortunately sugar believes in me." I took a loud sip of my coffee.

"Stop being so taciturn, sister dearest. I know you need to spill, so spill. Expound. Pontificate. Let your soul go to the wind, and I'll be here to help you gather the pieces. Blake?"

"Fine, it's probably the sugar and lack of sleep talking, but here's the scoop." I paused.

"Reese!" Ben pulled the donut box out of reach.

"Fine, fine. This is it—I don't know."

"What do you mean you don't know?"

"I mean, yes, I find him attractive. Clearly, he's a young Al Gore meets George Clooney meets Robert Downey Jr. with all the suave of Robert Redford from the sixties. And yes, we kissed. One time, right before I flew back here. But we were both slightly tipsy, maybe more than slightly, and we hadn't seen each other in three years. There were a lot of endorphins floating about."

"You mean oxytocin? And I'm not seeing the problem. Unless you think Mr. George Downey Redford will no longer find you attractive post your affair with these donuts?"

"Shut up. That's the problem."

"You eating too many donuts? I can see that."

"No, you dork, knowing if he's actually attracted to me. He hasn't said anything. For years we've only been friends. He broke up with his last girlfriend only a few months ago, actually. And she was basically Heidi Klum's hotter twin. So there's that. He doesn't even like brunettes."

"Oh wow. So we're reading a lot into one relationship. And in the twenty-four hours I've spent with the guy, he doesn't seem shallow. Plus, he laughs at all your jokes which is both disconcerting and adorable. He thinks you're funny."

"Funny doesn't put me in the life partner category—it almost exclusively guarantees me a seat in the friend zone for the next four decades."

"That's not true—Tina Fey happily wed and even had kids."

"Right, and I *am* as funny as she is, so maybe there's hope."

"Well, *that's* true. I'm just saying, he's cute. I think we should at least keep him on the options list. You're twenty-six now, tick tock." He ignored my glare and grabbed my coffee for a sip.

"And what about Charlie?" It made me sad to think about.

"What about him?"

"Ben. *You* know. I don't believe in destiny or sometimes even in love, but there's always been this thing between the two of us. This unspoken—"

"Sexual tension?" He nodded knowingly.

"Gawd, you're annoying. But yes, that. All I want to do is get Charlie naked, cover him in chocolate sauce and lick his body before I—"

"Okay, okay, stop."

"But I didn't even get to the whipped cream, and that's the exciting bit."

"Reese!"

"Okay, fine. I always imagined I'd end up with Charlie. There, I said it. It's been an understood for as far back as I can remember."

"But do you want that?"

"I think so. The thought of forever with Charlie exudes comfortable, like coming home. It feels known and happy and certain."

"But?"

"But he's never said one word. I did once, you know, a hundred moons ago. But he shut me down and we went right along being friends."

"The real question is—can guys and girls ever be *just* friends?"

"Don't get me started, Harry met Sally. I've seen him in diapers."

"For that matter, you've taken baths with him. So you're going to ask him out again?"

"I can't. He is the one guy on the planet I won't risk asking out because I can't stand the thought of wrecking our friendship if he says no. Can you imagine me showing up to work the day after he's turned me down? Uh, no thanks. Anyway, he doesn't want to be with me. But it's weird. Sometimes he looks at me in this way that makes the whole universe seem as if it's coming unglued. But he won't *say* anything."

"Words aren't really his thing."

"Well, you'd think if he wanted me, he could figure something out. And you know he's dated three other girls in the past five years. He obviously talked to them. None of them liked me, by the way."

"So you're counting."

"Yes, I'm counting. So I need to move on, try something new, forget about the romantic ideal of best friends finding a happy ever after. Not everyone is Gilbert and Anne."

"Is that Ann with an 'e'? I can't remember. But I do know there is a charming Irish dude who flew over an entire ocean to see you, and I think it wouldn't hurt to give him a chance."

"He flew halfway around the world to write a book; visiting me was an afterthought. Are you trying to get rid of me, Hamilton?"

"I'm only saying. I need to head out and actually make it to work on time today, but I'm happy knowing I'm leaving you in capable hands." He squeezed my foot. "Would it be embarrassing for you if I put these last two donuts down in the kitchen to be shared by the other three people in the house?"

"Do whatever you want. You always do." I pulled the comforter over my face with a groan.

Dad and Ben went out after work for one of Dad's appointments and wings at the bar, which left Blake with us ladies. We'd convinced him to stay a few extra days in Omaha before catching his bus to Chicago, so he insisted on cooking us a nice meal.

"I can work wonders in the kitchen if I'm creating shepherd's pie, chili, or a lemon meringue," he'd bragged at breakfast, and it was settled. I opted for shepherd's pie and sat with him for hours in the afternoon while he chopped away in the kitchen. When it was ready, Bernice brought out candles and a tablecloth.

"I must say, in your gray sweater and wreck of a bun, you shimmer by candlelight, Reese," he murmured as he walked past. I blushed and tore my gaze away.

"It's like an Irish casserole." Bernice looked pleased at Blake's meal.

"Yes, something like that. I'd like to imagine it's a bit more refined than a standard casserole."

"Are you saying my casseroles aren't fancy?" Bernice's hands flew to her hips. I made a face at Blake from behind my mother.

"Ahem. Bernice, I'd love to hear more about your, *ah*, your personal inspiration in the kitchen."

"You and everyone else, son. I am a culinary prodigy. I have ten secrets, and I will tell you one. It's all about the butter. When you think you've added enough, walk away, head to the nearest mirror, look yourself right in the eye and say, 'Amateur.' Then run straight back to your dish and double the butter. Double the butter, double the love, I say."

"I'm hearing you say the butter is important?"

"Bless your heart, of course it's important. So many people these days talk about fat and calories but they're barely living, are wisping about as if they can thrive on tofu." She gave a puff. "Eat the butter—live today and no regrets tomorrow, I say."

Blake nodded. "Thanks for sharing your wisdom, Bernice."

"I assure you there's more where that came from." She squinted at me. "I tried to give Reese some pointers last week but little good it did either of us."

"Hey now. You know *you* trying to teach *me* anything was a bad idea in the first place."

"You mean, it was a great idea but you had a bad attitude." Bernice pressed her lips together.

"Yep, I definitely had a bad attitude." I grinned.

"You should bring this chirpiness to the kitchen, missy."

"No thanks. But I think Blake could do with some special time in the kitchen with you."

"I've thought of that myself." She peered pointedly at him.

"Aha, well, thanks, ladies, but as you know, Chicago is calling. I'll certainly take a rain check though. And let me go grab the bottle of wine I left in the kitchen; I believe we all need it." He scurried away, returning with the pinot noir.

"Are you sure you're Irish?" Bernice squinted at him as he opened it, scattering the rich berry scents.

"Yes, I'm Irish."

"Where'd your accent go? It's pitiful. Did it wander off the edge of the flat earth?" She giggled, and I gave him an apologetic smile.

"Well, my mom was American, and we lived in the States until I was twelve."

"Oh, so you're American born and bred." She nodded and piled her fork high. "Good."

"My da is Irish. He went to Northwestern University." Blake put his fork down, looking resigned to the fact his food would get cold. "He planned to go the four years, graduate, and head back to Ireland. But he met my mom there in Chicago, fell in love, and didn't leave after all."

"Well how in the Sam Hill did you end up in Ireland then? Did your parents get divorced, did your dad steal you away?"

"No, they didn't get divorced." Blake pushed back from the table. "I'm sorry. I don't want to be rude, but I'm not exactly in the mood to talk about it. I never am."

But Bernice didn't stop, and Blake couldn't keep avoiding her insistently direct questions. "Well, I don't understand. You had a mother, so you have a mother. Mothers just don't disappear into thin air."

"Or do they?" I coughed into my napkin.

"My mom died," he finally blurted, and the room fell silent and awkward. Blake cleared his throat and softened his voice. "She had Lou Gehrig's disease, or ALS. I was twelve."

In all the time and all the letters Blake and I had shared over the years, we had focused more on the present and the future than the past. He'd told me very little about his mother. When I imagined Blake telling me about his complex former life, the conveying was under a myriad of stars as I nestled my head into his chiseled chest.

I would hold his face, lined with the narrative of his tragedy, between my hands and his heart would melt under the pressure of my kindness. He would tell me all. I would mend his past with my touch and sympathy. My tender care would mitigate his every agony. The inky night would be velvety and star songs would reach from heaven down to earth as we sank in each other's embrace and his heart would open to me alone.

I'd imagined this very scenario at least a dozen times, yet here we were. Bernice wiped the corners of her eyes with the bottom of her apron and shot Blake a lingering look of pity.

Blake tugged at his collar and muttered, "So yeah, after she died, Da and I moved back to Ireland, reportedly to help Gramps with the farm, but mostly to get away."

"You poor thing." Bernice's sigh filled the room.

"I miss Mom. After she died, I locked myself in her room for two whole days. I sat in the middle of her closet and hugged her smell. That's where I found the baseball cap I've worn ever since." Bernice had insisted Blake come to the dinner table sans hat, but now he pulled it off the seat next to him and shoved it down hard over his eyes.

"Well, then." Bernice patted Blake's hand and went back to eating as we swam through the uncomfortable quiet. She got up two minutes later and thrust his face into her bosom, ferociously patting the top of his head. I could see one of his eyes pleading with me for help, but I shook my head and daintily ate a bite of the shepherd's pie. It really was delicious.

I shot him a smile I hoped was meek. I'd ask him more questions later, under the stars.

"That is not how you spell xenophile." I heard a hint of childhood whine in Ben's voice as I came down the steps the next morning.

"It's how your recovering Dad spells it." He instructed Bernice to write down eighty-three points as his score.

"Eighty-three?" Bernice checked the board. "Your sick days are officially over. You can stop pretending now." Her voluminous curls didn't move an inch as she wagged her head.

"Yes, dear." He squeezed her hand. It was weird hearing Dad employ a playful tone. "Two double letter score plus a triple word score." He did a victory fist pump into the air and everyone laughed.

I grabbed the chunky mug from the cupboard and poured myself a steaming cup of coffee. I inhaled the warmth and the black as I looked between the kitchen clock and Bernice, Dad, Ben, and Blake gathered around the table. The Scrabble board in the middle had several words across it already.

"Why are you up so early on a Thursday, and how come no one woke me up to play?" I folded my arms across my chest.

"Stop pouting, Reese. It's very unattractive and you don't want any young men in your life to see you like that." Bernice's head looked like it would snap clean off as she nodded in Blake's direction.

Heat crept up my neck.

"Everyone said they didn't want you to play because they didn't want you to win." Blake smiled. "But I'm not frightened of your extensive vocabulary."

"Be afraid Blake, be very afraid." Ben moved the board to face him. "She started beating my parents when she was seven."

I laughed and picked up my camera. The morning light peeking through the French doors curled around the quorum concentrating on their tiles at the table. From behind my camera, I mocked Ben's attempt to spell intransigent. "And why aren't you at work?"

"Reese, for your information, I took off work this morning to hang out with the family. I head out next Tuesday or Wednesday, you know."

"I think I'll fly out then too." I decided on the spot. Bernice and Dad both turned to look at me, but I couldn't see myself staying here alone with them, and I avoided eye contact. "Until then, Blake, you do not want a piece of this." I pulled my fuzzy robe around me and leaned into the cold counter.

When the timer went off, Bernice jumped from the table. Dad sat and watched everyone dance around the kitchen in a sort of caustic waltz as Ben grabbed the plates and Blake got the cups for orange juice. My stomach growled in time with the mayhem. I knew casseroles were the devil for my body, but Bernice made a breakfast fit for royalty, and in the presence of her buttery goodness, I lost any ounce of self-control I once possessed.

In all of the commotion Blake leaned close as he walked by and whispered loud enough for only me to hear, "Oh Reese, yes. I most certainly want a piece of this."

In slow motion, he continued past me, touching the small of my back as he went.

Tingles.

Tingles.

Tingles.

I wasn't sure I could ever move from this spot.

12

Reese

Blake had been in Omaha a handful of days, and Ben and I had dragged him around the perimeters of the city twice over. On his last day in town we'd spent the afternoon at the Henry Doorly Zoo, and Bernice was marching across the front porch when we arrived home.

"Have you seen your father?" She turned and continued pacing without waiting for our reply.

We looked at each other. "No?"

"Dadgummit. He raced away to the doctor's this morning without me, and he's been gone all day. You know he refuses to own a cell phone so I don't know where he is. I called the doctor's office and they won't tell me a thing, just that he made it to his appointment. Now he's probably lying dead in a ditch somewhere. Or he's been kidnapped, we'll get the ransom call any minute. I should go be by the phone." She looked at us with wild eyes. "We'll find the money to get him released. We will."

"Mom, he's an adult, he's fine." Ben plopped on the porch swing.

"You're right, I'll go call the police." The door slammed as she entered the house.

I sat at the steps and leaned into the post as the afternoon sun played along my arms. Blake settled opposite me.

"So what about those Cubs?" Ben rocked in the swing.

"I could tell I was in the presence of a fellow Cubby. How did you decide they were the team for you?" Blake's smile broadened.

"Okay, first of all, we don't use the vernacular 'Cubby' here in the States, and I hope you never use it again in your lifetime."

"Ben, stop being a snob and treat our guest with some respect.

Besides it took your Cubbies over a hundred years to win the World Series. I'm not sure why you're getting your panties in a wad."

He kept his gaze on Blake. "And *second of all*, Dad and I used to watch them all the time. I guess I became a fan by default. What about you?"

"My mom grew up in Chicago and was a diehard baseball fan. She wore the cap every opening day." Blake looked cute in his black T-shirt and shorts, and as he tipped his cap toward us, I tried to ignore the butterflies inside.

"We've been handed so much from our primogenitors." Ben made a mock toast.

"Sometimes I think you use words out of context." I threw a pebble at my brother.

"Are you jealous?"

"As jealous as Jacob was of Esau." I rolled my eyes at him and ignored Blake's face turning in my direction.

"Give the girl some sunshine and she gets sassy." Blake shook his head at Ben.

"Right? Maybe we should change the subject. It's sacrilegious to be discussing our, ahem, 'Cubbies' in front of someone who so obviously doesn't understand their value."

"Actually I have a good premonition about them this year." I raised my eyebrow and dared them to disagree.

"To the Cubs." We cheered with pretend beers. Blake held my gaze for a few extra seconds before I had to look away. This would be a good year indeed.

"We should cook the family dinner tonight, what do you say—you and me and that kitchen? I won't try to give you any lessons, promise. It's our last supper, after all." My stomach hurt at the thought of leaving him at the bus station the following morning.

"Alright, da Vinci, I'll create with you." I blushed as I thought back to the previous night's kiss, hoping we'd find time for another between the meal preparations.

"And I will be on beer duty. You're welcome." Ben saluted.

"I need all the beer I can get."

"What's up, sis?"

"It's just that..." I didn't make eye contact with either of them. "It's sad we're all leaving this week."

"Um, sad and wonderful."

"You know what I mean. Who knows when we'll all be together again?"

"Ben, I hear her saying she likes us."

"I hear it, and I like it."

"I do like you, you dopes. But you need to go write your book, and Ben, you need to get back to the most sane part of your life."

"She is that. Maya's a wonder."

"Clearly. Maybe I need that beer now. Do we have any left?"

"Reese, has anyone told you you're probably a locational alcoholic? I've seen you drink more in the last two months here in Omaha than in the rest of our adult lives combined."

"I'm not denying it."

"Let me go see what I can find. Blake, protect the lady whilst I'm gone."

"More like she'll protect me."

We waited until Ben was inside before we turned and looked at each other.

"So you're heading back to Atlanta?"

"Yeah." I was scheduled to leave in less than a week and needed to message Charlie to sort out the details, but I was less than inspired to move even an inch in that direction. "Or maybe I can't."

"Why not, Reese?" When he said my name, sincerely and without accusation, something inside me broke.

"It happened again." I wasn't making eye contact with him anymore. "It?"

"Never mind. It's nothing."

"Okay, Reese. But know you can tell me if you want." He scooted closer.

"I failed. That's it. That's all."

"I think maybe you should start at the beginning."

"There was a shoot I did on my own, a week or so before I came here, and I handed everything over to Charlie right before I flew out. He finally told me the clients weren't happy with it, and he had to re-shoot it last week. It was hugely inconvenient and expensive for him, not to mention embarrassing for our company."

"Forgive my ignorance, but that happens, right? A barista makes a drink wrong and they re-do it. Voilà."

"It's hardly the same thing."

"I'm sorry if I sound cavalier about this. I'm an artist too, so while I don't understand everything, I know I always have to re-write stuff. It's part of the job description."

"Have you ever been in business with someone who shines so brightly you don't need the sun? I'm not sure I told you, but I tried to go out on my own. Once, a long time ago, I called up all my contacts, let them know I was available for shoots. Ten minutes into our conversation, they'd ask about Charlie. 'Oh, he's doing his own thing too.' Afterwards, they didn't call me. They called Charlie."

"Sexist bastards."

"Right? Only I wasn't jealous of him. I get it. It's Charlie. He *is* the best, and we all want him, we all love him."

"Not *everyone* loves Charlie."

But I was in no mood for his charm. "I don't need advice, believe me. I joined forces with him, and he was adorably happy to have me. The funny thing is, he says I'm a better shooter than he is. But a good half of our clients assume they're getting the second-best if I'm the shooter, and at the end of the day, sometimes it's easier to let him shoot. So I don't know if they're sexist or simply right. Either way, it's exhausting."

"Aha. I'm sorry, Reese. Don't you think—"

"I'm sorry, too. If Ben comes back with that beer tell him I've started my AA group. I need to go for a walk. I'll meet you in the kitchen afterwards."

I needed to walk off the ends of the earth. But as I stood, a honking orange apparition pulled into our driveway. Dad jumped out with a flourish as Bernice and Ben joined us on the porch.

"I've made a decision," Dad crowed and pounded the hood of the beast.

And just like that, I knew we were in trouble.

Bernice

"Carl, what the Sam Hill? You left me all day without so much as a note. You, you—" But he was dancing around the van, not listening to me at all.

"What's up with the van, Dad?" Benjamin moved to thump on the hood of the bright orange VW.

"I've been scouring the newspaper sale section and calling all over Nebraska to find a VW, but didn't find one until today. It is circa 1975 and was very affordable. It belonged to an old lady who'd only used it to visit the grocery store and church for the past forty or so years. When she died, the van only had 20,000 miles on it." Carl stuck out his chest. "I bought it from her grandson."

"A steal, Dad." Reese looked unsure.

"Let's circle back around to why you bought a van," Benjamin said.

"We're taking a road trip, kiddos." Carl beamed at the twins and then moved his gaze to me.

I bolted down the steps. "Carl, I love seeing this raw, decisive you. I told you my cooking was good for the body *and* the soul!" I swooped beside him and ran a manicured finger over his cheek. "You bought our VW," I breathed into his ear, and he squeezed my hand. "And it's so... *orange*." I tried to hide my shudder. I'd always imagined a nice blue. Or a pink. Even a fun green. Orange was so, well, orange.

I watched their faces as Carl outlined his plan—The Grand Adventure, as he called it. "We'll take a simple two-day trip over to Mt. Rushmore and then back east to Chicago for a Cubs game. A week's adventure, something special and bonding for the lot of us." He made it sound so enticing with his quivering voice.

"Because we need another cliché in our life, right?" Reese looked put out. "Bucket list has already been done, Dad."

"Reese, honey, I don't know what that means, but I'll pay for your change of ticket and write Charlie a personal note of apology for stealing you for an extra few days." He dabbed his eyes. "We need some quality time together."

"Because we haven't spent the last two months breathing the same air? What if you have a relapse, Dad?" Reese crossed her arms.

"Ah, well, as a matter of fact, I did go see the doctor today." Carl leaned against the van.

"And?" Benjamin and Reese spoke together like they used to do when they were little.

"Well." Carl cleared his throat. "He told me I am in fact cancer free. I have a follow up appointment later in the month because there was one little—"

"WAY TO BURY THE LEAD," I shouted and he twirled me around.

As Reese and Benjamin hugged their dad, I sobbed. It was like I didn't even realize the weight we'd all been carrying until it lifted. I don't know how long we stood there shouting and crying—it could have been an hour, maybe three. I focused through my tears to see Blake shake Carl's hand. "Congratulations on the good news, sir."

Carl smiled. "Time is a slippery bugger. It gets away from us." He mauled his eyes with the back of his hand and put his arm around me. "If you want something, go for it while you have the chance. Which is why I'm taking you all on this trip. I only wish I would have done this sooner."

"Dad, you just told us the news of the century; let's not talk about your trip."

"It still feels too soon for you to be away from your doctor." My stomach knotted at the thought. "Just in case."

"You're all invited so you can stitch me up if I fall. Blake, you too, we'll drop you off in Chicago, no need to take a bus." Carl rocked back on his heels.

"I'd forgotten how stubborn you can be." My voice quivered.

"Do you think we should have a family talk about codependency?"

Reese's mouth pressed into a smirk.

Carl smiled. "I'm leaving the morning after next at dawn. You don't have to come with me, but I sure hope you do. I'd hate to relapse on the road while I was all alone. We'll take the VW."

"Dad, you're playing all this a little over-the-top."

"Reesey, after my dance with death, there is a need to make a statement." He kissed the side of her head. "Besides, I learned a few things from all my years with Bernice." He gave me a pointed look and moved past us to the house.

"What should we name it?" Blake drifted reverentially to the van. "Lee? As in the poet, Li-Young Lee?"

"As in Lee Harvey Oswald or Robert E. Lee? Uh, no thanks," Reese said.

"As in Harper—"

"Buddy." Benjamin leaned close to the van. "He says his name is Buddy."

"That's funny, because she told me her name was Evangeline." Reese blew the van a kiss.

"I don't know why you're all making such a fuss," I said. "His name is Ernie." I pointed to the name which looked as if it had been Sharpied on the left side of the bumper. "Must have been her grandson." I scooped up Rocky and headed to the house. I had clothes to pack, brownies to bake, and nails to manicure before we hit the road, because if we were going to do this thing, I was determined to do it in style.

The morning we left, I was up before anyone and sat on the porch with my tea. Carl joined me on the steps, while the purple-hued edges of the horizon still sank dusky.

"I told the kids I wanted to celebrate this second chance at life. I didn't tell them I needed this hoorah to extend the hours with my family."

"I don't think you needed to tell them." I rubbed his back.

"Even the last of my rage at you faded after my last visit with the doctor. It gave me some perspective on what really mattered."

"Well," I cleared my throat. "That's good." *What about my feelings?* I wished I had a recipe to dissipate the layers of hurt we'd buried between us.

"I was so, so angry at you, but when I zoom out and look at the whole of my life, that anger isn't worth holding on to." Carl sighed and studied the distance. He grabbed my hand. "I have some things I need to do. I don't need to race through our entire dream list; a few well-chosen activities will do. And now is the time. I'm growing my hair out, for one. True, you can't tell yet, but soon enough there will be a silver mane on top of this old horse."

I ran my hand through his growing locks. "You've never looked more handsome."

"This is the Trip of Carl, and there is no time like the present to jump into my destiny."

"Let's jump away." I patted him on the shoulder and left to finish packing before I started to cry again.

An hour later, Benjamin and Blake strolled into the kitchen wearing bow ties.

"I thought we were supposed to dress up," Benjamin said as Reese entered in a cap, baggy jeans, and tank top. "I guess it was a different memo." She shook her head at them and grabbed a travel mug for coffee.

Even in her horrifying clothes, she was striking. I watched Blake swallow hard. As Benjamin wrestled my two suitcases out the door, she and Blake lingered in the kitchen. She brushed her bangs aside and lightly touched his arm. "Thanks for coming along with us. I know there are some high maintenance ones amongst us," she nodded with a cheeky smile to where I was putting away the last of the clean dishes, "but having you here is sweet."

I watched their hands graze as they walked outside. I followed them out to where Carl stood embracing the long golden rays of the rising sun along his body like a cat. "This is the first day of the rest of my life," he announced to no one in particular.

"To celebrate I have a surprise for everyone." I pulled a stack of shirts out of my bag and held one up. "I put personalized decals on each." I handed Blake his sheep tee with a smile. "I thought it would be fun to wear these."

"Oh, what did I get?" Benjamin asked. "Please tell me it's a tiger, my obvious spirit animal." I handed him his cookie shirt without comment—Mama knew what he needed.

"Is fun the word we're going with here?" Reese wrinkled her nose and unfolded her shirt. "Uh, why does mine have a horse on it?" Reese's head was cocked so hard I thought her ear would touch her shoulder.

"I don't neigh, er, know." I kept my face blank.

"Why are they pink?" Benjamin asked. "And I thought you didn't wear T-shirts?"

"A lady can change her mind. And fuchsia is my favorite color," I said. "I even made one for Rocky." I slipped it over his cute head. His had a crown on it, of course. King Rocky.

"Your mother spent your entire childhood trying to convince me the kitchen needed to be a bright pink with flamingo accents," Carl said displaying the shirt I'd handed him, a pink flamingo shining on the front. I'd made myself a matching one. His and hers.

"Like the Caribbean every day," I said. "I wish we had shows like *Property Twins* or *Fixer Upper* back then. I would have been a contestant for sure. It's easier for them to work with people like me who already have a refined sense of style."

"*Property Brothers*, Mom."

"That's what I said."

"We need to get on the road; let's finish packing up the van." Carl wrestled on his shirt.

"Packing up *Ernie*," I emphasized.

"Ernie?"

"That's his name."

"How do I not get to name my own van?" He squinted at me.

"We all voted; I thought you were there." I kissed him on the nose and moved to claim the front seat.

"Fine, we can call him Ernie after Ernie Banks," Carl said. "Best ball player the Cubs have ever seen."

"If that's what you need to tell yourself," I called from my perch. "Either way, his name is Ernie and Ernie is ready to get this show on the road."

"'Home is behind, the world ahead, and there are many paths to tread,'" Reese said in singsong tones and threw an arm around her dad. Carl didn't acknowledge her outwardly, but from the look in his eyes, I knew he was melting inside.

"'It's a dangerous business, Frodo, going out your door,'" Benjamin said.

"Especially for you. I don't know if you've noticed, but you tend to be a bit of a klutz." Reese peeked at him over Carl's body.

"'A wizard is never late, Frodo Baggins. Nor is he early. He arrives precisely when he means to.'" Blake flung his bag over his shoulder and Reese smiled at him.

"Way to keep up for once."

"For once? I set the pace here, baby." He blew her a kiss and strode to where Ernie and I waited, blissfully unaware of all the trip would bring.

13

Bernice

Carl insisted he drive the first stretch of our trip and good Lord, who agreed to that? Don't get me wrong—he was a safe driver, always has been, always will be. But he was a little *too* safe if you ask me. Carl believed it was about the journey, not the destination. Great balls of fire. If the speed limit was sixty, Carl went a cool fifty-five and thought he was living it up, spreading his wings, letting himself go, and all that crap. I'm a lady; a lady with places to go. And this old man was holding me back.

When Carl announced his Grand Adventure, his Trip of Carl—or a glorified "road trip" if you want to know the truth—I had to cancel a few appointments to get on board with his spontaneity. I swear that man will be the death of me. But, then again, I couldn't help but think it was cute how seriously he was taking his second chance at life and love with me.

"I'll be the first to admit my idea of a good time includes you sitting next to me on the beach with cocktails." I patted his arm as he drove.

"That sounds nice, honey."

"Or a couple's massage in one of those huts where you can see and hear the ocean." *Not* a van stuffed full of three twenty-somethings. But no matter, sacrificing our dreams is what mothers do. It seemed we were all making up for lost time.

"Oh, yes. I like the way you are thinking." He grinned and tapped the brakes as he noticed a bird a mile away. I rubbed my temples and exhaled so they could all hear.

Carl got under my skin like there was no tomorrow, but I loved him like no one else on the planet.

We were sixteen when we met, all starry-eyed and wild. I'd moved up to "The Good Life" from the golden land of Mississippi, and I was immediately the most popular girl in the school. He was the star of the basketball team, and by my junior year, I was the head cheerleader. Carl was tall and thin, but not too skinny like those other boys. He had hair as black as onyx and dark green eyes, with teensy streaks of gold. We had three classes together that first year—English, Biology, and Advanced Math.

He looked at me as I walked into class on my first day, and I marched right up to the second row and plopped down beside him. I was one of four girls in the latter two courses and without conversation or planning we sat beside each other in all our classes. We were like magnets, he and I, destined to be each other's centering in the cold, lonely universe.

He was sick with the flu the third week in October, when the trees were their most vibrant shades of yellow, red, and orange. I felt sick too, desperate to have his quiet self back by my side because he was always the best part of my day. I wore all my prettiest dresses to school that week, day after day, wanting to look my finest when he returned. Each day was a battle royale for my mother to let me wear my Sunday best, but it was worth it, knowing I'd be shining when I next saw him. I hoped he'd be excited to see me too, that he noticed my absence like I did his.

When he didn't come to school for the fourth day in a row, I showed up at his house in the afternoon, in my blue dress, with my hair curled within an inch of its life. I scrunched my toes inside the leather patent Sunday shoes I'd snuck out of my house from under my mother's ever-watchful eyes. My stomach ached and my head too, but when his mother answered the door, she took the pile of jottings and books and sent me away without inviting me in to see him.

I hoped she wouldn't see the note I'd stuck between his math homework. *I miss you. I'm blue.*

He never said a word about it, but after that, we took up walking home together. He rarely talked, but he looked pleased as I chattered and explained and told him my stories. He was too shy to ask me out, but I could see the desire in his eyes and so one day, when we were walking down 52nd Street, I grabbed his hand and kissed him on the cheek.

"I couldn't help myself," I hummed into his perfect ear, undone.

We were inseparable for the next two decades.

We did homework in each other's living rooms, applied for all the same colleges, danced under the stars almost every night, told secrets for hours on end until I knew him better than he knew himself.

He was mine, completely.

And I was his.

I was too young to realize a love like ours was rare, beautiful, something to be cherished.

I was too naive to understand how complicated life can become.

I sighed, I fanned my fan. Highway 29 North didn't offer much in the way of scenery. I changed radio stations even if others were singing along. I was restless, a little bored if you want to know the truth.

"Do you want me to drive, sweetie?" I fanned him too.

"Oh, no, no, no. I will carry this burden." He squeezed my hand and missed my grimace.

"I need to pee."

"Bernice, we left the house ten minutes ago." Carl looked wary.

"Well, that's the problem, I peed before we left."

"So you're fine."

"Carl, I am *far* from fine. Once I open the floodgates in the morning, the floodgates stay open. I don't know what to tell you."

"Can you hold it?"

"We shall see." I caressed Rocky and rolled my eyes at the state of things in general.

"I'll stop in the next ten minutes then." He sighed.

"Make it five and make sure you stop where I can get one of those fancy coffees too."

"But—"

"Carl, I need it." I licked my hand and slapped it on a stray wisp of gray atop his head.

"Okay, kids, who's been reading the news?" His voice was ten shades of happy. "Capital of Romania?"

Carl used to be that parent. The one who interrogated them on current events or geography over dinner. He gave the kids extra reading assignments on all their summer breaks and ignored their complaints because he said they'd thank him later. Of course, teaching our kids they should be independent thinkers led to Lord knows how much sass over the years, which was plumb annoying. But he liked to think they secretly loved his foray into academia, so as the sun climbed hazily behind us, he continued.

"Tell me what you know about the Bay of Pigs."

"What year did the United States become a nation?"

"How do you feel about America's current foreign policy?"

"Where do I start?" Blake pulled at his baseball cap. "How much time do I have?"

As the kids talked over themselves, I glanced in the visor mirror, and the clock wound backwards, whirling through dozens of moments like this, years of my kids' laughter and love. I loved every second I heard my children's voices, though they were adults now, far too old for this foolishness.

Carl must have been feeling it too, because he looked at me with tears in his eyes. "My Trip of Carl is everything I wanted. My kids have grown into adults."

"Might as well call it your Trip of Sappy." I rubbed his hand and looked out the window. That decade of lost years with my family haunted me daily of late, and I couldn't think about it anymore today. I refocused on pleasant things, like Margarita Mondays.

Half an hour later, all traces of nostalgia were decidedly lost in the chaos of the flat tire which greeted us within minutes of our post-pee break reentry onto the highway.

Blasted heat.

Blasted high spirits.

Blasted flat tire.

Reese thought the flat was hysterical and took photos of the whole thing. She ignored me when I told her my hair was too flat, and I couldn't be documented until a full twenty-four hours after I digested last night's burger. The swelling from that meal was unbelievable. Even my hands puffed up.

"Reese, that camera of yours adds twenty pounds to my fabulous figure. Stop!"

Click.

"I love my curves and your Mama's got the body of a goddess but your blasted camera makes me look like a pile of lard, a bowl of mashed potatoes—not my tubers, the lumpy kind."

Click, click.

Blake, Benjamin, and Carl all worked on the flat. *How many men does it take?* One by one, they took their shirts off, claimed it was too hot under the hood. I'm sure Carl thought it was sexy and masculine over there, but I assure you, besides Blake's abs, which were a happy surprise, it was not. And Benjamin, well, I'd clearly been too lenient with the cookies. Carl gave me a wink between his sweating and grunting. His hands had Lord knows how many layers of grease on them, and I looked away with a shudder.

Fifty percent of the tools they needed were missing. Fifty percent, people. Did they not think to check the spare tire situation before we left Omaha, all in a rush, in a tizzy? But they insisted they could make this happen.

I glanced at my watch.

Did I know how to change a flat tire in no time at all, without breaking a sweat?

Yes sirree I did. Did they think to ask me?

They did *not*.

These people were driving me crazy.

I looked at Reese. "You know the two of us could have had that tire changed in ten minutes flat."

"Five." Reese smiled at me before she fired another frame.

"Babies, I can't be in this heat anymore. I'm calling a cab. Y'all can pick me up at the first bar you see in Modale, Iowa." I waved my phone at them. They could catch up with me and my margarita when they were done. Story of my *life*.

"Bernice, it's ten in the morning." Reese tilted her head.

"You're right. I might want a little snack too."

When the taxi pulled up, I glanced back at her. "Well, are you coming or are you not?" Rocky barked his invitation from my arms.

"I am," she said, and she did.

Reese

Modale, Iowa must be the smallest town in America.

"Bernice, didn't you look to see if anything was even here?" I asked as she paid the driver in the middle of the quietest street in the world. "If I'd blinked, I would have missed this place."

"Word is that the whole town is a single square mile," the driver added.

"Why didn't you say so in the first place?" Bernice raged at him, making Rocky bark. "I picked the closest town. I'm not from here, I don't know—" But the driver zoomed off before she finished her rant. She shook her head at me. "No one has manners these days." And off she marched.

I was taking a photo of a duck crossing the street when she yelled at me from in front of a yellow building. "Reese, this place looks like a restaurant. It's called the Sour Mash and will open soon." I'd just taken my last frame of film, so I sat with her on the hot sidewalk to wait.

"How's Charlie?" she asked.

"Great." I'd talked to Charlie at 2 a.m. before we left and explained about Dad and Ernie and everything. "So I should go with them," I'd finished in a rush.

"Uh yeah, keep notes of all the craziness," he said. "I'll need to know everything that happens. And I do mean *every* detail." It wasn't until after I hung up I realized I'd forgotten to mention the insignificant fact of Blake's presence, but it really didn't matter. I told myself filling him in on everything else would take enough time.

Bernice looked at me. "What is it like—" But a honking Ernie drove up before she could finish.

"We might as well stay here and grab some lunch. They open at eleven," Bernice called to the guys, unmoving from our sidewalk seat. "And I can tell you one more thing: we're going to need to make this a short day. I'm ready for some pool time."

After lunch, we managed to drive two hours before Bernice decreed we were done for the day. We pulled off at the next town that had a hotel with a pool and spent the rest of the day recovering from day one of our road trip. I made a couple of notes for Charlie in the notebook I'd brought along before going to bed early.

The next morning Bernice greeted me with a "Hey, baby," and rubbed my back when I showed up for the hotel breakfast. I moved beyond her reach, and the men waved their coffee cups at me, all looking as if they'd been up for hours.

"I really wish you wouldn't call me that."

"*Sugar*," she enunciated her syllables distinctly, "I have an announcement." She stood with Rocky and adjusted her brightly-colored scarf.

"Oh boy." I reached for Ben's coffee.

"We are related to *the* Hamilton?" Ben looked between everyone expectantly.

"I won't throw away my shot!" I crowed.

"Well, I *am* young, hungry, and pretty scrappy," he said.

"You're adopting a second Rocky to give to Ben?"

"Now that *is* an idea." Bernice moved Rocky close to her face. "Do you want to play with a new brother or sister?" Her voice was high and fake.

There was a sharp kick on my shin as Ben asked, "What's up, Mom?"

"We'll have her give Charlie a dog," I whispered to Ben out of the side of my mouth, and he gave me a thumbs up.

"Yes, honey, what's on your mind?" Dad had acquired a rancher-style hat from one of our many gas-station-pee-stops the day before, which he'd perched atop his salt-and-pepper hair. He hadn't stopped smiling since we left Omaha.

"As I was *saying*, I have an announcement. I am taking us on a retreat. Last night after dinner I went through the rack in the hotel lobby and found a brochure for a family retreat center. I made some calls; the rest, as they say, is history." She looked pleased. I ingested the news and waited for the punch line.

Nothing.

I looked at Ben, who was halfway out of his chair from laughter.

"It is called The Center for Family Relaxation and Inner Healing. There is a lake at the retreat center and some complimentary sessions with a guru, for inner family healing. We will go for three days and two nights."

"Absolutely not. I'm not going." I was already shaking my head. "Hashtag, boundaries."

"You want hash browns, Reese?" Bernice frowned at me.

"Uh, sure, I'll eat some hash browns. But this is me doing a sit-in." I crossed my arms and smiled. "My peaceful protest to your family retreat."

"Could it at least be a silent sit-in?" Ben leaned back in his chair, and I gave him the stink eye.

"Oh Reese, it's healthy to get out and about and see the world." Bernice waved her arms to demonstrate. "It's two hours from here, in South Dakota, only two hours further north than we need to go, so it's right on the way. It will be a big worldly experience for all of us."

"Mom does have a point there." Ben was almost crying from glee; Dad nodded as if this wasn't the craziest thing ever proposed in the family.

"Guys, three months ago I was in Ireland with Blake. I live in Atlanta. I see the world."

Bernice ignored me. "I was surprised they had such last-minute availability, but as they say—serendipity. So I booked two cabins. Reese and Benjamin: you are sharing. But then there is the problem of Blake." She pursed her lips in his direction. "We're heading there today, and he clearly can't come on our *family* retreat weekend, but he can't stay here." She looked peeved, and I grimaced an apology at my friend.

"Bernice, don't talk about him as if he's not two feet away from you. And fine, I'll stay back with him." I grabbed an orange from the basket and peeled it with precision.

"Young lady, you will do no such thing." She twirled a piece of hair around a perfectly manicured finger. "It's not proper."

"Oh Lord. What is happening to you? I'm going to grab some food, and we can discuss this like rational humans when I return." As I drifted to the food bar, I heard Bernice's giggle.

"Maybe I should take you men with me and leave Reese at a spa in town. Lord knows she and her high horse will make the two days all about her and her eye rolls."

"I can hear you." I turned and granted her a glare.

"Oh, sorry." She winked at Blake.

"You need to rein her in." I wagged my finger at my twin.

"I'll see how I feel this afternoon. It's never too late to drop her off on a doorstep along the way."

"Bernice!" I slammed my plate of fruit onto the table, but she ignored me.

"Take a look at these." Bernice patted Blake's hand as she passed out brochures. He looked at me beseechingly, but I ignored him and moved the pamphlet where I couldn't see his eyes.

"Conveniently located northwest of Aberdeen, South Dakota." Ben waved the glossy paper.

"I've always imagined myself shining in a place like Aberdeen," Blake drawled.

"Can we take a moment to note that, according to this 1970s-esque brochure, the retreat center says we are allowed to bring our journals, pens, and two changes of underclothes. Are we not worried they used the word 'underclothes'?"

"Nope, I'm not worried at all." Ben's face was blank. "Besides, we can also bring organic soap, glitter, and cash."

"Glitter is on the list?"

"Arts and crafts."

"Great! So we can explore the childhood we lost. I have a stash of popsicle sticks begging to be used."

"Ahem, we are *not* allowed to bring anything else, which includes cell phones, computers, e-readers, chargers, extra clothes, extra food, non-organic soaps, aluminum foil, batteries, video cameras. Reese, why aren't you taking notes?"

I pinched his thigh under the table.

The Do Not Bring list filled two entire sections of the leaflet. The retreat was obviously going to kill us. That might explain Bernice's excitement over the idea.

"We all need our rest and relaxation. Self-care, people. Reese, if you want, I will pay for a mani and pedi for you on the way this morning—not the gel kind of course, those are expensive. But the plain, straightforward kind. A woman needs to be a woman and having a pedicure is part of it."

"No thanks. To all of it." I handed her the brochure.

"You are all going and no complaints. It is the last request of a formerly dying man," Dad said.

"You know you can only use that card so many times, right?" I eyed Dad. "Besides, we need to get Blake to Chicago. We promised."

"Right, well, I can book a room in a town outside your retreat center and work from a coffee shop." Blake smiled, a little too good-naturedly. "Really, I can write here as easily as I can write in Chicago. It makes no difference to me."

"I'm sorry about this inconvenience." Bernice offered him a limp shrug. "But you can see this is so important for our family, Blake. Thank you so much for understanding and being willing to change your plans. You all need to be ready to go in an hour." She jumped up from the table and grabbed Dad's hand, pulling him out of the room before I could protest further.

Ben tipped back on his chair with a shake of his head. "Well, Mom has done her share of wacky things throughout the years, but even she outdid herself this time."

"Where were you with this astute assessment two minutes ago, Dr. Howser?"

"Reese, who are you kidding? Saying 'no' to Mom is like trying to negotiate with Che Guevara. It's simply a dead end."

"Uh, it's like fighting Stalin and Mussolini's love child."

"It's like—" Ben's dark eyes gleamed as he leaned toward us.

"It's like the First Battle of Athenry." Blake tapped the table with each word. We stared back at him.

Right.

"Yes, maybe. There has been some recent controversy about the details of said battle, didn't you hear? It's scandalous." Ben nudged him.

"Oh right. Americans only study American history. I forgot." Blake pressed his lips and reached for his coffee.

"Speaking of being American, we're rather steamrolling you into this little change of plans. Can you handle the heat?" Ben made a face of mock terror.

"Well, I suppose I could take the bus over to Chicago from here, though my uncle's house is empty and waiting for me, so it doesn't really matter when I arrive." Blake looked at me with a question in his eyes.

"Ben, Blake, do you hear yourselves? Earth to my martians. We can't go on this retreat. We're setting ourselves up for failure."

"Oh, I'm going. You're going. We're all going. Dad said!"

Despite the detailed packing instructions, Bernice rolled three suitcases into the "take" pile for our 10 a.m. departure.

"You have a lot of journals." I waved toward her flashing trio on wheels from my station by Ernie's door.

"Actually, it's glitter I collect."

I made eye contact with Ben as he shoved a beer from the cooler into his pants.

"I'm leaving my phone." He made a show of handing it to Blake.

"Let me know if you want to sneak away in the night," Blake whispered in my ear when we dropped him off in Aberdeen, leaving a sea of butterflies in his wake. But the feelings were soon eclipsed by our arrival at The Center for Family Relaxation and Inner Healing. Bernice hopped out of Ernie and wheeled her largest suitcase up to where a man dressed in a white robe waited on the porch outside the main cabin.

"Carl, grab my other two bags, dear," she called over her shoulder.

"Someone's excited," Ben said. We watched as she ignored the man's outstretched hand and went in for a hug. When he moved to extricate himself, she didn't let go. He said something we couldn't hear.

"Now that wasn't very nice," Bernice spoke loudly and held the robed man at arm's length. Rocky ran to where they faced off and barked at their feet.

"Like I said, Fidel Castro's double. I have twenty bucks on the lady in red." I calmly popped a piece of gum into my mouth. Ben and I hung back with Ernie as Dad wheeled over her two other suitcases.

"Actually, you said no such thing, you said—" but before Ben could get warmed up, the voices on the porch escalated.

"Ma'am, you need to remove your nail polish, leave at least two of your fifty-pound suitcases in the vehicle and 'robe up' or remove yourself from the premises."

"I will do no such thing, young man!"

I snapped a couple of photos and stuffed the camera behind my back before they noticed.

"I wonder how one becomes a guru," Ben said.

"Is he the guru?"

"Reese, he's wearing a white robe."

"Touché, brother. Okay, well, in this case becoming a guru was easy." Bernice had called on our drive over with a "few" last-minute questions, and I'd listened in on the conversation. "Apparently, he is a self-proclaimed guru." I was proud of myself for holding in an eye roll. "Bernice said she was happy to champion his dreams."

"Wait, you can appoint yourself a guru?"

"Well," I waved at the scene before us, "no one is stopping him. And apparently *some people* even pay him money for his so-called guidance."

Bernice proceeded to empty her suitcase across the front lawn as the guru looked on. One after another, she tossed her items into the air.

"I think I will need my eyeballs bleached," Ben said as she threw a tiny green nighty high.

"And to think I almost didn't come." I sat cross-legged on the dirt. Bernice marched in circles in front of the guru, pumping her hands into the air. Dad made a move toward her, and I thought she might punch him. There was really no telling how this weekend would play out.

Dad eventually corralled Mom into a compromise, and an hour later we all stood in front of the white-robed man. He stroked his beard as we contemplated each other. He was tall with red hair that he'd tied into a man bun, looked as if he was in his mid-thirties and ate tofu three times a day.

"Alright, we shall begin with introductions," he murmured and stuck out his hand to Ben. "Good day, sir, what are you called?"

Ben leaned and kissed his hand. "I'm Sir Alexander Hamilton: the first of his name, ruler of Knoxville and the southern kingdoms. And you are?"

"I am one with the earth, with your family. I am your guru." He stuck out his hand to Dad. "What is your name, good sir?"

"Carl," Dad boomed. "It's nice to meet you…?"

"Carl." The ginger granted him a small smile.

"Yes, he said his name is Carl, and mine is Bernice." Bernice leaned close to his face and enunciated slowly. "What's *your* name?"

"You may call me Guru Carl." He gave a small bow.

"I'm Reese, and I'm going to take a nap." I gave a small bow in return and shuffled backward. Guru Carl moved to block me.

"Young Reese, Alexander Hamilton, Bernice, *Carl*—welcome to The Center for Family Relaxation and Inner Healing!" Guru Carl thundered with his arms open wide. "I hope your time here does indeed bring family healing, inner healing, and relaxation."

"Ohhhhh. So we get family healing *and* inner healing here? Sign me up!" Ben grinned, and I held in a giggle as Bernice pinched his elbow.

Guru Carl patted him on the head. "Your time here will be scheduled and I will lead you as I see fit. We will enjoy any number of group activities during our three days together. Pretend you are at camp, but open up your hearts. You all have demons to battle during your stay, and I am here to lead the way. I hope you, especially, Carl, will find a role model in this place."

"Why me?" Dad asked, but Guru Carl was already floating ahead, motioning for us to follow.

That first morning Guru Carl instructed Bernice and Dad to hold hands and jump into the lake in their matching transparent shifts ten times in a row. It was my favorite memory to date.

I ran to Ernie, grabbed my camera, and took a few pictures of them bopping around in the calm blue waters before Guru Carl noticed me. He chased me, but I raced back to Ernie and locked my camera away. That was one line Guru Carl was not allowed to cross.

My least favorite memory was the lengthy moments it took Bernice and Dad to remove their bodies from the water, encased in the soaked, diaphanous garb, after each jump. "I can't unsee that," I muttered to Ben, who looked like he might cry. Those images, though not captured on film, would haunt me for the rest of my life.

Bernice glowed.

Literally glowed. I attributed it to all the enlightenment she received until Ben revealed that instead of dabbing a drop of peppermint oil behind her ears, as Guru Carl instructed, she had emptied the rest of the bottle on her chest and neck.

She spent the day beaming, adding suggestions to Guru Carl's plans, and smelling minty. When he asked us to hug each other in turn, she insisted we hug each other thrice. When he wanted us to throw a rock into the lake, she dictated that we all yell a dream to go along with it.

"I want to fly to Jupiter." I heaved my rock into the lake. I was quite enjoying myself. Now that we were here, it was better than I could have hoped, complete with a fake guru and a mandatory schedule. No one else associated the details with a cult, but by the way Guru Carl spent three hours over our first dinner explaining *his heart*, I'm fairly certain he was out to get new recruits. But for once, the rest of the Hamiltons had decided to be placid.

By nightfall, we sat around the circle stabbing our fire with sticks.

"Where are the marshmallows?" I was hungry. I'd always loved fires and thought I might actually enjoy the evening until Guru Carl opened his mouth.

"My children, now is not the time for sweet treats. Now is the time to listen to our hearts." Even sitting, Guru Carl looked tall by firelight. "This is one of my favorite moments with any family. The moment of truth. The moment to dive into the unknown and make it known." He stood and walked behind us, waving his hands over our heads.

"Geesh." I slouched on my stump.

"I think you, young Reese, are called to go first."

"Um, if anything I'm called to go find another sweater. Or another family. But thanks." I didn't even pretend to make eye contact with him.

"Reese, tell me about your family. About your family's strengths. About your family's weaknesses. Tell me what is *within* you Hamiltons."

"Okay, first of all, this is definitely more of a whiskey conversation. Second of all, that's definitely more Alexander's department. Third of all, I'd still like that whiskey."

"Oh, soul. You know the here and now is not a space to dabble with inebriation. Squire Alexander. It seems the call of truth is something with which your sister is uncomfortable. Perhaps you could speak to the sinew of the Hamiltons?"

"Well, now that you mention it, I have a few thoughts on this subject." Ben leaned toward the fire.

"Of course you do."

"Did you say something, Reese? I see us as a family of stallions, of elephants, of any wild beast." Ben stuck his tongue out at me behind the guru's back. "Our spirits are being reborn, even here, even now. And I think this is the moment to reveal our deepest darkest secret so we can move into our new creation. Reese, do you want to tell us all about the time you stole $20 from Dad's wallet?"

"I was borrowing it, and no."

"What about the time you streaked down our street on a dare?"

"I don't know what you're talking about."

"What about the time you made out with our cousin, Jonathan?"

"I didn't. It was Marc and how did you even know about that?"

"It's alright, Reese. This is a safe place." He rubbed his hands together over the fire.

"At the time, I didn't know it wasn't okay to hook up with second cousins."

"Now when you say 'hook up,' do you mean first base or third?"

"I was fourteen! I'd had a glass of wine *you*'d stolen from the adult table."

"Woah, sister, woah. It's okay. Calm down. No need to rile yourself up."

Guru Carl cleared his throat loudly. "I believe we're getting off topic."

"Not necessarily. I firmly believe the sexual explorations of the young reveal so much about our inner angst." I'd never seen Bernice look so sympathetic. "I've read about this in the magazines."

"Bernice! There were no 'sexual explorations.'"

"Bee, I really don't have a need to talk about anything sexual with our kids." Dad and I spoke over each other.

"Or *do* we need to talk about this?" Ben asked, and I glared at him. This was becoming a nightmare.

"Ben, you're such a nob."

"Who's Ben?" The guru looked around.

"Use some respect when addressing my penis."

"Gross. I'm not addressing it. I'm saying you are one."

"You hung out with it for eight months in utero."

"That's true, Reese, you did. Eight months and one day. And the mere fact you bring it up while concurrently denying the need for a sexual discussion is interesting and something we should certainly explore. Those eight months were a time of—"

"A time of what, Bernice? A time when you couldn't escape us?" We were eons past Too Far.

"Okay, okay, baby girl. I know you're angry."

"Let it out, young Reese." Guru Carl looked at me with kind eyes. I wanted to punch him. "Why don't you ask her a question and try to understand?"

"Fine," I snarled. "Why did you leave us, why didn't you ever once try to come back, what in God's green earth makes you think it's okay to waltz back into my life when you ran out of it so long ago and never once tried to see me again?" My throat went tight and ended my screams. *Why did you leave me, why did you leave me?* It was the only question I ever heard, always on repeat. I shoved it so far down I couldn't see it anymore because to hold it too close would mean my heart breaking all over again. Through the wet of my eyes I could see Bernice's shoulders slump.

"Okay, Hamiltons, I think we need to take a collective breath." Guru Carl looked pleased. "And remember—"

"This is stupid. I'm done." I stormed off toward the cabins, throwing my stick as I went. I heard someone, presumably Ben, hurrying after me, but I slammed the cabin door so he'd get the message.

At six the next morning, Guru Carl sounded a cowbell outside our cabin doors and herded us down to the water like cattle.

"Sit," he commanded the four of us, indicating a circle of stumps in the sand. "You failed last night, and now we try again. I've never lost a family, and I'm not about to start with you."

I glowered at him and hugged my gray robe close. Bernice, resplendent in a silk nightgown, moved her stump next to Dad's, where she snuggled into his side. Dad's salt-and-pepper hair stuck out in clumps beneath his rancher hat, and Rocky settled between us.

Crickets.

"Somebody ask a question. Any question." Guru Carl folded his arms. "No one gets their breakfast rice until we make some progress here."

"Rice again?" Bernice squinted. We'd had rice for lunch and dinner the day before.

"Yes, the white grains have spiritual, cleansing powers," Guru Carl said in hushed tones. "It's all we eat here. Now somebody ask a question."

Bernice stroked Dad's face, I looked away, Rocky barked at something in the middle of the water.

"Fine. Where are the other families, the other people?" I waved my hands toward the otherwise empty campground. "I've counted a total of seven cabins and five humans. Besides us, there isn't another living soul."

"I only take one family at a time so I can give them the whole of my attention. Unless I decide to allow in two or three families. It depends on how much attention family number one needs." He gave me a pointed look.

"But how do you know—"

"Shh," he said and glided away to stand by Dad. "We're going to look into each other's eyes and think nice thoughts. Alexander and Reese, partner up first. Carl and Bernice, you do the same."

I sat across from Ben. *This is dumb, this is dumb. This is dumb.* He crossed his eyes.

"Good, good," Guru Carl murmured beside me. "I feel your energy, Reese. It's beautiful."

"Isn't it though? And thank you, Reese," Ben said.

"Huh?"

"For telling me how much you admire me and want to invest all your savings into my dreams. You won't regret it."

"I—"

"Okay, now we switch." Guru Carl clapped. "Ladies, pair up and look into each other's eyes. Men, you too. Ask each other a question from your heart, with your heart."

"Should we hold hands too?" Bernice peered anxiously at me.

"I don't think—"

"Yes," Guru Carl said as Dad shot me a look. She grabbed my hands, and I looked at my feet.

"Look into her eyes," Guru Carl instructed, and I dragged my eyes to her face. Guru Carl moved to stand beside Ben and stared at Dad. I felt a laugh in my stomach. Bernice made a face at me and the laugh inside me grew. Out of the corner of my eye, I watched the guru inch his face closer and closer to my father's.

"Well, don't kiss him, he's mine!" Bernice jumped up and raced to the men and my laugh seeped out, slow and sweet and didn't stop for a long, long time.

Time with Guru Carl was equivalent to dancing on the moon or living in southern California—it simply didn't add up to the reality in which the rest of the planet existed.

I stayed all three days at The Center for Family Relaxation and Inner Healing with a resignation I didn't recognize. I hated it at first. The forced talks, the push to resolve. And yet, in some seemingly horrific parallel universe, when I let myself relax, our time in the woods—our weird, freakish, overpriced time in the woods—was more wonderful than I could have ever imagined.

I grew to love the simplicity of living in the moment with no distractions. I enjoyed the days without external pressures and lingering through each hour.

We continued doing the dumbest things with Guru Carl—painting by numbers, sitting in the lake for an hour straight, going for walks while holding hands. I suspected he made up his curriculum as he went along and experimented with how nonsensical his commands could become before we revolted.

We didn't revolt.

"Guru Carl and Bernice together have broken me," I whispered to Ben as we sat beside the lake watching the clouds as per the guru's instructions.

"Yep, it's too much to resist them both at once." Ben nodded and sketched a cloud onto the paper Guru Carl had given him for that particular purpose. "We will never speak of this again."

"What will we tell Blake when he asks about our time?"

"We'll tell him it was fun and change the subject."

"And if he pushes us for details? It would be great material for one of his books."

"If he wants more information, we tie him up and leave him in the badlands of South Dakota," Ben said. "It's as simple as that. This," he waved his hands, "can never be common knowledge."

"Guru Carl is simply *The Best*. How is the world lucky enough to have two strong Carls in it?" Bernice batted her eyes and sighed contently. She'd insisted we take some girl time in the lake as our last activity, and while I wasn't keen on the idea, my options were limited to having lake time with my mother or helping Guru Carl paint cabin four—an activity he called "bonding." We'd been luxuriating in the cold pond water for the hour.

"Uh, I think the whole 'my name is Carl' thing is all for show."

"What?"

"He probably names himself after one of his guests each go-around." Our self-proclaimed guru never answered when I called out "Carl" and I could certainly see him as the type of wackjob who imagined Dad would feel a kinship with a teacher who bore his name. It was a theory I was perfecting, but I knew I was headed in the right direction. "I found multiple name tags shoved in a shoebox in the common room, but no Carls. Interesting, isn't it?"

"He's so wise, so grounded." Bernice ignored me. "I've never before seen a young man who overflows with so much enlightenment. Being around him makes my spirit come alive like nothing before." My mother's hair floated about her smile.

"Right." I really didn't have the energy. When she looked crushed, I added, "Your spirit does look lively." I wondered how the guys were doing with the painting.

"This was exactly what we needed as a family. I have been watching the light come back into everyone's eyes, and I like it." The beam she offered could have filled the lake. "I have waited for moments like this with my family for so long, and I am happy to be the one who made it happen," she simpered and floated closer to me.

"Well…" I bobbed away.

"I really thought we got somewhere this morning during the Family Love session, when we went around saying something nice about each person. I liked it when you said, 'Bernice taught me if I can't say something nice, to not say it at all.' I did teach you that. You remember, don't you?"

"I said I did."

"But you don't have to call me Bernice. You can call me Mom." Her eyes were shiny, full of hope.

I splashed her. "Okay, Bernice."

"You are far too big for your britches these days, but I see the ice cracking." She tilted her head, grin growing. "Crack, crack, crack."

"Time to go, girls," Ben called from the shore, and I swam out fast. We packed up and before we piled into Ernie, I threw my arms around Guru Carl's neck for a hug and a quick selfie with him before he could say no.

As we pulled away from the retreat center I watched GC, as we now affectionately called him, wave, and turn to go.

"Dad, stop!" Suddenly, I was certain we'd left something behind. Ernie screeched to a stop and, panicking, I jumped out with the others trailing behind.

"What did you leave, Reese?"

"I don't know."

"Reese, think. We don't have all day. Blake is waiting for us."

Ben and Bernice circled me, growing louder and more insistent with their questions. The cabins turned up empty, and when I couldn't put my finger on exactly what we were leaving, what we'd miss if we didn't stay, they boarded Ernie and pulled me in after them.

As Dad sped off, GC faded smaller and smaller into the distance, and I tried to convince myself it would all be okay. But I couldn't shake the chills on the top of my head, at my spine. We had left something that mattered there, and I wasn't sure we could ever get it back.

14

Reese

We picked up Blake—who looked as cute as he ever had—from a coffee shop where he was working.

He looked between us. "How was—"

"How was writing?" I jumped in.

"I'm struggling," he admitted. "I know I want to write, but every time I sit down, the words remain elusive."

After that, we all fell quiet and managed to drive an hour west before Bernice decided she was hungry.

"Rice was probably a good diet for some people," she looked at me, "but Mama needs a steak. We can call today Bernice's Day."

"I thought every day was Bernice's Day," Blake said mildly.

"Nowhere, South Dakota looks as good a place as any to stop," Dad said as we pulled off at the next exit. "I'm sure we can rustle up a steak somewhere."

After dinner, we all piled into one hotel room, trying to find something to watch, because even after the long day of activities, no one except Dad was sleepy. But after three full days of nature's silence, the commotion of the television jarred.

"Can't you picture me as Santa?" Ben said, shutting off the television. Bernice and Ben had spent the greater part of dinner weighing the pros and cons of throwing a Christmas-in-July party on the road and were apparently re-opening their dialogue. "I'm a natural." Ben flapped his hands while Bernice laughed and walked in circles with him as if they were in a parade.

Blake looked intrigued, and when he started asking them questions, my hasty departure went unnoticed.

When we were little Mom and Ben had 364 days of the year to enjoy their special bond, but Christmas had always been my day with her. From October onward, Mom and I geared up for our celebration. We baked cookies, lavished the house with tinsel, played Christmas music on repeat for weeks on end. We bought matching Christmas sweaters and visited Santa in the mall to get our photo taken, year after year. She'd sit me down for twenty minutes under the harsh lights of her bathroom and transfer upon me the ritual I'd watched from afar over the years. A dusting of blush, a swipe of mascara. We even spritzed on the Chanel for such an occasion. The year I was twelve, mere months before her exodus, I refused to go with her, and she went alone. We'd argued, and I was angry at her, wouldn't indulge in her merriment. I had never been able to remember why.

I woke up the next morning to find a giant framed photo of her and Santa watching me sleep. She was like that.

Growing up with Bernice was like living every day in a candy store. She believed in treats, in fairy tales, in all that was enchanting.

She often woke us up at midnight on our birthday with a cupcake and a song.

She spontaneously mesmerized our entire third grade class with her rendition of *Thriller* when she stopped by to drop off a jacket I'd left at home.

When we had crazy hair day at school, she crimped and dyed our hair with Kool-Aid. For crazy lunch day, she made me a peanut butter, apple, and bologna sandwich, the perfect blend of delicious and disgusting. Ben got a fried green tomato and apple mix. All the kids thought we were the coolest.

We lost part of her when she was promoted to partner at work; her co-workers received so many hours of her love and attention there was little left for us when she got home, tired and full of fury. I resented them, the unknown associates who got her cookies and her smiles. I battled to win her assiduity, but there was no going back.

When she left us, it rained for three days and three nights on end, the sorrow of the heavens in one monstrous upheaval of misery, the firmaments dislodging the thousand tears I could not.

I went to visit Santa alone the year she left; the photo shows bright pink cheeks and lipstick outside my lips. I'd found her old makeup at the back of the bathroom cabinet, dusty and cakey. I didn't believe in Santa anymore, but I hoped she'd be there waiting for me, that some osmosis would draw her back to the place where anything could happen. I went every day for a week and when she didn't show, I walked home and threw away all her makeup. I hadn't had much use for the stuff since.

For all those years she'd made the ordinary extraordinary, and when she left, whole pieces of me exited too. I was transported from the land of whimsy to the land of acrimony, almost overnight.

I hated her for it. I hated her because I loved her and sometimes the line betwixt is so fine the tiniest wind will blow one over the edge. And the currents of her escape carved a wake so vast it left me capsized. I hadn't quite walked sturdy on my own two feet since.

When I let myself back in the room, Bernice and Ben were leaning toward a "no" for the mid-year Christmas celebration.

"Since we can't have Christmas cookies and they're half the fun." Ben pulled his hoodie over his hair.

"Benjamin, are you pouting?"

"No."

"Right then. No cookies, no party." Bernice clapped her hands and with a resounding tinkle, it was decided.

I ignored them all and went to bed without a word.

The next morning, I convinced Dad to relinquish control of the wheel for our late-late morning start. Thanks to the flat tire, the countless bathroom breaks, the stops to eat, the so-called retreat, and Bernice's multiple requests, we were already on day five. It could have been a lifetime.

Four days to drive 200 miles, people, I lectured them in my head. But with me behind the wheel, we should be there by dinner. All three men piled into the back and were sleeping within minutes.

"Reese, I can only sit in this vehicle for ten more minutes today," Bernice said and from the corner of my eye, I could tell she was staring at me.

I turned up the radio.

"Wowee. Mama needs a break. Make that a double break, with a side of double wine. I'd share my bottle with you, but then we'd need someone else to drive. I vote for anyone except Carl," she cackled from the passenger seat, but I didn't respond.

Apparently she didn't need me to reply.

"Well, then. I am going to keep the map on the dashboard in case you want me in a pinch, Reese baby, but I need these vents pointed at me so I can sleep in peace."

Everyone was asleep, and as I watched the road ahead, I became inspired. I checked the passing signs to make sure I was correct and changed lanes to take the connecting highway.

Two hours later, Bernice was the first to wake. "Reese, where are we? I don't see any signs for Rushmore. You promised we'd be there pronto. What's happening? I demand answers." She checked her appearance in the mirror.

"Of course you do, Bernice." I looked over my left shoulder and changed lanes.

"Watch that tone with your mother," Dad called from the back. "But do you need help with your directions?"

"I'm no expert on U.S. National Parks or geography, but I know something isn't right," Bernice said and Rocky barked in agreement as she grabbed the map.

"It's fine, guys. I'm only changing the itinerary." I kept my eyes forward and held in a grin.

Bernice

"We are 157 miles off the route, Reese! Take this exit. Okay, fine, take the next one and we'll only be five more minutes behind schedule. One sec, I'm rerouting." Benjamin brandished his phone near our mutinous driver's face, shouting directions patiently, then impatiently.

Reese ignored his commands, one after another.

"It's about the journey, right, Dad?"

And then it was pandemonium, pure un-calculated chaos. Still Reese kept her lips sealed and wouldn't divulge her master plan.

"This is your doing, Benjamin." I shook my head at him.

"In what universe, Mom?" I'd never seen him look so frustrated. "Take this exit, Reese, or there's not another one for miles."

"Well, you are always encouraging Reese in her independence. But I can see where this could be a result of *your* DNA, Carl." Carl laughed until he cried and only shook his head.

"Or you, Mr. Blake. Flying to Omaha on a whim, as if the world can be built upon the spontaneous. Reese, where *are* you taking us?" Despite her sass, my baby looked so pretty behind the wheel, cheeks flushed, head held high.

Finally Carl said, "Enough. This trip is about the journey; not the destination."

If I'd rolled my eyes at Carl declaring "it's about the journey" once, then I'd rolled my eyes at him a thousand times. But sometimes it's not about the journey. Sometimes we need to get to the darn place. As it turned out, the darn place Reese wanted to get to was the Grand Canyon.

"The Grand Canyon, people, is north or south of Mt. Rushmore, not the way we're going. Any fool with two cells in their brain knows that." I crossed my arms over my chest. "I need to pee."

"Mom, *Reese*, the Grand Canyon is southwest of Mt. Rushmore."

"That's what I said." I taught that boy how to use a map, basically how to do everything he knows.

"Reese won a prize for geometry in the eighth grade, not *geography*, but she still thinks the fields of study are related," Benjamin whispered to Blake behind us. "I'm not sure when she thought the Grand Canyon cheekily moved north to Canada."

"*Geo*graphy, *geo*metry. You're not the only brainiac in the family, Ben. Besides, no one else thought to seize the day and take a pit stop by the Grand Canyon since we're so close anyway."

"*So close.*" I fanned myself. "Bless your heart, sweetie, I'm going to buy you a globe."

"You already did," she said, and I was shocked she remembered, but before I could say anything, she continued, "Blake lives in Ireland; he hasn't been this close to the Grand Canyon in at least a decade. Come on, people! Where's your sense of adventure?"

"I suppose Chicago will still be there next week," Blake said. "But Ernie says he's hungry, Reese."

"We're all hungry," Benjamin added.

"If I pull over, will you still let us go to the Grand Canyon?" Reese asked.

"No," Benjamin and I spoke forcefully together.

"Exactly." She sped up.

While she was distracted, I grabbed Reese's notebook to add some notes.

Do not forget... To tell my mother I love her today.

Do not forget... I should NEVER wear orange. This is a BAD IDEA, Reese. DON'T do it.

Do not forget... That my mother loves me too.

Do not forget... That I am horrible with directions.

I closed the book with a sigh. Bless. I had done my duty, I was plumb wore out and closed my eyes.

My phone buzzed. Benjamin.

Mom, do you care about the journey or are you hungry? Maybe it would be good for you to get out and stretch your legs. You know, find a clean hotel to rest. Text me back.

Good plan, son. Ernie's good for a few things, but comfort isn't one. I will wait for your move. Wink at me when you're ready. I added a cute smiley face and hit Send.

The wink didn't come, but the gas did. It was lethal. I fanned myself and Rocky and thought about daisies.

"Who did that?" Benjamin spoke indignantly toward the group at large. "This rudeness is downright distasteful." I looked at Blake suspiciously, and Benjamin gave me a wink. I slapped Blake's knee and turned around with a snort.

"Though no one would expect anything less from an Irishman," I muttered and hoped he heard me.

Reese looked at Benjamin in the rearview mirror with disgust, and I watched him shoot her a shiny look of innocence.

"Blake, are you an ale man or do you prefer a nice lager?" I thought Benjamin was planning an uprising, not their next beer tour. I rolled my eyes.

"Reese, why haven't we had much Italian food while we've been at home? I have been craving manicotti all week."

"I know what you're doing."

"But also, a big spinach salad sounds delightful. Oh, or freshly-seared salmon."

In less than an hour, Benjamin had caused enough anarchy in the confines of our vehicle I was surprised Mr. "It's About the Journey" Carl didn't climb into Reese's lap to pull Ernie over himself.

Finally Carl spoke firmly, "Reese, we will let you take us to the Grand Canyon—Mt. Rushmore can wait—but you need to pull over now."

Reese pulled over at the next exit without a fight.

"And that, my beloved sister, is how you stage a mutiny," Benjamin said as we drove along the strip of restaurants.

"Whatever, Ben. You're not the one who just get a whole stop added to the trip." She turned off Ernie's engine and threw a peace sign over her shoulder as she hopped out. I gave a nod to no one in particular and heaved myself out of the seat. She did make me proud.

Reese

I may or may not have miscalculated the distance to the Grand Canyon, and the morning after my hijack we were still 1,000 miles away. As Ben drove, I pulled out my notebook and added some notes for Charlie.

Do not forget... the feeling of this road trip.
It is summer break, Fridays in high school, taking my first car for a spin.

It tastes like coconut popsicles, a root beer float, green apple Jolly Ranchers, strawberry bubblegum, a Jones Bros. vanilla bean macaron.

It smells like sunrise, rain, like stale and new, old and green.

It looks like bright spectrums and sunset, a blank page in a journal, a brand new map.

It sounds like laughter and fights, tears and silence, Taylor Swift, Johnny Cash, and Bob Dylan.

It feels like Family.

Do not forget the way Blake looks at me, like I hung the moon.

Do not forget the sensation of his hand brushing the back of mine in passing—rough and silky and a thousand tingles in between.

Do not forget, do not forget.

I swear, I won't.

He is kissing me, kissing me and I trace kisses down the side of his cheek to nuzzle into the warmth of his neck. I soak in the danger and safety of him. I move my hand up and down his arm and he—

The snores startled me awake, and I looked around Ernie in confusion. Ben drove and Bernice prattled on about nothing beside him. Dad dozed in and out of sleep in the middle section which meant the shoulder I slept upon belonged to Blake. I turned.

With his mouth gaping, his snores were as obnoxious as a freight train. The haze of romance I'd so palpably experienced between us evaporated into jagged pieces with each objectionable bellow he sent in my direction.

Confused, I sent Charlie a text before I changed my mind.

Blake stirred beside me, and I watched a smile spread across his face. Those snores must be doing something for him. His breath was ripe. I gave him a rough shove and scooted to the opposite window to feign sleep.

After the next stop for gas and lunch, Bernice nabbed the driver's seat, and I maneuvered my way up to the front passenger seat before anyone else could claim it.

"People, we have thirteen hours between us and the Grand Canyon. Let's make it happen," Ben called from the back.

"Benjamin, baby, Mama's got you," Bernice said as she looked between the rearview and side mirrors and pulled onto the road. A small laugh escaped my lips as I peeked at the speedometer, but I said nothing. I was learning to stay silent. Through the years I'd watched her checking for cops as she zoomed about. She'd never once been in an accident, but her legendary lead foot had gotten her pulled over for speeding on numerous incidents. In true Bernice fashion, she talked her way out of every single ticket.

She attributed her reigning success to the flirting, of course. She was a terrible flirt, and I honestly think she wore the officers out with the sheer deluge of her words.

"So, Blake, you're a writer." Bernice switched lanes without looking.

"That's the word on the street." He leaned forward from the row behind us.

"Are you going to write under a pen name? You look more like a Wilfrid Xavier, something more dignified."

"Thanks…I think."

"What are you writing? A red-hot romance I'll need to read with an icy margarita?" She sped up.

Blake's eyes bulged. "I'm more of a creative non-fiction guy." He'd once told me it was the genre of serious, legitimate writers.

"Creative non…what?"

"I've been trying my hand at a story about my mom's family, but I've been stuck, which is why I'm heading to Chicago. I'm hoping being at the scene of the crime, if you will, will act as a sort of reset button for my writing."

"Maybe I'll write a book too. One about myself. What do they call it? A biography?"

"An autobiography."

"That's what I said, an autobiography."

"No, Bernice. Ernie says there are already too many writers on board." I was surprised at the firmness in my words. I don't know why her jumping on the writing bandwagon annoyed me, but it did.

"Fine, well I could at least write the foreword for your book, Blake. Let me check my schedule," she simpered, and I stifled a snicker.

Blake and I made eye contact in the visor mirror and smiled at each other for weighted minutes. He broke our trance first and pulled his Cubs cap low over his eyes until I could only see his smile. It stayed there for a long, long time.

I never thought we would be those people, the ones yelling at each other in the parking lot in Page, Arizona at 3 a.m., but so much that summer was unexpected.

I wondered, if we dissected it later, if either of us would even be able to remember how it began.

By pre-arrangement, Blake and I had snuck away to the State 48 Tavern once everyone was asleep. After they called last drink, we ambled through the blackened streets, talking about our school days, tests we'd cheated on, the worst kisses we'd ever had.

And when we kissed, standing under a cold row of streetlights, the future flickering around us and the distant hum of cars, I forgot everything else. One leisurely kiss that left me breathless, longing for more. He wasn't wearing his cap and his thick clean hair curled around his ears; I reached and touched the half crescent on the edge of his neck.

Walking with Blake was happiness, like anything could happen. And safe—being with Blake was perfectly comforting.

In the cool of early morning, under the moon, he clasped my face between his rough hands and gave me one soft kiss after another. I broke away first. "Race you to the lodge!"

We sat on a stone wall outside and played "Would You Rather" under the stars and made promises we'd never let the other pass into obscurity. Life was too short, we said. It seemed so easy then. We kissed some more.

"Reese, can we talk about us?"

"Shh," I murmured and kissed the curl right under his ear. Tonight was for kissing and believing none of the hard questions mattered.

Later, mid-laugh he asked, "So when do you plan to start your own photography thing or whatever it is you want to do in life?"

"What's that supposed to mean?"

"Maybe I said it wrong; I wasn't trying to be harsh. I've watched you the last three years, Reese, and I know enough of the backstory to believe there's something more inside you." The supernatural powers of the night evaporated in seconds and left behind an Arctic I'd never known.

"Because I wrote you some letters?"

"Okay, I'm going to ignore that you said that. Reese, you know you have always stood in Charlie's shadow, answering to him even though you are as good as he is, if not better in your own way."

"You know nothing about it."

"Reese, you want to go out on your own again. I know it. I see it in you. I believe you can do it. I believe in you."

"Oh, you know how to be a photographer now, to run a business?"

It seems insane it spiraled so completely from there, but it did. He tried to hold me, to calm me, but I would have none of it. I let the anger take me in waves and if it didn't exactly feel good, at least I felt something.

"Your family believes in you too." He grabbed my chin and I twisted away.

"Don't talk to me about my family."

"You have an incredible family, Reese, but you barely appreciate what you have."

I glared at him and spun to stomp off.

"I think it would be good for you to get on with your own life, to embrace the family you have, to live your own dreams."

"What do you *really* think?" I spit out the words, let them ring with bitterness.

"I know you need to stop letting Charlie tell you what to do. You are enough, Reese. You have what it takes. Be *you*."

I snapped back around. "Be *me*? What does that even mean? And you don't even know Charlie."

He shrugged. "I think maybe you are amazing at life, at taking risks, except when it comes to Charlie and photography." It felt too close to everything I feared.

"And *I* think you're bossy, an Irish boy who is too scared to leave the farm and try your hand at real life. You say you're a writer, but when was the last time you wrote a bloody thing? You're waiting for life, for the world, to come to you, and you pretend you can't do anything because your mom died." And then I stopped, horrified at what I'd said.

"Reese." He ran his hand through his hair.

Even I knew I'd gone too far. I couldn't even say sorry, just turned and ran away like a ludicrous little baby.

15

Bernice

"This should have been our number one stop all along." I held Carl as we inspected the view. We'd made it to the Grand Canyon and wowee, she was a beaut. I visualized Carl and me building a little mansion right there on the edge, sipping our coffees with the warm tones of the Canyon around us each morning.

"I'd take that with a side of pie."

"You want pie, sweetie?" Carl squeezed my hand. "I could use a big slice of chocolate myself." He kissed the side of my face.

"I'm dreaming over here." Maybe not so close to the edge, in case Carl started to sleepwalk in his old age. I pictured him wandering about, shuffling in his slippers and naked under his robe, right over the edge of the Canyon at 2 a.m. That would be that, my dear. I imagined the white wood against this bronze background and my smile zoomed past the sides of my face.

"Live here with me forever?" Drat, that's not how I wanted to say it. Carl's face wore a peculiar look, but he nodded and clung to my hand.

"Oh yes, let's live here." His words were so low I almost lost them in the air between us.

We were never the mushy type, but maybe we were turning over a new leaf. People do that, you know. Carl and I clasped each other for an hour right there beside the Canyon, letting the dust drift into all the inches our words left empty.

This place spoke to me.

Sometimes I imagined telling my children my side of the story. I dreamed I sat on them and made them listen until they finally understood.

He stopped seeing me, stopped trying. He wasn't there for our family. Everyone told me that was the way of it, that all marriages grew cold and dull. But not with us, not with him, I couldn't stand for it.

I'd almost left once before when you kids were little, two screaming babies, a mountain of diapers, and hardly three hours of sleep each night. Carl had been so excited to have children but something happened after your first birthday and he mentally checked out. He'd come home from work, sit on the couch for hours, not lift a finger to help. I begged, I pleaded, he stared past me. When I found five minutes to shower, I cried. When I went to bed, I cried. I was at the end of my tether, met myself coming and going. I thought I was going to lose my ever-loving mind. It lasted for six months and when spring came, Carl came back to me. I don't know how to say it other than that. He'd left, he came back, and I almost imagined it had all been a bad dream. Until it happened again.

The second time, I persevered for two years until I thought my very being would implode from agony. But he wouldn't hear me. Now I think he couldn't. So I did the one thing I knew would snap us out of it, the one thing I could do to save myself from going crazy: I left. At the time I told myself either my sanity or my body needed to have a time out, and I chose the latter. It was supposed to be for thirteen days, not thirteen years.

I'd been parenting solo for two years. I thought that two days managing on his own would wake him up. And the man I knew and loved couldn't be a day without me. I swear I thought he'd come after me. He'd find me, fight for me, no matter where I hid.

But he didn't.

He didn't fight for us, and I hated him for it.

My phone calls were met with acid and disdain.

When I gobbled my dignity and showed up at the house he slammed the door in my face, told me I wasn't welcome, wanted, or needed. I hated him almost as much as I hated myself for not taking you kids with me.

I'd lost him and lost you; with that, I lost myself. Now it all sounds crazy, but then it was all we could see. We lost our way, which was much more complicated than it sounds.

And now I lived with my decision in the eyes of my children, two grown adults who acted like strangers though I remembered the intricate details of them.

I knew them.

We all grow and change with time, but not that much. I told myself they were old enough to realize there were two sides to every story, the only consolation to which I could cling.

For now, Carl and I had let each other back in and that was all that mattered. This extra chance at happiness was a lifeline, a second chance to dance and Mama was ready to tango. And maybe someday, when I had wrinkles around my eyes and held my grandbabies tight, they would listen to what I had to say. They—Reese—couldn't shy away from this love forever. I would tell this to myself over and over until it rang true, until it let me sleep at night.

We'd gathered our kids and Blake at the best vantage point we could find. My anticipation doubled by the minute.

"Your father and I have something to say, and we'd like to say it here—"

"So you can pre-visualize," Carl interrupted me with a squeeze of the hand. "But, I'll let you take it from here, honey."

"Picture this." I drew them all to the view with a wide sweep of my hands.

"Yes, we're seeing it." Reese plopped onto a rock.

"Well, we'd like to renew our wedding vows right here. Tomorrow. At 5:12 a.m. So our love can shine with the brightness of sunrise, the new day."

All three kids stared back at us with glazed eyes.

"And you're all invited!" I wiped the corners of my eyes and went between them doling out hugs. "Do you have any questions? Need to know your assigned roles for the day?"

"Um, congrats?" It sounded like a question. Blake shook Carl's hand

and gave me a small hug.

"I hate to jump in here, but you have to be married before you can renew your vows," Benjamin said.

"Oh, that's no problem." I moved beside Carl.

"I mean, I suppose you can do some sort of symbolic vow sharing and then take care of the legal paperwork later. You can probably go the day after we return to Omaha. Unless you want to wait and have your big wedding there?" Benjamin removed his glasses to mop the sweat from his forehead.

"I mean, it's no problem because we're not divorced. We never filed one single paper."

Carl was giddy. I was giddy. Benjamin looked back and forth between us. "Huh."

"Come on, Benjamin, get excited with us." I beamed at my son.

"I'm trying. I'm just—" he shrugged and twisted toward me. "Okay. I'm having a vision of you arriving in a limousine." He widened his hands to paint the picture.

"That would be classy, and you know Classy is my middle name."

"I thought it was Sassy, but sure."

"Son, you've officially been promoted to my man of honor. We've always had a special bond, and this is my way of saying thanks."

"It doesn't sound as nice as bowling."

"Oh Benjamin, I'll have a list to you by 3 p.m. today."

"Fine, I'll do it as long as I can wear a top hat, black tie, and tails."

"Baby, we'll talk details later." I caressed his head.

"Can we go now?" Reese sighed. "This was funny, haha, but I'm hungry."

"Reese, sweetie. You do know this is real, right?" Carl reached out to give her a hug.

"No!" Reese stood, eyes on fire. "I thought this was all some sick joke Ben put you up to."

"I wondered why you'd kept quiet for so long." Benjamin edged closer to his sister.

"So this is actually happening?"

"Yes," Carl and I chorused together.

Dust flew from Reese's heels as she stormed away. Carl and I studied each other, then looked at Benjamin.

"This is your bed, parents." He shook his head.

Carl squeezed my hand and headed toward our baby girl.

Reese

They'd managed to shock me again.

Dad held me while I cried. When he finally spoke, the thunder in his voice surprised me.

"Reese, I love that you are a strong girl." He paused and cleared his throat. "You are a strong *woman*. A woman who knows her own mind and has well-formed opinions."

"Dad, stop."

"You remind me so, so much of another beauty in this family. Every day you remind me of her in a hundred ways. Mother and daughter with stares so defiant, mirror images of determination."

"You've got to be kidding me."

He ignored my grimace and held me as I struggled to get away. "But you are wrong about your mom."

"Dad, I'm not wrong—"

"I know your heart is closed off toward her, but you don't know her half as well as you think you do. Yes, your mom left me all those years ago. But I don't blame her; I would have left me too."

"Dad, don't be silly."

"Back then, we didn't have labels, but mine may have been depression. Bernice tried to help me climb out, but I pushed her out and locked the door."

"Dad." I bit my lip.

"For so many years I didn't even know how to reach her, but she's here now, and I love her. I never stopped loving her."

I shook my head so hard it hurt. "No."

"I always have, and I always will. I know you don't understand what happened between us—heck, I don't understand all of it either.

177

But what you need to know, Reese, is that your mom forgave me and I forgave her."

I couldn't meet his gaze.

"Celebrate our happiness with us. After her love, you and Benjamin are the very best gifts your mother ever gave me." Eyes glistening, he reached out for a hug. "And I need to tell you one more thing—"

But I turned and headed to the horizon.

"This was a bad idea." Two hours later my shirt had darkened a full shade with sweat, and I sat down in the middle of the trail. Mom and Dad were on a wedding planning date this afternoon, so Blake, Ben, and I had voted to take on a section of the North Kaibab Trail. The Arizona sun beat down on us without mercy. "I give up. We've already hiked, what, eight miles give or take?"

"Try take. Reese, we started half an hour ago." Ben pulled his Superman T-shirt over his head and slung it across his shoulders.

"No, I don't believe you; I already have blisters."

"He's right, Reese." Blake sat on a boulder several feet away and wiped his forehead with the back of his hand. I didn't look in his direction—we'd hardly talked since our fight.

"Are you guys giving up? I can leave you two here and sojourn on alone," Ben said.

"No!" Blake and I were in agreement for the first time all day.

"Come sit down for five minutes, Ben. Help me plan how we're going to stop the wedding."

"I don't want to stop the wedding. I think we should leave them be."

"Leaving it be is not exactly my forte."

"Not exactly?"

"Why is it so easy for you to get on board with them and their insanity? Why aren't you angry too?" My words ran together and I kicked the dust at my feet.

"Reese, you're obviously upset. Let's all get into a yoga pose. On the count of three: one, two—"

"Stop it, Ben."

"Okay!" Blake's worried expression was almost endearing. "Cersei, Jaime, you need to stay on opposite sides of the trail, and we can all enjoy a nice time out."

"I suppose there is always The Red Wedding route." Ben fanned himself with his shirt.

"That's a bit harsh, mate." Blake leaned forward. "Side note: did you know they filmed a lot of those episodes in Northern Ireland?"

"Yeah, I was reading that."

"Uh, guys. Please stop geeking out on me and focus." I threw a pebble at each of them.

"I'm a Tyrion man, what about you?" Blake said it like a challenge. "Though of course I'm a Snow fan too."

"You know nothing, Jon Snow. What about Daenerys? Since book slash season one, Maya has been shouting out theories about the two of them getting together, even though she says they're surely related—you'd know something about that, Reese—and ruling forevermore."

"Guys!"

"Are you caught up?" Blake squinted at Ben.

"Nah, I'm a couple of seasons behind. I read the books before I watch the corresponding season. It's annoying, but it's my thing. I wish winter would come *now*." Ben mopped his forehead.

"Are you guys talking about *Frozen*?" I glanced between them.

"Or imagine if Daenerys could storm in, pun intended, and take over all seven kingdoms in one fell swoop. She doesn't need a man to help her rule." Ben could talk about his nerd stuff for hours. "I know I'm enough of a feminist to write that in, but what about George? I have my doubts."

"I like what you're thinking." Blake looked amused.

"Maya was so proud when I told her I'm a feminist. She tells her girls every time they come over for wine."

"Seriously, can we have one adult conversation?" I sprang to my feet.

"What, are you upset because you're not the only feminist here?"

"Right now I'm a *silent* feminist. You should try it. I'm never really in the mood to wave my bra around, and besides, I loathe labels." We were so far off topic.

"Reese, what are you talking about? Bra waving can be so freeing."

Blake poked a stick into the dirt. "In my world, feminism is so much less about the bra demonstrations and so much more about the world believing a girl is as intelligent and capable as any dude in the known universe. Girls can kick arse out there, if they'd let themselves." His words were tight, clipped. "Or if others would let them."

"Maybe it's not always a sexist issue, maybe sometimes the girl isn't as good." My jaw stuck out on its own.

Ben cleared his throat.

"Or maybe she should try and see what she's capable of creating." Blake's voice held an edge, and we were definitely close to uncovering a nuclear war.

Ben cleared his throat again. "Okay, okay, feminism is a huge issue. We can answer any questions you may have, sister."

"Whatever, Ben. Let's just hike. And when your parents come crawling back to us in three months because the adrenaline has worn off, and they realize they've made a dreadful mistake, I will conveniently be out of the country. You get to help them sort the pieces."

"Reese, don't you worry your pretty little head. I believe in a thing called love."

"Just listen to the rhythm of my heart!" Blake fell to his knees.

"Fine. My family is clearly mad."

As I huffed down the trail, Ben called after me, "I honestly think this is their happy ever after. But please make sure you shower before the ceremony tomorrow or you'll kill the mood."

Bernice

I am a goddess.

I'd purchased one hundred candles the previous night and I prepared myself by their golden glow through the morning hours. I swiped on layers of purple eyeshadow as Vivaldi's "Four Seasons" played with majesty. I asked Reese to join me, but she preferred her beauty sleep. Carl and I had agreed to wear our matching flamingo shirts, and my last look in the mirror told me my cheeks were pink, my lips shiny.

We arrived separately at the Grand Canyon, the old-fashioned way, and I handed Rocky to Benjamin as I floated out of the taxi. "Don't let him fall over the edge, and don't let her throw us over either." I nodded at Reese who'd surprisingly shown up, but didn't look like she was ready to go all Shirley Temple on us either.

I glided toward Carl. Despite its early hour, the morning was hot, like our first time around the marriage corner, only not as humid. When I reached his arms, we both breathed a sigh of relief and let the tears gather in our eyes. I'd been terrified he would change his mind at the last minute.

"Well, here we are all these years later—second chance at my life, second chance with my wife," he murmured.

"Let's do this, sugar." I rubbed his bicep, and he offered me his arm.

"Okay, since we agreed to write out our vows, I need you to stand there so I can see your eyes, and you can know I mean my words." Carl moved me to face him. "Sharing my feelings has never been easy—"

"Don't I know it."

"I remember the days when I could grunt and walk out of a room. I miss those days. But maybe they were part of the problem too, at least to hear you explain it." He rested his hand on my shoulder. "So here we go, hold on tight." He fished two folded pieces of paper from his front pocket. "Bernice, I have two pieces of paper here. This one right here has been on my person since you gave it to me over three decades ago. Do you know what it says?"

I already had tears in my eyes as I shook my head.

"It says, 'I miss you. I'm blue.' This has been true every single day of the last thirteen years without you."

I miss you. I'm blue. I mouthed the words back to him as the tears coursed down my cheeks. I grabbed his hand and out of the corner of my sight, I noticed Blake furiously rubbing his eyes.

"Here we are, Bee, and here are my vows to you." He waved the second piece of paper. "When you sashayed into my high school, over thirty years ago, the whole world turned technicolor. From the monochrome of my life, I could see blues and reds, even some fluorescent pinks."

"Flamingos," Reese muttered.

Carl pressed on. "I suddenly heard all the wonder of the world, in everyday, seemingly dull, minutes. You gave me birdsong and the roar of the ocean. And when you left, you took all your songs and your colors and your wonder. Yet by some miracle, here we are, together once again."

I'm sorry, I mouthed, but he kept going.

"Bernice, you have always been my love, you are the mother of my children, the most beautiful wife of my youth. I don't know how to say all the flowery stuff. But this is what I do know: I know I love you. I know you are beautiful, on the inside and out. I know you are the better half of us. I know I want to spend every moment of the rest of my life with you. I know you sometimes drive me crazy; I know I drive you crazy too. I know even when the world seems fuzzy, our love is enough. So I re-offer you my love and my commitment, for whatever time I have left on this earth. You are my first love, and you will be my last. I promise to be faithful to you alone. I promise to listen to you. I promise to be the very best husband I can be and to stick around for as long as I can."

This was more than I could ever have wished for. I tucked a graying piece of Carl's growing hair behind his ear and unfolded my written promises. "Carl, you were not the man of my dreams when I met you, but you have since become more than the man of my dreams."

Lord, I could have written a book of vows. Mostly because I'm an excellent writer but also because I love this man so gosh-darn much. Since my time was so limited between making our clandestine plan and executing it, my vows were much, much shorter than they could have been.

"We have been through hell and back, and you are the only cowboy on this entire dazzling earth with whom I want to ride this rodeo."

The first time around, Carl and I got married at a courthouse, at high noon in the middle of August. The day was sweltering, but the courthouse was cool inside. We stood before the judge and tried not to watch the blob of mustard moving on his upper lip as he addressed us. I registered the slickness of sweat on Carl's hands as, drunk on love, we said "I do" and flew straight out to the daylight to celebrate with champagne and strawberries by the river.

We had a massive wedding planned for the following spring, with twelve bridesmaids and half a dozen groomsmen, with bows and bells and whistles, but we couldn't wait another day to commence our life together, so we married on a whim, in a fever.

We planned to tell our parents that night but stayed in the abandoned field with our love and strawberries until long after the sun went down and the stars came out. The stately yellowed grass was itchy and the field beyond was full of white flowers. Carl picked me a bouquet. The insects buzzed insistently about us, the faint smell of something ripe clung nearby. We held each other closer still, until I thought my heart would need to be sewn into my chest.

I never knew a love like this, and I drank it in like summer wine, like the river's flood, like it was my dying breath. I'd already told him all my secrets but as he held me and kissed me, rocked me under the moonless night, I told him deeper things still. I told him I was afraid of the dark, of death, of being insignificant. Deep in his arms where he couldn't see my gaze I confessed that I didn't understand God, had some questions about hell, and didn't like Frank Sinatra's voice.

He kissed me and listened. He listened and kissed me.

The dew settled over us and I smiled, knowing we'd found our happily ever after and no one else had a love like ours. We never did tell our parents; we went right on being married and running around like chickens with our heads cut off, planning our big wedding with smiles because we had a secret no one even suspected. We'd found each other and there was nothing more we wanted.

"You know all the parts of me and you love all my ways. Thank you. Through the years you have learned so much from me, and you've taught me a couple of things too. You drive me crazy. You make me laugh. You gave me two beautiful children that look like me, thank the

Lord. You are my sunshine and my rain, my river and my flood. You are the dance to my song, the jelly to my peanut butter, the flowers to my spring. You are the dull to my wild, the spellcheck to my novel, the toast to my breakfast. I am the spice to your soup, the jalapeño to your burrito, the amusing adjectives to your sentence.

"Carl, there was a time when I thought I would never see you again and I was glad. I was glad, Carl, because I'd let my heart grow bitter. But now I'm joyous you came back to me, and we can get this next party started. I am your sunshine. I am your rainbow. I am your princess. I am your darling. I am yours forever plus forever plus forever times infinity.

"Carl Clifford Hamilton, you complete me in one thousand and one ways and together we make the world a better place. I'll write you a book of vows on our next anniversary, when I have more time, but I hope you get the idea for now?"

He nodded, his eyes glistening. "I love you too, Bee."

All I could see was Carl. The Grand Canyon itself paled beside this man. I moved close to my groom and stood with him, forehead to forehead, breathing in our mixed scents of Chanel and spearmint, of clean and optimism. I could hold him like this forever. I never believed in second chances until now, but these days I clung to them like a drowning woman. This was the story of forgiveness, a story of hope. This was a story that would never grow old.

Our kids came to hug us after the vows.

"Can we sit here for a few minutes? I want to remember this." Carl was already heading to a nearby rock. Reese wandered off, but Benjamin and Blake stood near enough for me to overhear. Carl wasn't listening—he was oblivious—but I was all ears.

"So, that was special." Benjamin threw an arm around Blake's shoulder. "Dude, are you crying?"

"Standing here in dawn's primal greeting…It *was* special and now my handkerchief is a sopping mess."

"It isn't the only sopping mess I see."

"So much love." Blake sighed, and I wriggled out of Carl's arm to lean closer.

"Indeed, Romeo. Even the ice maiden looks as if she's melted."

Blake paused, as if considering something. "I had a crush on Reese when I surprised her you know, and said crush is snowballing into something more, something fierce. Danger personified."

"Stranger danger."

Carl exhaled contentedly and pointed to a bird. I rubbed his knee. "Shh."

"It makes me miss Maya. I wish you could meet her, dude." I peeked to see Blake staring at Reese in the distance. "You are batty over my sister, aren't you?"

Blake eyed him warily.

"She's crazy too, you know."

"Every morning when I see Reese, my mind is electrocuted." Blake's voice was clear, decided.

"I can see where the dramatic tendencies would draw the two of you toward each other."

"I see her, and I realize she's more beautiful than she was the day before."

"Okay, Pablo Neruda, this isn't the kind of stuff you should tell other people."

"What can I do?" Blake shrugged.

"All I know is you'd better say something soon. You don't want to miss your chance."

They drifted away, leaving me to figure out what I should do. When we could finally move again, we left the kids at the Grand Canyon to explore, while Carl and I went back to the hotel alone. Wink, wink.

It was early in the day, but I closed the curtains. "It's hygge," I explained and lit the sea of candles.

"Who?"

"It's all about the ambience." I grabbed the front of Carl's navy robe and drew him to me.

Later, we ordered room service and champagne and decided to jump online to book a real honeymoon. We lounged on mounds of pillows with our legs intertwined, his hair tickling the length of my legs.

"Honey, I'm sorry we never got a honeymoon the first time around, but I'll make it happen this time for you, my darling bride."

"Oh Carl." I smoothed his grayed temples.

"In all those years, I never wooed you, Bernice. That is about to change."

I kissed the bridge of his nose.

"Should we do Spain? Dominican? Name the place, darling, and I will take you there."

"I like the way you're talking, sugar." I ran my fingers up his arm, and he kissed the top of my cheek. "What about the Greek islands, in August?"

"But baby, you live with a Greek god every day of your life." He pinched my derriere.

"Oh, Carl."

"I should probably actually work for more than two days in a row, so let's make it September, but you can consider it done."

"I'll sell my condo in Toronto, and we can go crazy with the money." I propped another pillow under my head.

"Baby, we can go for the entire month and spare no expense. We will make up for lost time; heck, we can take a month away a year for the rest of our lives. Spain. The Caribbean. The moon, for all I care. Let's remake the dream list from our first go at this marriage thing. Nothing, absolutely nothing, is too much for my bride." He kissed me again.

"We can take the kids sometimes too. Maybe every other year they can come for a week."

"I have to tell you something." His face turned serious, gray, and my stomach clenched. "About the kids. About before."

"Oh, tell me tomorrow baby." I could tell it was going to be bad.

"I have to tell you now, as we're restarting, I have to—" He pounded a fist on the bed.

"No." I knew a sudden resolve. "Don't tell me at all. Let's each start

186

with a clean slate."

"Bee." He looked sad. "You might leave me again once I tell you." He started to cry, hot wet tears that fell from his cheeks onto my hands. Without meaning to, I started crying too.

I thought back to the pregnancy I'd kept secret. About all the babies he wanted and the ones I didn't, and how I'd been so angry when I found out I was pregnant that second time. I thought about the miscarriage I'd had the morning I left, and how I must have willed it into being. About how I'd wanted that baby so desperately as soon as I'd lost it, but nothing would ever bring it back to me again, and how I hated myself for it. And how I hated him too.

I thought about how I'd done the very worst to him and he to me. I thought about what else he could have done, and then I stopped myself.

"No matter what it is, I forgive you. Don't tell me at all. Let's move forward, not backward." I took his face into my hands and kissed him over and over again. Sometimes the only way through is to walk into the unmarred future, a new grace, an absolution in itself. Sometimes the only way to forgive is to force yourself to forget.

16

Bernice

"Let's recap for a minute: we're on day nine of our little 'five-to-seven-day road trip'." Reese made air quotes. "The upside is that we've met a self-proclaimed guru in South Dakota, been to the Grand Canyon, and renewed your vows—insert eye roll parade here." She pursed her lips as we regrouped at a diner in Utah for lunch the day after our vows.

"I feel the need to remind everyone that Mt. Rushmore and the Cubs were *the only stops* we scheduled for this trip," Benjamin grunted into his cup.

Carl smiled around the table. "Well, son, it's about the—"

"No, Dad. No." Reese shook her head.

"We can hit up Mt. Rushmore next year." Carl rattled the ice around in his cup. "Now that we have Ernie, we can take a trip every year. We'll fly in style, kids."

"Yeah, I can't wait to see photos of you all traveling about next year." Reese slurped her water.

"You're coming, Reesey. Ben too. And Blake. Maybe even Charlie." Carl put his arm around me. Benjamin choked on his gulp of soda and shot Blake a look that I'm pretty sure only I noticed.

"So what about those Cubs?" Reese swirled her straw around her drink.

"Okay, so here's the deal," Carl said, running his hand along my thigh under the table. "Our Cubs have upcoming away games so we need to stick to a schedule and get to Chicago before they leave. And no one has time for that. I've got some things to do."

"Ew, gross," Reese said, her eyes on his moving arm. "Yeah, nobody has time for that."

Carl removed his hand from my thigh, smiling. "So, the Hamilton plus Blake plan is this: Today, we continue driving east, toward home."

"If you let me drive, Ernie and I will have us there by tonight," I said and Rocky barked in agreement.

"It's another thousand miles. Let's aim for getting there tomorrow night," Benjamin suggested. "As long as we're in Chicago by the weekend."

"Right. The day after we arrive in Chicago we can watch our Cubs game. The day after *that* we must leave Blake in The Windy City and return to our respective corners of the world." Carl looked up as the waitress approached with our food. "Sometimes even the best of journeys must come to an end."

"So you people are promising me we will be in Chicago in under three days?" Blake made eye contact with each of us in turn, and Reese bit a French fry instead of responding.

Carl nodded. "You of all people need to get to Chicago, Blake, so let's get you there. Your book is waiting."

Two mornings later, we were briefly back in Omaha, waiting for Carl so we could get back on the road. Before we left for our trip, Carl had booked his "follow-up" doctor's appointment and our extended time on the road nearly made us miss it. Of course, I wanted to go with him, but he said I should sleep in, and I let myself be lazy. As we woke up, the kids and I grabbed coffees and wandered out to the front porch, one by one.

"If Ireland had a Mt. Rushmore, I'd vote for the face of Colin Farrell," Benjamin said from the porch swing.

"Oh, and Liam Neeson." Reese whipped her hair into a bun.

"Rory McIlroy, and—"

"Harry Potter." I filed my nails from the steps.

"Um, Harry is English," Reese said.

"Are you sure? I've seen a lot of red-haired people in that show."

"Sinéad O'Connor!" Benjamin pushed his glasses up on his face.

"Yes. Good one, brother."

Blake shook his head at the two of them. "We Irish would never desecrate Mother Earth with a Mt. Rushmore. *But if we did*, the Irish Cliffs of Moher would consist of Oscar Wilde, Benjamin Guinness, James Joyce, and—"

"Bono!" Reese hadn't been talking much to Blake, but she smiled at him then—whole and unassuming.

"Never Bono." Blake shuddered. "C.S. Lewis."

"The Narnia dude? I thought he was English," Benjamin said and Blake's face contorted.

Carl drove up, honking, and handed me a chai from Hardy Coffee Co. with a kiss. We clamored for the report.

"I'm fine. There had been one little abnormality from before. But it's gone."

"It's gone?" I eyed him suspiciously.

"Yes, Bee. One hundred percent fine and dandy. But right now, I need to run one quick errand. Blake is coming with me." Carl clamped his hand on Blake's shoulder.

"What, is he your favorite now?" Reese frowned.

"Daughter, you know I don't have favorites, but yes." He tugged her bun. "Come on, Blake, race you to the car." He sauntered past Blake, who widened his eyes at Reese and followed.

The kids and I were still on the porch an hour later when Carl pulled in the driveway ahead of Blake and one giant piece of crap.

"Carl, you have got to stop doing this, we're not a junk yard," I called. Why did they bring that monstrosity to my home? I could tell it was going to die on my lawn and want to be buried there too. I leapt up to let Mr. Blake know exactly how things stood.

That rust pile had to go.

"Happy Birthday, Ben! Merry Christmas! Happy Easter!" Carl yelled and before I could say another word, the three men commenced whooping around the car.

"Good Lord. You all like it?" Benjamin and Blake inspected every square inch of the beast as if it were pure gold. They patted it, rubbed it, grinned at it from all angles.

What was happening?

Carl grabbed me for a twirl right there in the middle of the yard and that was that. "It's okay, Bee. This is another thing I needed to do."

"I hope nothing else on this list of yours looks like buying a decaying pile of rust. It's getting passé." But my husband's strong arms pulled me into his familiar warmth, silencing my protests.

If I was going to be wild with anyone, it was with this man right here, and the road ahead beckoned.

Reese

I actually thought Ben's face would split in two.

A car.

No. *The* Car.

A 1964, rusted-out blue Mustang.

"Forget the Cubs. I can't leave my girl. I can't wait to get my hands under the hood." He'd circled it ten times.

"Ew, Ben!"

"I can't drive her all the way to Knoxville in this shape. I'll have to take trips back here to work on her with Dad, which I'm fairly certain is part of his master plan. And I love it." He ran his hands over the hood. Blake stood to the side with his arms crossed approvingly while Bernice and Dad danced around the lawn.

"You're almost cool enough for this car, brother." I opened the door and sat in the driver's seat.

"I can't wait to tell Maya. She's amazing at working on cars; she'll want to come too. Can you take a photo on my phone so I can send it to her?"

Ben couldn't even stand still for the photo, he kept twisting to inspect his new toy.

"Ben, focus!"

"Focusing is your job, get it?"

"Ben!"

"I shall call her Dolly. Or Mabel. Or Pumpkin. No, something sexier."

"Are we going to do this Cubs thing or not?" Bernice's yell jarred Ben out of his trance.

He shook his head. "Okay, so maybe let's not forget the Cubs."

He snapped a selfie and kissed her hood. "Goodbye, my Samantha." He didn't turn his back on her as he climbed into a waiting Ernie, and we drove on down the street.

After our eight-hour drive over to Chicago, Bernice insisted we go to a karaoke bar. "We are only this young once. We need to live it up."

Right.

Blake attempted a swift exit, but the parents were unanimous in their insistence he stay with us until after the game.

"Welcome to my life," Ben said as we passed a tired-looking Blake in the hotel hallway.

An hour later, at the moody bar, Bernice ordered tequila shots for the table. When half of us turned up our noses, she shrugged and downed the three extra shots.

"Now we sing," she proclaimed from atop her stool. "Blake, as our guest of honor, you're up first." When Blake protested, she came over and sat in his lap, as if the sheer bulk of her could convince him otherwise. He stood, dumping her to the floor and bolted left.

I waited half an hour before barging into the men's bathroom to find him huddled on the squalid floor. "I have my counselor on standby; do you need to schedule an appointment?" We'd been rather unsociable since The Fight, so I knew it wasn't so hard for him to ignore me now. "Look, Ben's on stage with Bernice. You can come out, I swear you're safe." I held out my hands, but he didn't meet my gaze. "Blake, I'm sorry about the other night. I shouldn't have said those things."

He finally looked at me. "Truce, Reese, I think we were both out of sorts." He shook my hand and stood. "I didn't mean to hurt you. I never want to hurt you." He pulled me in for a hug and I melted inside.

We finished making our peace in a hidden corner of the bar and two beers later, we sang a duet. Afterwards we went back to our stories and kissing in the corner. When he told me about the accident he'd had at sixteen while cycling, and that he hadn't cycled since, I invited him to a bike ride and coffee early the next morning.

Ten hours later, we whirled willy nilly on bikes through the busy streets of Chicago.

"You have to go faster," I called over my shoulder. "You're strong. You can do it."

We pulled over and sat under The Bean. The air itself was sweet, a slight breeze danced between us. Tourists milled about, but we hardly took note.

"You did so good." I grazed the back of his hand and tried to ignore the sentiment in his eyes.

"You didn't feel the daggers I was shooting at your back?"

"Oh, I felt them all right." I couldn't hold back the grin.

"Everywhere I looked, I saw large objects. Tall buildings, pedestrians, poles which called to me, begging me to run into them. Vehicles passed me helter-skelter, and I saw the nearness of death at every turn." He sighed.

"Now you're sounding like Bernice."

"Reese—" He looked at me so tenderly, I wilted inside. His gaze terrified me, and I spoke fast.

"So I was thinking we should each pick one thing this year, one challenge to work on. Maybe yours is riding your bike." I punched his arm. "Maybe mine is, I dunno, inventing something." I wasn't yet ready to speak what I was actually thinking. I told myself this could be the year of Reese, of courage, of dreams coming true. Maybe I'd grow out my hair; maybe I'd get a tattoo. I needed to figure out a way to stick to doing the hard stuff, without Ben, without anyone. And that was daunting on a whole new level.

"So *I* was thinking." He looked shy.

"Yes?" I shoved my hair behind my ear, heart thumping like it wanted out of my body.

"I'd like to take you on a date. Tonight, after the game. Tomorrow morning, sometime in the next twenty-four hours before we say goodbye."

"I'm not sure if—"

"I'd like for you to dress up, and I know you're capable of opening your own doors, but I'd like to open the door for you like a gentleman. I'd like to tell you all the things I've been thinking. I'd like to have one chance to woo you."

I couldn't meet his gaze. "Blake, I don't know if—"

"Reese." He lifted my chin. "Reese."

I looked into his kind face and my insides twisted.

"Please, give me one chance. I think we could be something great, and I think you know it too."

Between the tightness in my throat, I couldn't find words, but I accorded him a short nod.

"Okay, tonight then. I'll make it count." He leaned in close until I could see the smile lines around his eyes, smell his soap. "One date."

"One date," I said, and hoped it wasn't a mistake.

"And then hopefully a million more." He gave me the lightest kiss on the side of my face and my insides exploded. If I'd known what the rest of that day held, I might have lingered there with him a moment longer, but instead I said we should leave.

I thought about our pending date as he continued to watch me, as he ran a finger over my cheek, as he did a cartwheel when we stood to grab our bikes. I thought about our date as I reached for my bike and as I slide my phone from my back pocket to put in the bike basket.

But when I saw the text, I forgot all about him and sped away without a word.

17

Bernice

"Finally. After years of watching them on the television I have arrived. In Wrigley Field. Ready for an afternoon with my Cubs." Benjamin stood trance-like beside me.

I shook my head. "Oh Benjamin, you make it sound like they hung the moon."

He didn't answer but snuck down to the field. I watched him bend over and touch his cheek to the grass. As the security guard huffed over to our son, I smiled at Carl and ran my fingers through his hair. "So last night was…"

"Incredible. It was incredible, Bee."

It had been my shining hour and the music roared out of me. Once I got Benjamin off the stage, I crooned "It Feels Like Home" and focused on keeping the tears at bay. "Brick House" was for Carl. He knew what I meant. "Stand by Your Man" was for all the loves I turned down to come back to Carl. "Coal Miner's Daughter" was for Baby Bernice and Baby Carl.

This was it, my encore for my love, and I would not let it be cut short by even one syllable. I found myself growing sentimental again, but it was instead cut short by Benjamin's reappearance in the stands.

"What did the guard say?" Carl leaned over me.

"He was in a huff, told me I couldn't be down there."

"Well, that's silly," I said.

"I told him I'd waited my entire life to be here. He told me he'd heard it all before."

"You know what I say. Son, *live today, no regrets tomorrow.* Go back down there." I wanted more time with Carl.

"I told him he didn't understand the lengths it took for me to get to this patch of grass. And after I went into a five-minute commentary, in which I mentioned the trip was the last request of a formerly dying man at least three times, he turned a blind eye."

"Good job, son. Make your own destiny."

"Go Cubs Go! Go Cubs Go! Hey, Chicago, whaddaya say? The Cubs are gonna win today." Benjamin wasn't listening to me at all.

"I don't know what all the fuss is about. It's a bunch of sweaty men in unflattering uniforms. They toss the ball, they miss the ball, they stand around." I fanned myself.

"Mom, this is America's game!"

"Boooooooring."

"Mom!"

"If they would get some uniforms like those police officers, let's say it would be a step in the right direction. Whatever happened to top hats and tails? That Rhett Butler knew how to dress. My, if I could get my Carl to dress like him for one night, dot, dot, dot."

"Mom, stop!"

In response, I spritzed wisteria at his face. "Well, if you hadn't insisted we leave the hotel room before noon for a three o'clock game, we wouldn't have so much time for the chit chat." I pulled lipstick, a nail file, a book, two pairs of sunglasses, gum, snacks, a pen, and a notebook and placed them in a row on my lap. "Stop squirming, son, I'm going to work on my To-Do list." I waved my pen in his face.

"This really isn't the time or the place…" He shut his mouth.

"I also have Scrabble on my phone. I'm prepared for anything."

"Really, Mom?"

"Yes, if you download an application on your phone, you can carry it with you absolutely anywhere. It's the niftiest thing."

"You will not take this from me; I won't let you."

"Benjamin, what in the world are you talking about?" He ignored me and headed back to the ground level. "It's okay, don't mind me," I called to his back. "I'll just sit here like the princess I am and wait

196

for Charlie." He didn't even turn around at the mention of his friend's name.

Reese

I biked back to the hotel in half the time it should have taken, hardly noticing if Blake was keeping up or not. Charlie was there waiting when I arrived, taller than I remembered, broader too. I fell into his hug and his scents. He smelled like Old Spice, like clean, like home. I didn't realize how much I'd missed him until he was in front of me.

We sat and talked over each other for hours, and when it was time, I was transported to Wrigley Field—I floated, didn't take a step. Briefly, through a Charlie-induced fog, I noticed Blake arrive, then sit, watching me. But I couldn't tell what it meant, what any of it would mean.

And then, during the seventh inning stretch, there were a series of gasps as Charlie knelt in front of me. "Will you—" but before he could finish, I jumped backwards and ran up the stands. I swear, I don't think I even knew what happened until I was ten blocks away.

Charlie was back.

And he had proposed.

I began a steady spiral to somewhere outside my known universe.

I didn't even realize where I was heading until I was already there and when I arrived, I sank to the ground and waited. I knew he would find me.

We were still connected, even after all that time and all those miles. Charlie found me an hour later tucked away in that ferocious metropolis, and he claimed it was the first place he looked.

Once, when we were sixteen, we flew to Chicago for a school trip. We'd both placed in the school art competition and went with our friend, Alisa, for the Nationals. That night, after Charlie placed first and I didn't even get an honorable mention, we snuck out of our hotel and explored the streets of the city until dawn. We took hot chocolates and apple tarts from Mindy's down to Lake Michigan and told our dreams to the wind and the stars and each other. That was the first time I knew I loved him, that he was more than a friend. I tried to kiss him that night, reclined in close, intoxicated with the light of the moon and the smell of him. But he pulled away, and we've never spoken of it since.

When he appeared post-proposal, he brought me hot chocolate and an apple tart (*gawwwwd, how does he do it?*) and sat beside me in silence for an hour before he broke the stillness.

"So, I guess that was a bad idea?"

Instead of yelling at him, calling him a moron, I laughed. He always does that to me. He was my best friend, the keeper of all my secrets. He got me.

I'd always loved him.

"I was worried you weren't coming back to me. I was about to do something drastic," he said and grinned with both his mouth and his eyes.

"I definitely think this counts."

"Your mom kept me posted on the trip schedule." He ran his hands through his blond hair. I'd always love his hands, almost delicate but rough enough to be manly.

"Are you kidding me? Why do you talk to my mom?"

"It's not a big deal. She messages me constantly, but sometimes it works out. Like in this situation."

"It's still weird."

"Reese, I couldn't wait another day, another minute before seeing you." He caressed me with his gaze. "And I heard I might have a bit of competition." He came in for a kiss, concentrated and sweet, with a yearning I'd never seen in him. I'd ached for this entwining for so long, and I met his advances with an embarrassing eagerness. I'm a big fan of kissing, and it turned out he was a good kisser, a great kisser.

I extracted myself to hold his face, to pinch myself. "I've dreamed of this moment my whole life." Falling in love with my best friend—maybe clichés were nicer than I liked to think.

"Have you now?" He kissed my collarbone. His hair was soft beneath my fingertips. I drank in the experience of him. I'd waited for this meeting of hearts and lips since I was sixteen, but something felt off. I craved for this magic to taste credible, but when he kissed my neck, everything else went black.

We lingered there for hours. Once again we watched the distance and the lake, lying side by side on the tired dock, waiting for something, everything, nothing. After the initial silence, then the kisses, we couldn't stop talking. After years of avoiding the topic of "us" we escalated into story after story of wanting, not wanting, mixed signals, confusion.

"I've had a crush on you since our freshman year in high school, but I lost hope after you talked about Seth Stevens for months on end."

"What? No you didn't!"

"And the night you tried to kiss me right here, a decade ago, I was too nervous. And figured you were delirious from lack of sleep."

"Stop."

"All through university you were on a 'I don't ever want to get married' diatribe." He reached for my hand.

"I only said that because I knew you'd never be interested in me. And all those other boys were boring."

"Clearly." He smiled.

"Clearly." I smiled back.

"So I finally gave up all hope. I thought you actually meant it."

It was the most confusing, exhilarating untangling of stories and lives I could imagine. I kept still, all warm on the deck, under the blanket of revelation and mulled it over again. This is what I'd wanted for as long as I could remember and now I wasn't sure I knew quite what to do with it.

After long moments, even more questions, lingering kisses, and wandering hands, as the heat left the deck and the long, long lines of sunset appeared, I said I needed to think. When Charlie didn't respond, I realized he'd fallen asleep, and I kept my own company. The night turned orange, pink, purple. It faded into gray, then black and still we stayed back. I knew everyone was probably worried, wanted to know where we were and what happened. I knew Blake would be gone, at his uncle's at last, but I didn't let myself think any more about him.

I didn't dare move because I couldn't help but think if we shifted one tiny inch the illusion would shatter.

"So we can talk about it tomorrow?" he whispered so softly it was easy to pretend I didn't hear him. Instead I buried my face deep in Charlie's chest and willed myself to believe we would forever be this happy.

Bernice

"Mom, is there anything you'd like to tell me?" Hours after the game, Benjamin and I waited for Carl in the hotel lobby for our last night out.

"Benjamin, I've been dying to let you in on my secret. This is my effulgent moment. I invited Charlie here because I could see the way Blake looked at my Reese, because I started to see it echo back from her eyes too."

"Look at you, throwing out big girl words, while doing childish things," he said, and I could tell he was proud.

"I have another phone application for my words. I work on learning a new word a day. Effulgent was from two days ago."

"Right. Let's focus here. You don't think you could have left well enough alone, let the cards fall where they may, let destiny take its course?"

"Hogwash." I folded my hands in my lap. "You should be thanking me, it's Charlie."

"Mom. It's Reese's life. Blake's a good guy too."

"Don't get me wrong, I like the kid well enough, and I didn't mind the idea of her married to some foreigner so I have an excuse to travel and a place to stay. But Ireland? No thank you. If I can't have the Cabana boy, well, don't get me started."

"Right." He pulled out his phone.

"Besides, Reese and Charlie were made for each other. Since they were little tots, Leah and I talked about the dresses we would wear at their wedding. Leah would have killed me if Reese had wandered away to another boy under my watch. I've had a host of stellar ideas in my lifetime, but I must say this one is my tasty cherry on top."

"At the top of the charts, Mom." He gave me a thumbs up.

"I already sent a text to Leah, so she'd hear the good news from me first. Blake is a hot catch for someone, but only Charlie is good enough for my baby girl."

"Unbelievable, Mom. You are absolutely unfreakingbelievable."

"Well, Charlie and I are best friends—I had to do something." I clicked my heels on the tiled lobby floor and looked around for my husband.

"You had to do nothing." Benjamin rubbed his temple. I reached to smooth his hair, and he cringed.

"Benjamin, need I remind you Charlie's dad was a movie star and his mom was a swimsuit model? He got all the right genes, and I would eat cake off that backside."

"Mom!"

"I'm just saying. Oh, the grandbabies they will make me; a Mama has to think about these things. You're fine—Maya is a sweetie. I'm never worried about you."

"Thanks."

"And the proposal at the game? I wasn't expecting that. That was all Charlie. That boy is pure genius when he goes off script." I rummaged in my purse for my lipstick.

Benjamin walked away in response.

I watched his back blend into the crowd and shook my head. Everyone seemed so tightly strung. We were here to celebrate baseball and love and summer. If you ask me, what we all needed was a little time to kick back by the pool, to work on our tans and watch the drama between the lifeguards. It was like watching daytime soaps in real time.

Last week I pushed my cocktail hour to four instead of five, today I made it three. We were only there for one more day, and Mama was living La Vida Loca. I used to be such a teetotaler, but it was tiring.

So here am I to live a little. *C'est la vie*—I'll have no regrets.

Reese

I barged into the room sometime after midnight and sat on the massive pile of blankets.

"What, what? Stop. Zombies, I kill you." Ben thrashed his arms as I turned on the lamp.

"We need to talk."

"I kill you dead."

"The zombie apocalypse happened while you were asleep. I saved you, and you're welcome. So now it's time for a wee tête-à-tête."

"Did you use a bazooka?"

"A hand knife. We need to chat."

"Really, there's no other moment we can have this conversation?" He rubbed his eyes.

"No." I slipped my feet under his covers. "Ben, it was too much, too soon."

"And by *it*, you mean…?" He tucked another pillow under his head.

"Okay, here's the thing. Dream Proposal Scenario 1: My best friend wakes up and realizes he's madly in love with me and proposes out of nowhere in the middle of the street, in the middle of a laugh, in the middle of doing what we do best—simply enjoying each other. I cry and hug him and can't stop saying 'yes.'"

"That is beautiful indeed. Should I be taking notes?"

"Maybe. Okay, or Dream Proposal Scenario 2: My best friend wakes up, realizes he's madly in love with me and plans a surprise midnight picnic at the top of a mountain, or at the beach, or in Central Park and tells me I am the best part of his life and he never wants to be apart from me again in this lifetime. He loves me, he wants me, will I walk with him forever? I cry and hug him and can't stop saying 'yes.'"

"Right. Do all girls think about it this much? I'm starting to feel worried. Or maybe it was the curry I ate for dinner."

"Here's the kicker. Dream Proposal *Never*: After barely talking to me for months, my best friend surprises me by showing up to support me after my Dad was sick (yay!) and proposes in front of thousands of screaming strangers. My instinctive response is tears and immediate flight."

"It would have been awkward, except I barely noticed since I had the Cubs distracting me."

"I didn't want his proposal. I wasn't scared or angry or happy or sad. I wanted to run away."

"You *did* run away."

"So, what should I do?"

"Reese, I can't tell you that."

"Oh, but you can."

"Well, first of all, you could start where most people start—dating."

"Don't be coy, little man. We are light years past dating."

Ben grinned. "I figured I should at least give it a shot."

"So, where do we go from here?" Impatience percolated from each syllable.

"I mean, sure, if it were me, I'd be ecstatic to wake up next to Charlie's golden face every morning for the rest of my life. But that's me. You need to ask yourself if Charlie is it."

"How do I *know*?"

"Well, all Oprah and I are saying is this—if you can see yourself with Charlie forever, then marry him. If you think you won't run out of things to talk about fifty years from now, then marry him. If you can get into a fight with Charlie and come out on the other side stronger, then marry him."

"When did you become so wise?"

"Sugar, I was born this way," he said with a Southern drawl. He changed his tone and added, "And if you can look past Blake and where that might have gone."

I willed my expression to remain noncommittal, even if my heart skipped the smallest beat with the mention of his name.

"Keep it simple, Reese. Go find a quiet place and ask yourself the hard questions. For once in your life, don't make this dramatic."

"Ouch."

"The truth hurts, baby. Also, don't ever wake me up at this hour again." He folded back into his covers. "Oh, and sis?"

"Yes?"

"I love you. You'll make the right decision."

So I said yes.

Charlie had given me the key to his room, and I galloped inside around 2 a.m., expecting to have a long conversation. He was dead to the world, so I poked him repeatedly and said, "yes" in as many languages as I could remember, which only consisted of "yes," "si," and "oui," but I figured it would be good for our later retellings.

Yes, I would marry Charlie.

Yes, I would finish the story we'd started together oh-so-long ago.

Yes, I would follow him to the ends of the earth—hadn't I shown that already?

Yes, I wanted this.

Yes, I was being true to myself.

Yes, yes, yes—this was the only answer.

The more I said it, the more sure I grew. Yes, of course. The irony it took me half a day to sort it out was not lost on me. I had time to roll my eyes at myself between one more prod and "yes" before Charlie launched himself at me with tickles.

"This is my vision." I spoke quietly, since his face was inches from mine. "One day next week let's drive up to the peak of a mountain and say 'I do' in front of the clouds and wind and a handful of our closest friends."

"You haven't had enough time on the road of late?" He tapped my nose. We'd been engaged six hours, and I was loving every minute of it. Every hour with Charlie was another grand adventure, and he had whirled me to a quaint café first thing this morning. The other Hamiltons were running around Chicago seeing all the sights in their last vacation day, and Charlie was all mine.

I clasped the warm latte and held Charlie's gaze. "Okay, right, let's wait two weeks. The Rockies? The Alps? I'm happy with either. Or the Himalayas, we've never been there."

"Does Ireland have any mountains?" he said, his voice a cool neutral.

"I don't know, we can ask." *If Ireland had a Mt. Rushmore…* I felt my face flood carmine.

"I thought it might be nice to have our wedding in Ireland, since it's *our* place. And then it's easier for your friend Blake to come."

"Oh, I don't know." I looked away.

"Reese, is there anything you want to tell me?"

"What, are you jealous?"

"I mean, just because my fiancée and her family spent the last two weeks jaunting about with some guy I don't know, just because you've apparently been friends with him for three years, and I've never before heard one word about him, just because he looks at you as if you are the light of his existence. So yes, I have my questions."

"Charlie, you and I weren't together. Nothing happened. I mean," I fiddled with the end of his shirt, "it doesn't matter." I took a sip of my drink to avoid his gaze.

"Reese?"

"Whom should we invite to our vows? Right now my whole list consists of Ben, whom I have dibs on as my person of honor, BTW."

"What? No way. Ben is my main man. You can't take him from me."

"I have embryonic rights, dude. Step down." I couldn't hold my smile.

"We'll rock, paper, scissors it later, but for now, I'll tell you *my* vision—pizazz and piles of it." He tugged at my hair.

"When you say 'pizazz' you scare me."

"Reese, we are only going to do this once in our lifetime, and we need it to be a showstopper."

"Now, when you use the word 'showstopper,' you mean…?"

It turned out Charlie hoped for next year in Europe or Australia. I liked the idea of something sooner and although I couldn't say it, I was thinking of my dad. Even though he was out of the woods, his recent scare left me skittish, with the need to live at 120 miles per hour, cramming in moments as if they were going to expire.

"You know you are more perfect than I remembered." His face was beautiful.

"What did you remember?" I murmured, frozen.

"I remembered you were scrappy in a way I'll never understand, but forever admire. I always want to keep you close."

"Scrappy, huh?" I sank into his gaze.

Charlie always said his first memory of Ben was the two of them fighting over a baseball. It was Charlie's ball, but Ben wouldn't give it back to him, wouldn't let go. Charlie ran and jumped on him, and in response, Ben punched him right in the face. Charlie grabbed his hair, and that's when our mothers walked in to their cries. Ben launched into his side of the story right away, and when they looked at Charlie, he couldn't find the words to explain the injustice. That day, Charlie got a time-out and Ben got the baseball. I believe we were all six at the time, and the two of them had been best friends, brothers ever since.

I don't remember that day.

He said his first memory of me was probably two years later—the year I loved wearing dresses. I do remember that day. Bernice was taking me out for the morning, and I'd dolled myself up in an offensive purple ensemble. I sat on the porch steps, waiting, and the boys taunted me as they rode their bikes up and down the driveway.

"Stupid boys." I moved to stand on the bottom step.

"You're not supposed to say stupid." Ben looked hurt.

"You are. You're mean and stupid." I moved to the edge of the driveway.

"You're only mad because we're starting a club, and you can't be in it." Charlie stuck his tongue out at me.

"We are?" Ben biked to Charlie's side, and I heard him whisper, "We should let her in. She's cool."

"No, we can't. Only boys are allowed." Charlie offered me his best look of superiority.

I was in the middle of the driveway by then, hands on hips. "Girls are better than boys."

Charlie zipped over to where I stood, and stopped an inch from me. "Says who?"

"Says everyone, ever." I jabbed his bike with one hand, and his shoulder with the other. He was caught unawares, and we both fell over in a heap.

"Reese Mae Hamilton, get your tiny bum over here right now." Mom glowered from the porch. "And you boys, go bug Leah. I don't have time for this. Go now." My dress ripped as I extricated myself from our pile. I kicked his bike with my shiny black shoes before walking away.

We fought off and on for the next few years and enlisted Ben as our moderator. It was only when we found photography that we found our friendship too.

"Uh huh, our mothers called us Trouble 1, Trouble 2, and Trouble 3." Charlie's voice brought me back to the coffee shop. "But I knew the truth. I was the charming one. Ben was the smart, funny one." He pressed his head next to mine, filling my breaths with hints of coffee. "And you, Reese, you are the wonderful one."

I'd memorized the pattern of the streaks through his eyes ages ago—since when did I feel shy meeting his gaze?

"Reese, you are the strongest person I know." He reached for my hand.

I cleared my throat. "So we'll come back to the date question sometime next week."

"You know I'll do anything in the world for you, Reese?"

"So I'll meet you in Calgary on Saturday." I grinned.

"I only want bells and whistles and a little bling because you are the kind of girl who deserves the whole world. You know that, right?" He kissed the side of my head.

"And I only want one little mountain, which I'd say is pretty low-maintenance of me, all things considered." I cupped his face, and he laughed.

"Reese, I never imagined a girl as out of my league as you would ever see me, let alone date me, let alone love me, let alone marry me. You've made me," he paused and kissed my right cheekbone, "the luckiest man," kiss on my forehead, "on the entire planet," kiss on my neck. He pulled back, and I couldn't meet his look, but my heart pounded in time to the music playing above us. "*And*, I want to catch you up to speed on the shooting schedule. I have to fly back to London tomorrow and we should figure out if you can get on the same flight."

"I need to fly out of Omaha." I offered him a rueful smile.

"Reese, what are you talking about? It's logistically easier on every level." He tapped the table with his thumb, a telltale sign he was on the verge of annoyance.

"Some of my stuff is still at Dad's. It wouldn't fit for the trip." I bit my lower lip.

"Fine, we'll ask your parents to ship it. I'll buy you anything you don't have." His grin squeezed the parameters of my heart. "Reese, I need you there. I've missed working with you."

I was distracted by the atramentous places in his eyes, flecks more familiar to me than my own face.

Charlie stroked my cheek. "I should have told you a long time ago how much I loved you, and I'm sorry I never did. I should have told you every day. You are the best thing that has ever happened to me."

I couldn't help but wonder what else, even after all these years, lay unspoken between us.

Blake called the hotel a couple of times, but I never called him back. I couldn't. I'd hurt him, and I didn't know how to fix it, how to fix any of it. But the next morning when we were set to leave, he showed up at the hotel with a fancy bottle of champagne.

"To celebrate you two." He handed the bottle to Charlie and avoided my gaze.

"Let's find you a girl here in the States so we can go on double dates." Charlie slapped him on the back, and my insides cringed.

I pasted a smile across the lower region of my face as he hugged Bernice and shook Charlie's hand, then Dad's. Ben pulled him into a hug and pounded him on the back.

And then there was only me. I saw him through a tunnel, and as he went in for a sideways hug, I became increasingly aware of our curious audience. I shook my head. "I'll walk you out."

We ambled down the street in a quietude he broke first. "I considered dramatics with a nice midnight picnic, a tale of love where I got on my knees, proclaimed you were the best part of my life, and begged you to give you a chance. I didn't mind the embarrassment of it, but I now fully see Charlie has your heart. I didn't believe it before." He stopped and looked at me, daring me to disagree.

"Blake."

"But I'll do the midnight picnic thing if it will make a difference."

"Blake."

"Reese, you could go on a date with me. One because you promised. I know he has your heart, but maybe—"

"Blake, stop." I forced the words out of my mouth.

"Reese, please." He tucked a strand of hair behind my ear. "Please."

"I can't." The whisper scraped my throat. "I'm sorry."

"Then goodbye, Reese." He put his hands on my shoulders. "Don't forget all the things we talked about, about how great you are, all on your own."

"Blake." I looked down. "We can still write?"

"No, we can't." He shoved his hands inside his pockets. "Not right now. That's not how this works. Right now I can't be 'just friends' with you."

"That's dumb." Tears pricked my eyes though I knew he was right. "I care about you, I do."

"Then give me a chance? Reese." He leaned and whispered in my ear. "Reese, you know we'd be great."

"I can't." The words came from somewhere else, someone else who was demolishing this moment. "I promise I care about you. But I can't be with you."

"Right." He stepped away. "You're engaged to Charlie."

Despite myself, I pulled him close, covering my grief with a hug. I shouldn't feel so sad, couldn't acknowledge what it might mean. So I held him, in that strange place, with the mad swirl around us. For a minute, two, I lingered in the *what ifs* between us. He smelled like laundry detergent, felt like the only goodness I'd ever known.

"Reese, I've got to go."

"Okay, bye." My voice sounded callous, but the ache in my throat went deep. We watched each other for a moment longer and smoothed our expressions into something impartial. "I can't wait to read your bestseller."

He kissed the side of my head and walked away.

Choosing to pretend was the only answer I saw, the only way any of it made sense. I could feign I hadn't liked him, not even a little. Pretend we weren't on the cusp of some wild and unexplored universe the day Charlie arrived. Act as if I hadn't found scribblings from him in the back of my notebook, which I'd fallen asleep reading and re-reading the night before.

It started with nothing really, unless you count an unintentional brush on the back of the hand followed by a sideways, rather ungraceful tumble toward her lap. I'd grabbed the bus on Synge Street, with the Lantern Centre opposite, and I was very, terribly late.

She had eyes that flashed, a sea of fire and storm, and I couldn't catch much else because after my murmured apology, she looked away. I know I didn't mean to choose a seat with her sublime profile in view, but I did and I have often wondered if that made all the difference.

From my vantage point, on the aisle seat and three rows back, I could see the impatient way she brushed her fringe aside and the straight line of her shoulders. She had a curious air about her—the way she looked out the window, inspecting each passing street as if it were her first time in the city.

I closed my eyes and forced myself to think about the lecture I'd recently attended on Modern British Literature. Wordsworth, now there was a fellow worth noting. I'd almost brought myself to the field of daffodils when I heard the insistent rustling of papers, zippers, and more zippers. She fished out a city map.

"Where is it you'd like to go? I can help you." I kept my voice neutral, friendly. In all my retellings of this story, I would keep it glib, make myself sound noble.

She met my gaze with a bold, quiet stare.

When it came, her voice surprised me.

It was, quite simply, the most wonderful sound I'd ever heard.

That's when I knew it would end in everything or it would end everything. Either way, it was everything.

He moved his fingers in a half wave. And with that, he caught a cab and rode away like it didn't even matter.

18

August

Bernice

We were back in Omaha. It had been two nights since Benjamin drove the four of us the 500 miles straight from Chicago to Omaha.

The four of us shared the Hamilton house for one whole day, ending the chapter as we'd begun it, with hours spent around the dining room table and out in the garden. It sounds romantic but it wasn't. We were all out of sorts, exhausted, and short with each other.

Benjamin had left late the afternoon before and should already be back home. Charlie was back in Europe, ramping up for his next photo session, and Reese would follow in a couple of days. My friends had told me it was always this way with kids—they needed you voraciously until they didn't. I told myself it would all be okay, it was time for Carl and me to make our new life once and for all. He'd arranged for two dozen roses to be delivered to me yesterday, and promised he would follow it up with a nice dinner on the town after Reese left.

"But, seriously, we need to get this snoring under control," I said once Carl woke up. "I need to consult Maya about her oil stash. I could lather it on you."

"That would be fun." Carl ran his finger over my arm.

"Or maybe I can sew you a mouth harness to wear at night."

"But then how could I do this?" He pulled me close until all the inches of me fit into all the inches of him. He clasped my face and kissed me so deeply moonbeams shot out of my head *and* my toes.

"Carl, I love you too."

"I'll take an early retirement; the payout will be small but what is money compared to the hours I will have with you? I need to make the time count. We have years of life to catch up on, and not enough time to do it." His eyes held sorrow.

"We do. We do." I couldn't meet his gaze. It was still difficult to imagine all we'd missed.

"We can set our sights on making each day better than the last. By the time we're eighty, we'll be sailing up the Seine."

"That sounds lovely."

"The kids won't be able to catch up, even if they tried." He kissed me, and I snuggled closer. When we were young, but still adults, we thought we knew what life was about. Now that we were heading toward old, we were realizing we'd barely begun to sort it. But one thing I knew for sure—I'd found the one my soul loved. All I'd ever wanted was right here in my arms, and I wouldn't take him for granted ever again.

"I'm heading to work this morning," he said into my hair.

"Stay with me a few more minutes."

"I can't. Too much to do over there at the office." He moved to kiss my head. "I promise I'll spend all weekend in bed with you if you want." Another kiss and he was gone before I could protest further.

When I dragged myself out of bed, I headed straight to the kitchen. I'd missed cooking. Reese joined me two hours later, drawn in by the smell of baking butter.

"I remembered you wanted hash browns so I made you a hash brown casserole." I waved her to a stool.

"I did? You did?" Reese sat at the kitchen counter and slumped her face onto her hands.

"Yes, back on our road trip—on one of those first mornings at breakfast." I forced myself to be patient.

"Okay, right. Nice, thanks. Can you please give me another scoop?" She adjusted her bun and accepted the plate I held out. She was lucky her figure had held up decently for this long, but if I'd warned her once about the future, I'd warned her a thousand times. She had Aunt Naomi's genes, and I'm sorry, but there's no running away from that.

Bless her heart.

"Just make sure you're getting some fresh air and exercise today, baby." I eyed her plate. Rocky barked in agreement at our feet.

I pulled more bacon out of the oven and studied my daughter until she spoke. "Hey Bernice, let's go out and get coffee. I feel out of sorts and could use some caffeine."

Reese had always been an emotional eater, so I wasn't surprised when she devoured the embarrassingly large serving of casserole and then asked for a coffee out. The girl liked her treats. I was only surprised she asked me to join her. I hardly dared breathe. I would unpack, sort, and clean later. It was the first time in decades my Reese had asked to spend time with me.

"Baby girl, this is our day. Let's make it shine." My pocketbook was already in hand. "Rocky, you stay here. This is a ladies-only morning." I gave him a cuddle.

It was best to give her my wedding planning tips while she had something in her mouth anyway. She would be forced to listen and couldn't sass back. Her wit will be endearing when she's sixty, but now it's plumb indecent.

I also wanted to give her their first wedding gift: a Christmas wedding.

Yesterday I called the Waldorf in New York to ask about a Christmas Eve wedding. I planned on paying the deposit this week and would pay the remainder of the balance by late fall. Lord knows at their prices I was only able to secure a 10 a.m. spot on Tuesday, December 21, *not* on Christmas Eve, so we'd have to make do with a brunch wedding. It wasn't my first choice, but it was Reese's, so we would make it work.

Carl would wear his snazzy red bowtie and we would have "The Nutcracker" performed during their reception. Benjamin and Maya could wear the matching vests I'd sew them and pass out ginger cookies together. Everything in my gut pointed to this festive gathering.

Charlie had told me they wanted bling, so I would give them all the bling Mama could bring. I would let my baby know on our morning out and wait for the waterworks. My Reese has always loved Christmas with all the twinkle lights and bells, and when she was five, she told Santa she wanted a Christmas wedding. I haven't forgotten it for a single day since.

I grabbed the keys before she could waddle off her stool and headed straight for the door, knowing she'd be right behind me.

I remember planning my wedding with my mother. It was a fight every day of the week but Sunday, when we took a break from figuring out details. My secret weapon, of course, was that I was already married. Right when I'd be on the point of strangling her for sure, when she insisted that cream was tacky, only white would do, I'd take a deep breath and remind myself Carl was already my husband. If I needed to, I could walk right out the door and say, "Poo poo on you." I wanted my big wedding so badly, I held out for it, using every ounce of self-control I possessed. I told my daddy I needed him to run interference now and again, but he chuckled and said, "Fat chance, little lady. You listen to your mama and do what she says, or I won't be paying for this wedding of yours." And I knew he wouldn't.

I was excited about my entourage of bridesmaids so I snapped to the line she laid down for me.

I was the bride of the century: a blonde, classier Jackie Kennedy with a bit more tulle. My girlfriends and I talked about my wedding for the next ten years. We relived the glory of the petit fours, the fiasco of Aunt Loretta drinking three glasses of champagne. A girl's wedding comes once in a lifetime, and I would throw my baby a party that would make Scarlett O'Hara herself jealous.

This season of planning her wedding would be the yarn that wove us together, ameliorated the cavernous plain that stretched between us. Christmas was magic; weddings were full of love. Christmas was *our* happy place, and I knew in my bones this would be the bridge between me and my beautiful baby girl.

I blinked back the tears. I'd done so many things wrong through the years, but I would do this one thing right.

Reese

We jumped into Dad's truck. I'd grown fond of Ernie, but still—I'd be vetoing him for the foreseeable future. Bernice sat high behind the wheel as she navigated us into the drive-thru.

"What can I get for you?" To say the overly excited voice was two decibels above annoying was generous.

Bernice went first. "A grande two-pump sugar-free vanilla, two-pump sugar-free caramel, no water, extra hot, whole milk, no room, no foam chai." I bit my lip—it made me happy when others got to experience the complicated layers comprising my mother.

Bernice turned to me, and I leaned over her. "Tall Americano with whipped cream."

"Are you sure you want whipped *cream*? You do have a wedding dress to fit into."

I'd like to think my death stare would demoralize Darth Vader, but Bernice only boosted her shoulders. "I'm just saying."

I shook my head at her, relaxed into the seat, and closed my eyes. She put her hand on top of mine, and stroked my fingers with her thumb. Her touch was still familiar, even after all these years. I tensed up, but didn't have the energy—or maybe the desire—to fight her efforts. I didn't pull away. She still drove me crazy, but it felt more complicated these days. The fury was layered with something akin to fondness, mixed with a side of frustration and pity. I couldn't let myself think about any of it or I might grow sentimental.

We paid for our drinks, and turned back onto the road in silence. We drove two minutes before Bernice spoke up.

"Baby, I have a surprise for you. Do you remember telling Santa all those years ago you wanted a Christmas wedding?"

"I did?"

"Yes, when you were five." She glanced at me. "Well—"

There was a screech, a blazing light. There were yells all around and searing pain. All I saw in every direction were flashes of bright, humming, the chaos of a crowd.

Then, nothing.

PART III

19

Reese

Ben had been in Knoxville less than half a day when I called, and he didn't believe me, wouldn't believe me. When he dropped the phone, Maya picked it up to finish the conversation. "Uh huh. Uh huh. Okay. We'll see you soon."

They made it to Omaha in ten hours instead of the usual thirteen and raced to where Dad and I sat side by side, unmoving and unspeaking on the porch swing. Rocky lay on my lap uncharacteristically quiet, like he knew something was wrong. When he whimpered, I whispered, "Don't worry, I'll take care of you" into his furry ear. I hadn't yet cried. My arms were still covered in dried blood. Mine or hers, I didn't know which.

"I don't understand. How could this have happened?" It was all Ben could say, over and over when he arrived, as I stared past him. There had been a dog—or maybe a cat—and a swerve so fast I flung my scalding Americano in all directions. There had been pain, a slowing of time, and an escalating feeling of horror. There was the car speeding in the other lane, but mostly there was the mangled body of my mother beside me.

Maya hugged Dad. "It's horrible. I'm so sorry."

"She asked me to stay with her a few minutes longer, that was the last thing she asked me, and I couldn't even do that. My darling bride, my beautiful one. I wait for her return for hours on end, but she never comes home," Dad said, his eyes distant.

I longed to channel comfort from my twin, my other half, but he was decidedly withdrawn. Instead he made arrangements, answered phone calls, ordered food.

I retreated to our tree house in the backyard and waited for him to join me, but for once in our lives, he did not come. I was alone in the cold night.

Maya came instead.

"It's okay, you can cry if you want." She stroked my hair.

"It's not okay." Nothing would be okay again. My voice was raw from holding back the flood of tears, my lips were broken from all the bites where I'd held in the pain.

"I know." Her voice was a breath in the cold black, and I put my head on her shoulder. I had never loved her more.

"Why am I the one with only scrapes and bruises, and she…" I swallowed, stopped.

"Shh."

"But why?" I whispered a minute or a lifetime later, the question of my life.

"I don't know," Maya whispered back and wiped a tear from her own face. *Why, why, why?* All through the night, I sat with nothing left to give, and then she held me too.

Someone who claimed to be a doctor rushed over and shouted orders to anyone who would take them.

She was still alive, barely breathing, with wide eyes open, bleeding tears.

I wanted to go to her, hug her, hold her, but found instead of feet, only lead.

In those final moments, she had eyes only for me and I saw them say, I love you, I'm sorry. I love you, I'm sorry, I love you, I'm sorry *for all those minutes. A beautiful, horrible melody on repeat that was both exactly what I wanted to hear and nothing like it.*

In those moments when my feet were glued, my gaze stuck too, I sent her the message back, in perfectly mirrored form. I'm sorry, I love you. I'm sorry, I love you, I'm sorry. *And also,* This isn't how it was supposed to be. Don't die, stop it right now.

But she didn't stop, and to the end, until her eyes closed for the last time, I saw her tell me again and again. I'm sorry. I love you, I'm sorry, I love you, I'm sorry.

Or maybe that's simply what I wanted her to say.

I woke from the nightmare multiple times a night. The sweat was cold, soaking my sheets, so I moved to the couch and stared at the textured ceiling until the sun rose and the birds sang.

Night after night on repeat.

I need to go back. It was all I heard as we made arrangements with the funeral home for her cremation, as we walked around like zombies, as the hours crept.

I need to go back. I would put myself in the driver's seat, let my mother be the one who walked away with one small bump and ten stitches.

The doctor explained that although Mom didn't die instantly, the shock would have taken away her sense of pain. The details meant little to me; she still died.

Ben asked question after question. Dad chimed in with a few of his own, but I tuned them all out, staring over the talking mouths at the wall. When they wouldn't stop, I drifted off to wait by the car, squinting up at the bright sky, wishing I could crawl into bed and wake up in a different decade, in another lifetime, in someone else's body.

Ben called Charlie for me and it was a whole day and a half later when we finally spoke. He finished at his set and raced to the airport, with nothing except his phone, wallet, and passport. But after a delayed flight in Madrid and a security mishap which lasted ten hours, two more days passed. I told him not to worry, to stay put, and I'd come once we closed out everything here. He didn't love the idea, but I didn't have the energy to be around anyone. No one at all. I said "Please" and he backed down.

I couldn't stand still. I went for long walks, which turned into runs, which turned into sitting at the park, which turned into more long walks.

I wanted to crawl straight out of my skin.

"Bernice wanted her ashes thrown to the four winds, a sensational ending for her time on this earth. And I will make sure she gets her final curtain call." Dad had gathered us to make a plan.

They asked me what I thought, but I couldn't form ideas, let alone words. I shook my head and headed to the porch. After two hours of conversing about the logistics, Ben and Dad informed me we would spread her ashes at Lake Okoboji, a short drive from Omaha. It had been our cherished weekend getaway when we were young.

"We'll pack a picnic like old times and bask in the blue for hours on end," Dad said, words waspy.

Even though she always liked a show, we would forego a funeral as we didn't want to see anyone or talk more than needed.

On the appointed day, I stormed out to Ernie unapologetically in my pajamas. I had a passing thought about digging my skinny jeans out of my bag, but thought better of it. I'd woken abruptly from another nightmare and my heart wouldn't stop pounding.

When I reached the van I remembered again she was gone and the reason for this stupid trip.

Gone.

Gone.

I'd said it to myself so many times over the last few days the word itself started to look peculiar, like four strangers forced into a tight row of an airplane, awkward and unhappy about it.

She would leave first. I grew angry all over again.

Ben tucked me into the back seat beside Maya with a mound of blankets. He handed me a mug and commanded me to drink.

Was I three? Was I an invalid? I pushed the snarky comments back inside my clenched teeth and held the mug on my lap with no strength to bring it to my lips.

I was tired of the guilt. Tired of the regret that threatened to suffocate me.

I was simply tired.

When sleep eluded me, I pressed against the window and let the tears fall. The radio played, I cuddled Rocky, and Ben drove. When we arrived, we stumbled out of Ernie, rag doll style. The earth held still and the air rolled around us. For once, time slowed to a complete stop but at the one destination I did not want, would never want. I couldn't let myself believe the urn in Dad's hands contained all that was left of my mom on this earth. I didn't want to think about the fact we were about to scatter the minuscule bits of her we had left.

We stood in a line, unsure.

When Dad took us each by the shoulders and insisted we "take a moment as a family to say something nice," I puked. Heaving, grieving, I could not stop, and I didn't want their solace. The ground beckoned me, and I sank to it.

Ben didn't attempt to comfort me or anyone. Instead, he seeped with grief like a sieve under a waterfall. He clung to Maya's hand, reeked of sorrow and regret.

Eventually, he cleared his throat. "Mom, I want you to know that I loved you. I never said it enough. I want you to know I'll always love you. I want you to know you were a good mom, that I understand…" The sobs billowed through his chest, and he fell into Maya.

Dad put an arm around the two of them.

"Bernice. You were my best years. My shining star, so vibrant and full of life. I have never met anyone else like you, and I have loved you always. You have been the wife of my youth and of my middle age too, a double blessing I do not take lightly. I know you won't stop dancing, so please save a spot on your dance card for me. I'll meet you in some faraway dawn for our next masquerade."

He surrendered enough tears to fill another lake.

When I had a millisecond to think, I let the rage build.

I wanted to go back to Atlanta, to last year, to before.

I wanted to lie on the couch and sleep for weeks on end and not think.

I wanted to punch a wall, a mountain, a lion in the face.

I wanted to stop believing I could have changed this, to shake the sickening sensation that greeted me every morning and didn't leave me until I'd fallen into a restless sleep in the early hours of the morning.

I wanted a second chance to make things right.

They looked at me to speak, but I grabbed a handful of her and staggered away beyond their sight.

I gagged some more. I attempted gathering my thoughts into something coherent, but I found a depth of fury containing nothing but blackness in every direction. So I welcomed the nothingness in, and I exhaled it out anew.

The wind was light on my cheek, again and again, enough to bring me back. The sky was a shade of azure that shouldn't have been possible, and I squinted up, wondering where to begin.

I imagined she thought this goodbye would be poetic, theatrical, but there was nothing romantic or idyllic or anything, about this. It was only Death, and there was nothing beautiful about that.

Why did you leave me? I had nothing else to say to my mother, so I threw her at the sky. I turned before she fell back down, and I walked away fast, hardly breathing.

When I found Dad, Ben, and Maya huddled, I ignored them, and went and sat on the ground two feet away. I studied the earth around me and for a long time we stayed like that in silence, until I dared to look up.

The pain in Dad's eyes was unbearable. "She showed up at the house a few days after she first left," he choked out loud enough for us all to hear. "I shut her out. I wouldn't let her in." He exhaled, ran his hands through his hair, and I absorbed the revelation. "She wanted to talk. Maybe she wanted to fully hash it out, work us out. I'll never know what that day could have meant. It was complicated, and I was angry. I didn't even give her a chance, wouldn't listen to one word she had to say. I thought she'd been having an affair, and I was so pissed off at her. I can never undo the decision, and I hate myself now for that moment as much as I'd ever hated her."

"Well," Ben exhaled, "my therapist's wallet just thanked you."

Dad's mouth kept moving, but no words came out. Tears and snot ran down his face as he reached for Ben. "But I hated myself more because every time she asked to see you two, I told her you weren't home, didn't want to see her, despised her. She came and called, incessantly at first, but I told her it was better for you two if she stayed away, that if she loved you at all she would give you space, stop showing up on the porch every day. Eventually she believed me, eventually she got the message, thought you despised her...she was...I was so angry, and I..."

"No." I was crying, shaking my head, insides ripped in two.

"She hated me; I couldn't have you two hate me too, so I never told you. Then I didn't even know how to get ahold of her and tell her it was me, not you. The guilt, it's been—" Dad looked pleadingly between us. "I tried to tell her after we renewed our vows, but she wouldn't let me. Said the past was the past. But I should have told her. She had a right to know. I was a coward."

"No." *No, no, no.* I jumped back up and raced into the distance.

After we ceremonially said goodbye to Mom, life continued in a blur. There were more logistics with lawyers and calls about paperwork. I half heard and half saw everything unfolding before me. Someone from the Waldorf kept calling for her every day like some sick joke until I told them to shove it. Maya drove back to Knoxville, and the three of us hunkered down in the family house for a week. After his revelation, I avoided Dad as much as possible.

Dad decided to sell the house, the car, and everything in between. He only wanted to keep Ernie. He planned to travel to Canada to say a final goodbye to his bride.

After being inhabited by Hamiltons for three decades, sorting the house was a wreck. We only came up for air when absolutely necessary—to eat, sleep, and use the toilet. We ordered out every night and ate leftovers in the early afternoon. We didn't do a single dish or load of laundry.

We didn't talk because we had nothing left to say.

At night, haunted by what could have been, I sat on the front porch in my sweats drinking wine and Rocky cuddled beside me. "It's you and me now, buddy." Rocky barked in agreement. In Mom's absence I'd wake to find him curled up by my feet, and he'd stick to me like glue as I moved through the house, packing up a lifetime.

Every night, as I poured my glass of wine and wrapped myself in a blanket, Ben and Dad grabbed beers, studied the car manual, and worked on putting a new engine in the Mustang. And later still, I sat on the darkened porch alone and watched nothing.

The globe was the first thing in my "Keep" pile. It had been in my room since I was ten. Next, I pulled the box of unopened cards and the birthday package to the center of the room. I spread the envelopes in rows in front of me, but didn't move to open them. I reached for the gift instead. It was large, wrapped in kraft paper and tied up with a piece of ripped fabric. In bold letters across the whole front was written, *To The Best Reese in the Entire Universe and Galaxy and Beyond. HAPPY BIRTHDAY, baby girl.* There was a glittery gold heart beneath the words.

I opened the package carefully. The quilt inside was soft and covered the expanse of my floor when I spread it out. A note floated to the ground as I fanned out the folds of the fabric.

Reese, this is a quilt of our history, yours and mine. So you can find peace with the past as you dream about your future. You'll notice a couple of your old girl scout T-shirts in the middle, from when I was your troop leader, as well as fabric from the clothes I made you through the years. I cut up a couple of our beloved Christmas sweaters because, well, you know. There is a strip of my wedding dress here too, because I know you've always loved it. You'll find the dress itself altered for your figure and hanging in the back of my closet. (Watch the second servings of those casseroles, or it won't fit.) My gut tells me you're going to need it soon. Knowing you, you'll run off and get hitched without telling any of us, HAHAHA. I'm forward-thinking enough to give it to you now.

I shoved the cards back into the box and left them by my suitcase. I stared at the quilt long into the night, walking through my history, the steps that had brought me this far. In fabric letters over the top of the quilt it read, *Remember Us*. I traced my fingers over the stitching again and again but couldn't find the answers I craved. And it didn't bring her back.

There was a note from Blake:

Dearest Reese,

Ben messaged me, and I won't bore you with the commonalities like, "You will be okay," "With sympathy," etc.

To be honest, it will hurt in the deepest parts of you. I know it already does. I don't know what it's like to say goodbye without getting a real go at it.

I do know the horrors can take you to the worst places of yourself, to the ends of all you've known and at the exact moment you think you may never come back, you will lift your eyes and see a bit of hope. But you are not yet there.

Right now I imagine you are raging and confused and feel desperately alone. I think you must have more questions than answers and alternately hate your mother for leaving you like this and wish your ending with her could be different.

How I wish we could go throw rocks into the sea, and run miles on end, side by side, fuming against the skies. Thank goodness you have Ben or Charlie for that.

So while I wish I were there with you, what I most wish is that you are being taken care of on all fronts, and I know it's already sorted.

I won't write you again, but know I care.

I agree with Tolkien—"I will not say: do not weep; for not all tears are an evil."

Yours, etc.

Blake

I ripped it into a hundred pieces and then a hundred more. I'm sure he thought he was being kind, but he would never understand. No one would ever understand.

When we were done with the house, the garage, with everything, we passed the remnants to a real estate agent named Emily. The house would be on the market within two days, and Emily assured us it would be sold within two weeks.

The thought of selling our home distressed me, but Dad was

unwavering in his resolution. He sold it to a family who needed a quick closing. And just like that, the house I grew up in wasn't ours, and Rocky and I had no home.

Almost a week to the day after we'd sent Mom into the universe, Ben packed his belongings into the back of the Ford Mustang and drove away while Dad and I were still sleeping.

I rented a small trailer to move what I was taking to Atlanta. The day we were handing over the keys to my childhood home, I found Dad on the porch swing. We had to be out by 2 p.m. and we were alone in the empty house. Dad put his arm around me, and I snuggled in close. Cinnamon. Tobacco. Fire. My father smelled of all that was comforting. I hadn't sat with him like this in over a decade, but I think we'd both grown to need the proximity.

He held his left hand toward me and I placed my right flat upon it, staring at the differences. Little and big. Smooth and worn. Pale and weathered.

I'd always loved Dad's hands. Through the last few months, I'd found myself taking photo after photo of them, trying to capture the texture of their rugged edges forever. But no matter the lighting or the composition, the photo was a poor imitation of reality. It didn't stop me from trying once again, and so I reached for the camera beside me and focused carefully on our fingers. One slow *click* of the shutter, and it was documented.

Dad shifted and spoke, his words measured. "I remember when you two were born, you both had the tiniest hands, the most perfect toes. Bernice and I counted them again and again in those first few weeks."

I wiggled my fingers in front of us as my throat closed in on itself.

"Sometimes, when you're beside me, all I can hear is the story I want to tell you: I remember the first day I held you; you were minutes old and screaming so loudly. The sun was setting outside the window and I knew my life was forever changed. Thank you for making me a father. But I haven't been able to squeeze the words between my obstinate teeth until now."

His eyes leaked tears, and I couldn't meet his gaze.

"When we brought you kids home, there were many nights I fell asleep on the rug beside you, desperate for you to sleep, frantic to make sure you kept right on breathing. You two were perfect. And it was you alone, Reese, who held my finger for an hour straight, with a tenacity something so tiny shouldn't possess."

"Thanks, Dad." I patted his hand. My heart hurt.

"I'm sorry about keeping your mom from you all those years." He stopped and mauled his eyes. "She was a great lawyer, you know." He looked at me, and I nodded. "But I think she never filed for a divorce because she didn't want the finality of you two rejecting her. And I never filed because I didn't want to lose her and you kids. She loved you, she—"

I was still upset at him over his recent announcement, but I waved my arms to quiet him. For the moment, I didn't have it in me for that much anger. I was sure I'd need to ask him more questions later, yell at him eventually too, but for now I'd decided to keep the one parent I still had close.

"And I think we both know I owe you a second apology too. Since it's our last morning in this house, I need us to go to the kitchen, the original scene of the crime." I smiled, bewildered. We shuffled inside and he turned, putting his hands on my shoulders.

"Reese, I did make it to your university graduation, you know. I showed up two hours before it started and sat on the far left side. I looked for you the whole time, but I couldn't find you in the sea of gowns until they called your name. I told everyone in my section you were my daughter and as you marched across that stage, so proud and beautiful and good, my chest expanded two sizes. I wanted to find you after, but things were so awful between us I barely knew how to put two words together to talk with you."

"Thanks, Dad." I looked down.

"Bernice, hold me now, keep me strong." He dabbed at his eyes. "I'm sorry for not being around for so much of your growing up. And I was a fool that night at the dinner table. I was a fool years before that too. I should have believed in you. I should have been a supportive and present father. I didn't know how to do it, but I should have asked. And I'm sorry. I'm so sorry. And I hope you can forgive me."

My eyes went misty, and Dad plunged ahead.

"I'm proud of you, Reese. So incredibly proud. You've done more than I ever did, than I ever imagined. I don't know anyone else like you. You are a wonder." I nodded, overwhelmed and ready to be done with the conversation, but it kept coming, like Niagara Falls, the Mississippi, the Amazon. "I am proud of you, daughter, I am proud of you one hundred times over. I think you are beautiful, strong, and worthy of love. Because I never told you enough growing up, I will tell you until the day I die: I am proud of you, and I wouldn't trade you for a dozen Ansel Adamses or Dorothea Langes. You are better than both combined. I love you, Reese." And with that, Dad stepped back with a nod. "My baby girl is ready for the world."

I'd been numb for days, but something about Dad throwing around Dorothea Lange in the conversation perked me right up. I knew something akin to happiness, in the bittersweet edges of my body. I clung to the distraction like it was my only hope in a world gone mad. It was the strangest feeling, and I paced about Benson in the late afternoon, trying to make sense of it all. I bought a coffee, but only held it, aware of the burn in all the edges of my fingers. Before I poured it out, I noticed a homeless man sitting on the corner of a bench, and I ran to give it to him.

"Sorry it's not food. I hope you get to eat today too."

"Wait, I'm not—" But I didn't wait for him to finish, shooed aside his pending thank you and smiled at this new grace.

It was as if, after all these years, my sky expanded to limitless. The day was gray and the clouds hung low, the wind swept all around me, matching my mood.

I wanted to call Charlie. But again and again, I stopped myself. I wanted to hold the secret close a bit longer.

Instead I rode my bike out the trail behind our house and left him a note in our secret tree spot. Besides, he felt distant, and I felt, well…I felt a thousand different things.

20

October

Reese

I'd been back in Atlanta for two months when I turned Charlie's second bathroom into a makeshift darkroom. He was slightly annoyed, but I'd begun negotiating wedding favors with him for things I wanted. I gave him ten extra minutes of speech time at the reception in exchange for this baby.

We'd finally decided on a Christmas wedding. "Not this year, it feels too rushed. Feels too wrong. But next year." It was the only decision I could make for now.

"I'll marry you on every holiday for the rest of our lives." Charlie kissed me.

"Next Christmas will do." I found a half smile I didn't know I possessed. "I can't shake the feeling it's what Mom would have wanted." There was something in those last moments with her; I'd played them over and over again in my head. I'd had so many nightmares about the day she left, I was beginning to lose what was real and what was conjured.

"For your mom, then." He wrapped me into a hug, drowning my whispered plea. "And for us."

I had twenty rolls of film to develop from the road trip, and I was anxious to see my pictures. I started the process one Friday morning and by ten that night, Charlie had left the apartment. He said the chemicals hurt his brain. By midnight, I had the right wall of the living room covered in photographs. There was a selfie of Mom and me laughing, heads thrown back. Her arm was around me, but I didn't remember the moment at all.

It watched me, vexed me, so I turned my back on it, grabbed the road trip journal out of my bag, set it in my lap and skimmed over the pages. I glanced between the words and my photos without inspiration.

When the photos and the words couldn't make sense of anything, I gave up and went to bed.

It was after two when Ben called.

He didn't wait for my greeting. "Maya is the one."

"Of course she is. Are you drunk?"

"Hello to you too, Reese. I decided it before Dad became sick, before everything. I'd already waited a couple of years to propose. First it was because I needed more time to save up for the ring, then it was because she started a new job and said she didn't want any other big changes."

"We girls know what we want." I yawned.

"Somewhere along the way, we settled into life together without making it official."

"Okay."

"Here's the thing, Reese, it was easy. And when we found out about Dad, everything between Maya and me went on the back burner. And after Mom died, I held off on the proposal because the thought of her not being there to celebrate with us gutted me."

"I don't want to talk about it, Ben."

"But tonight, I had a revelation. I delayed all these years, thinking there would be an ideal moment to take the next step. But I now know, time is a bastard who shows no man grace. The time is here, the day is now. I don't want to miss out on any more life without Maya being my wife." It sounded as if he was pounding the table in front of him.

"How many drinks had you had for that little gem?"

"Only three beers."

"So you were basically sober."

"Exactly. Tomorrow, meaning later today, I will get down on one knee and promise Maya forever. I will probably throw in some of that stuff about time being a bastard too because it sounded good when I said it to you just now."

"You're a regular Shakespeare." I stifled another yawn.

"I will buy us a puppy. Should I do that today or tomorrow?"

"Uh, it sounds like today is already pretty full, so I'm going with tomorrow. Do you even know if Maya is a puppy kind of girl?"

"Of course she's a puppy kind of girl. Why do you think I'm proposing in the first place?"

"Okay, well, drink another beer to celebrate."

"Oh, big sister, I will, my happily ever after is mere hours away, and I plan to celebrate in style."

"Right. Night. Don't let the bedbugs bite."

Two hours later my phone rang again.

"I'm ready to discuss how this is going down."

"Are you seriously injured? I know that's the only reason you'd be calling me at 4 a.m." My voice held flint.

"Reese, I spent the last two hours collecting supplies. And practicing my Rocky Balboa dance around the apartment to maintain my momentum. I will wake Maya up with breakfast in bed. Nothing heavy and greasy. Something light and nice, like mimosas and my famous eggs benedict with music and a candle on the tray."

"Maybe bring her a toothbrush too? Maya's adorable, but who wants to say 'yes' with morning breath." I yawned.

"This is why I called you." I could tell Ben was pacing. "I'll throw in some nice quotes and bing, bang, boom."

"Sweetie, you need to get some sleep. We *all* need to get some sleep."

"I'm thinking of reading her a story about our love and ending on, 'will you join me in our second chapter?'"

"Oh Ben, that's good. I love it. And at the end of the day, it's going to be special, as long as you take a shower, ask politely, and focus on her, why she alone is the light of your world."

"Thanks, big sis. Maybe we can have a double wedding, like we had a double birth."

"Right, well that's about all I've got right now, except this: under no circumstances are you to put that girl through hours of LOTR before popping the question. Do you hear me?"

"I hear you. I'm supposed to show her the extended editions of *Lord of the Rings* before I ask her to spend the rest of her life with me. You're brilliant." I drifted off with his voice in my ear.

We jumped into Dad's truck; I would be vetoing Ernie for the foreseeable future.

Bernice sat high behind the wheel as she navigated us into the drive-thru.

"What can I get for you?" To say the overly excited voice was two decibels above annoying was generous.

Bernice went first. "A grande two-pump sugar-free vanilla, two pump sugar-free caramel, no water, extra hot, whole milk, no room, no foam chai."

She turned to me, and I leaned over her. "Tall Americano with whipped cream."

"Are you sure you want whipped cream? You do have a wedding dress to fit into... I'm just saying."

We paid for our drinks, and pulled back onto the road in silence. We drove two minutes before Bernice took a deep breath. I knew I was in for some sort of diatribe, so I jumped in before she could speak.

"Mom!" I might as well have shoved a rusty lead pipe through my throat.

She slammed on the brakes, and I hit my head on the passenger seat. Scalding Americano and sticky whipped cream sloshed over my hands and onto the front of my shirt.

"Reese! What the Sam Hill's the matter with you?"

I'm not sure why she was so fired up when I'm the one who almost died by passenger-ejection from the side window, and I knew my burns were at least third degree.

"Ow! What do you mean, what's the matter? I'm the only victim here." I held up my steamy, sticky whipped cream hands for inspection.

"Why did you just call me 'Mom'? I didn't see any cars about to ram into me, and I was definitely minding my own business." Her suspicious glare was so over-the-top, I giggled before I could stop myself, which only made her

puff up more. I was already on to the deep belly laughs when I saw the head a'wagging and knew a lecture was only seconds away, I pinched my arm as hard as I could to get my laughter in check, though it hurt my stomach something fierce.

"Mom. Mom. I was trying it on for size, seeing how it felt." I tried to keep my voice neutral, casual. I didn't want this to become a big deal, and I didn't want to get all chatty about it.

Well, that bought me another couple minutes of silence, though even after she'd pulled back onto the road, I did notice a few smiles in my direction. A few too many if you ask me. She was radiant.

Here we go, I thought. But it wasn't altogether a horrible thought. I rolled my eyes and looked out the window, wondering what version of the story Dad would hear.

I woke up trembling, unable to stop even when Charlie piled all the blankets in the room about me.

The summer I was ten, I waited on the porch every day for Mom to come home from work. I remember it because Charlie and Ben had made friends with our new neighbor, Jack, and daily zoomed off on their bikes without so much as a half invitation in my direction. I spent my entire break moping, building myself a fort in our backyard, reading Nancy Drew novels. And when it was time for Mom to get off work, I would bring lemonade out to the front porch and wait for her. We'd spend her first ten minutes home talking through our days or the problems of the world.

One day she brought me home a globe.

"It was in the window of the thrift store beside our office and it screamed right at me, it said, 'Reese needs me.'" She spun it around.

"Did it really?"

"Yep, it said if I didn't buy it, it would perish in its attempt to get here to you."

"Why did it want to see me so badly?"

"I imagine it's because it has a secret message for you."

"It does?"

"It does."

"But I'm right here, and I can't hear it."

"Shh, listen."

"I think it's saying hi."

"I heard that too. I also heard it say sometimes you have to go on an adventure."

"Yeah, an adventure."

"It's saying someday you need to travel to New York City and get on a train, in the rain, and get off at a stop you have never heard of before."

"Okay, tomorrow!"

"It says, maybe not tomorrow, but maybe the day after tomorrow or the day after that."

"Yeah, then." I smelled her wisteria, watched the sun peek back and forth behind her gorgeous self.

"It says sometimes you will need to forge your own path, to take a risk, go somewhere unknown. It says it will be scary, but also worth it."

"This old globe does a lot of talking."

"That it does. I think it knows you've had a hard summer."

"I've been sad because Ben and Charlie keep leaving me."

"I know it's hard, Reese."

"Do you go on adventures, Mom?"

"I used to imagine I'd hop on a train to nowhere, on a plane to a destination I didn't know. But then I got too old. Well, maybe not *old* so much as *adult*. First Dad and I got the bills, then I got the job. So here I am. Raising you and Ben is my Grand Adventure." She kissed the top of my head. "It's your time to dream big, little one. Those boys may be leaving you behind today, but they don't know it's your turn to leave them in the dust tomorrow."

"Promise?"

"Promise."

"Pinky promise?"

"Pinky promise. I can't wait to see the look on their faces when you do." She kissed the top of my head again. "Now I need to go see that father of yours. I'll see you at the dinner table."

April

Reese

It was bloody hot for April in Knoxville, but Maya looked beautiful.

Ben kept his arm around his bride as she thanked their small gathering of friends and family. She quickly blessed Mom for covering the cost of their wedding, and then it was Ben's turn.

"What she said." Polite laughter everywhere. He made eye contact with Dad, Charlie, and me.

"In all seriousness, we can all say this has been a long time coming, and I'm grateful you waited around for me, Maya." He kissed the side of her face, where her freckled skin met her blonde hair. She smiled up at him.

"My Mom always said..." Ben's face twisted and Maya rubbed his arm. "My Mom had this motto, for as long as I can remember: *Live today, no regrets tomorrow.* And while I waited too long to wed this fabulous woman, any future regrets will pale in comparison to the joy of living side by side with you, Maya. Maya, I adore you: thank you for your patience while I figured it out. Let's live today, baby."

"And tomorrow too," she said.

"And while I'm sad that my Mom..." Another pause. "My Mom can't be here with us in body, she is with us in spirit. Thanks, Mom, for showing me the way. Thanks, friends and family, for coming today—it means so much. Now, let's dance."

After Ben and Maya's first dance, they waved the rest of us to the twinkle-light encircled dance floor. I watched as Maya waltzed gracefully with Rocky, while Dad and Ben tromped together. I stayed in my corner, taking it all in.

Charlie gave me a dimpled wink from across the yard, bringing the pink to my cheeks faster than you can say Jack Robinson. I hadn't been surprised to discover he'd be Ben's best man. It was the obvious choice, but it didn't make it easier that Maya had asked me to be her maid of honor. We were the only two who stood up with them.

Dad, Rocky, and I had arrived in Knoxville two days before, on Thursday morning, to help with the last-minute details, but Maya handed us each a glass of white wine and pointed to the comfiest-looking lounge on her parents' deck.

"There are no details left that matter; we're here to simply be." She kissed my cheek.

We idled there, chatting, and enjoying wine for the two days leading up to the wedding. Though he called me twice a week, it was the first time in months I'd seen Dad, and I realized I'd missed him. He was out checking off his bucket list for the first time in his life and still growing out his hair.

"I need to go back to work soon, but right now I'm focusing on learning to carve wood, talking to strangers, and being present for my kids." He patted my knee.

When Charlie arrived Thursday night, in from Paris, all plaid and cute and still managing to smell like the sexiest man on earth, I hung back as he hugged Ben, Maya, and Dad in turn.

When he opened his arms to me, looked at me shyly and so full of love I thought I would faint, I folded right into his embrace. The others left us standing in the driveway, holding each other. Your best friend can't leave your heart no matter how many miles, how many closed doors lay scattered between you.

"How are things?" I broke the silence first.

"Oh you know, other than attempting to suture my broken heart back together..." He rubbed the scruff on his face.

"Stop!"

"I'm fighting the ladies off daily." His gaze asked me a dozen questions, blue eyes blazing.

"If only you were kidding, but I know you're not."

"I miss you," he whispered, and I was hot all over.

"Charlie."

"Reese, let's not talk about it now. Standing here with you is the happiest I've been in months. Let's not stuff it up. Can we pretend for this weekend we still are what we always were?"

"But do you understand at least a little?"

"I understand I should have pursued you sooner. I understand I should have been more vocal in my appreciation of you. I understand you're amazing and you can't do this now. Beyond that, I understand nothing. I'm angry at you. I'm angry at myself. I love you. I wasn't looking forward to this weekend, but now that I'm here I never want to leave this spot, this moment with you. If only you'd stop talking about the hard stuff. You're the worst for that, you know."

When he reached for me, I leaned in for another hug.

"Should we forget about this mess and go take care of Ben and Maya?" I choked out the words.

"Definitely," he exhaled into my hair, but he held me tighter still.

Three months previously we'd flown into Chicago on a Tuesday for a week of romance. Charlie pulled out all the stops. From flowers every morning to expensive wine every night, he knew how to make a girl believe she was special.

We sat at Millennium Park, takeaway cups from Intelligentsia between us, and discussed our Christmas wedding.

"A year from now we'll be husband and wife," Charlie said, resting his forehead on mine. I squeezed his hand. "I can't wait to see you in your dress. I think that's what I'm the most excited about for our big day. You'll look amazing."

I nodded, ignoring the pang inside. When I finally tried it on, Mom's wedding dress had engulfed me, so I took it to a seamstress for a fitting.

"I guess I stopped eating," I'd told the lady and looked away as my eyes filled with tears.

"Most brides do," she said and pinned the dress to my side.

Charlie and I shifted to talking about work, and my thoughts drifted as he told me again about meeting the famous designer, Tracy or Millicent or whatever her name was. Without meaning to, I started to cry, little tears forming everywhere and streaming down my cheeks in packs.

"Reese, what's wrong?" He put his coffee on the ground and placed his hands on my shoulders. I couldn't formulate the words to tell him what I wanted. I stared hard into those sea blue eyes I'd loved for so long, and just like that I knew I couldn't marry him. It was everything and nothing happening all at once, and I didn't want the goodbye to come so fast.

I so desperately wanted a different conclusion to us, to this journey.

"Charlie, I love you now; I will love you always. But I can't be with you." The wind blew, the clouds gathered, and I shivered.

"Reese, what are you talking about?" He kissed my forehead.

"You are brilliant, charming, hilarious. You are witty, wonderful, perfection."

"I love you too, baby." He kissed my collarbone.

"But I can't do this." The words caught in my throat, excruciating and true.

"I think we need to have some time to calm down." He ran his hands over my face and my breathing grew furious.

"No, Charlie. I can't. I can't marry you."

"I know we were getting married this Christmas, but we can push it back another year. I will wait as long as you need me to."

"Charlie!" My insides frayed. "I mean not at all."

I knew in some other version of the universe, we ended up together, he was my forever. Our stories would be intertwined for all time. I would care for him always; he had my heart first. He had so many of my firsts. I knew I would think of him a hundred times a year when I looked at certain photographs or listened to "Bohemian Rhapsody." I knew he was the best parts of me in so many ways; he was a piece of my story, a part but not the sum. In some other alternative ending to our tale, I ended up with him and lived happily ever after. In some other ending, but not in this one.

We walked down to our spot on the pier and he held me as we cried, all afternoon, as the sounds of the city went on and on beyond us and the clouds rolled in above. We sat, we kissed, and we cried, over and over on repeat. And finally I found the words, or a fragment of the words, to tell him goodbye.

He sat in silence.

"Charlie."

"Reese, shh. You are only doing this because you miss your mom."

"No." I couldn't look at him.

"Then what? Where is this coming from?"

"This last year was the first time we've ever had any substantial time apart, and I think it was what I needed to see how dependent I am on you, Charlie."

"Why is that bad?"

"*Charlie.*"

"We'll talk about it later, Reese. I'll wait until you're ready."

But I couldn't meet his eyes.

As it turned out, the location of our first kiss was also the spot of our last. Loving Charlie, kissing Charlie, was as sweet and perfect as I imagined it would be, and then it was over. Finally, I stood up and walked away without looking back.

I called Ben straightaway and told him what happened. "I don't know what is wrong with me."

"Me either. That was a bold move, Hamilton. Dare I say, dramatic. A bit like Gwyneth Paltrow."

"Poor Gwyneth." I giggled through my tears.

"Poor Gwyneth? Poor Brad."

"Brad Pitt is dreamy, but she wasn't ready for marriage." I was crying still, quiet streams of heartache and confusion.

"And neither were you. At least not to Charlie."

"Somehow I miss Mom."

"I do too. Is that why you said no to Charlie?"

"I said no to Charlie because it was the only thing *to* do. I rely on him too much and he lets me. He doesn't push me to grow at all."

"Maybe he doesn't know how, Reese."

"It's not what I need right now. I need to figure stuff out on my own."

"You'll always have me."

"Exactly." I kicked the ground. "Ben, I feel lost without Mom here, which makes no sense at all," I said through the ache in the back of my throat.

"It makes sense."

"I should have been a better daughter. I should have tried to understand, to have given her a chance." The pounding grew bigger, tight and furious in my chest. I was glad I didn't have to look at Ben in the eye. "I should have forgiven her."

"Reese. You were hard on her, but you can't beat yourself up. Mom didn't hold it against you, and you can't hold it against you."

"She could have been my Debbie Reynolds, but instead I made her Lady Tremaine."

"Lady who?"

"Lady Tremaine. You know, the wicked stepmother." Ben remained silent, and I groaned. "She was so selfish sometimes. Often."

"She definitely was."

"I wish she'd fought for us; why didn't she?" I'd asked Leah, Dad, and Bryony question after question about that time in our lives, but no one could satisfy my thick layers of hurt and doubt.

"I think she tried, Reese, remember? Dad told us—"

"But she was such a steamroller; how could she not have tried harder? It was always about her way, *her* plan, her—" As quickly as it had spiked, my anger dropped, and I stopped. "We'll never know and that sucks on a whole other level." I sighed. "I'm mad at Dad too, you know." But my voice lacked conviction.

"I know," Ben said softly and cleared his throat. "I'm trying to let it go. What are you going to do now?"

"I don't know. I've thought about trying out New York City."

"Remember when we met up in NYC over New Year's in college?"

His laugh filled the line. We'd been to Madison Square Garden, taken a walk in Central Park, paid our respects to the 9/11 memorial, skated at Rockefeller Center, and watched the ball drop in Times Square with a million other people.

"How could I forget?" We'd eaten hot dogs from street vendors, drunk cappuccinos from the local cafés, and waited in line for our cupcake from Magnolia Bakery in the West Village.

"We really did New York."

"It was amazing."

"I thought the whole experience was overrated." I could hear his grimace over the phone.

"And I loved it. The lights, the art, the people, the movement."

"It was totally you, sis. You know, Mom lived there once, for a couple of weeks, when she was trying to figure out life."

"No, I didn't know."

"I don't know any of the details, but she told me about it. You're so much like her."

"I'm going to take that as a compliment."

"You should."

"Ben…I think I might try to go out on my own again. I'm still young." The pit in my stomach grew three sizes as I said the words aloud.

"You are."

"And I'm adventurous."

"Then you should."

"Yeah, I should."

"You are indomitable Carrie Fisher." His grin shot through the phone.

Within a week, Rocky and I found a 200-square-foot studio apartment conveniently located around the corner from a subway stop, a coffee shop, grocery store, and a couple of local restaurants. Rent was $1,300 a month, the absolute cheapest I could find. Rocky thought it was hideous, and I quite agreed. I imagined it was my own personal Tardis—much larger on the inside than its exterior.

We moved in the following Tuesday.

I don't know who in their right mind thought parquet floors, a red brick wall, and yellow-tiled bathroom were a good combination. A tiny balcony with a fire ladder completed my space. Noise from the outside seeped through the cracks in the walls at every hour of the day or night.

A sanctuary it was not.

But this musty mess was all mine.

I painted the kitchen a lovely roseate in Mom's honor and didn't allow myself to think about the deposit I would never see again. Good riddance. A week after I told him, Ben mailed me a box of kitchen towels with a hideous host of pink flamingos printed across the white cotton. *A little housewarming gift. She'd be so proud*, he'd scrawled along the box. *Now go fly.*

I got a job as an assistant florist at a large local flower shop and put every last piece of my IKEA furniture together myself. I decorated my apartment the way I wanted with knitted throws and pillows everywhere. I bought candles by the dozen and anything that intrigued me at second-hand stores. I needed my home to be cozy. I hid all the photos I had of Charlie into my biggest shoebox, which I pushed to the back of the closet. I started saving to take more flying lessons.

Night after night, I ate dinner on the red plate I'd carried with me from Omaha and didn't bother buying extra dishware when I visited the thrift stores. I didn't want company.

Mom bequeathed upon me the legacy that was Bernice's Masterpieces and a few dozen boxes stacked taller than me showed up at my doorstep two weeks after I moved in. Her "empire" apparently consisted of her entire inventory which filled my already overcrowded living space with a host of hideous materials and a check that was my inheritance.

There was a note, dated five years before.

I know you'll find your own empire, Reese, but until you do, mine's big enough to share. Shine on, baby girl. Shine on.

We lived with the piles of cloth for a week, but the porcupine designs scared Rocky in the middle of the night. So I finally took the whole lot of it out to the curb, but not before I sewed myself an apron from one of Mom's patterns. It seemed a little short and had more lace than I usually preferred, but it would serve its purpose for baking the family sugar cookies. I'd promised Ben I'd bring six dozen of them to his wedding.

It took me thirteen loads to take all the cloth down to the truck to donate and by my last trip, there was quite a gathering outside my place. I saw two women in a brawl over a leopard print. Rocky and I walked past them without comment.

Ben and Maya kept their backyard wedding as simple as they'd promised. Maya wore a short ivory dress, a light fabric which swished with her as she moved. She and her mother had sewn it together. They told us the story the night before the wedding, mocking how frustrating the experience had been. Maya's mom Megan shook her head, saying, "You know mothers and their daughters," but her laughter broke off as I abruptly stood.

"*I'm sorry*," Maya mouthed behind her.

"I'll grab us another bottle of red." I cried in the bathroom for ten minutes straight, until Charlie came and found me. He moved me into the guest bedroom and settled me on his lap. He held me, cradled into his warmth, and let me cry. His rough hands wiped the tears from my cheeks, and we said nothing.

Dad sobbed through Ben's entire wedding and sat with me as the dancing wound down.

"I think I may have permanent snot marks on my tuxedo." He proudly displayed his rumpled suit. Ben told me he'd tried to convince Dad to downgrade to shorts and a T-shirt, but Dad would have none of it. He was determined to celebrate his son and new daughter-in-law in style.

"Good job, Dad." I offered a tight smile.

"Did you know your brother tried to convince me to wear casual clothes?"

"I heard a rumor."

"Bernice would have thrown a fit. And besides, I secretly loved the duds she always dressed me in when we were younger."

"You look great, Dad."

"Maya tried to set me up with her aunt, the one in the middle of the dance floor, flowing about in a green feathered dress, but I thanked her and grabbed a spritzer instead."

"Maybe you should dance with her." My throat ached.

"I will samba with the green dress lady, sure. But how could any other woman in the known universe compare to my bride? The memory of your mother is still better than the reality of anyone else."

"I know, Dad."

"I have a gift for you, Reese." He pulled a small, square package out of his suit pocket.

"Dad, it's Ben's wedding. Not mine."

"I found a planner of Bernice's and cherished the thoughts from my love throughout. She had an entire 'Note to self' section which I took to only reading on Thursdays, as a way of keeping our date nights alive. I think she would have wanted you to have it."

"Dad, I—"

"Go ahead, open it. There are lots of insights and too many questions." His eyes glistened as I unwrapped the book and flipped it open.

Note to self: Wear the purple dress to Ben's wedding and the red one to Reese's.

Note to self: Before making rash decisions on which dress to wear, at least go shopping and consider other options.

Note to self: Remember to tell Carl about the time I went skinny-dipping at Königssee. Give him a visual.

Note to self: I am beautiful. Tell my children they are beautiful.

Note to self: Research ways to cut Carl's hair while he is asleep. It's looking hideous. Just call me Delilah.

Note to self: Give Reese some extra hugs today. She's been prickly. Think up a cacti joke to share with her.

Note to self: Ask Carl about that red-haired lady who showed up with a pie for him when he took sick. I don't trust her.

Note to self: Find a way to incorporate the following into a gift for them—

Carl, you have taught me what love means, and I can't thank you enough.

Benjamin and Reese, you have been the greatest joy of my life. Thanks for making me a mom. I am who I am today because the three of you are in my story and are my three favorite people in the ENTIRE WORLD.

****make less mushy.*

I closed it with a sigh and laid my head on Dad's shoulder.

Charlie came over to ask me for a dance, and I held back the tears as I nodded. His hair was sun-streaked and, at Ben's request, he wore shorts and a button-down shirt. He swept me onto the dance floor, and I floated in his arms. "You're beautiful tonight," he whispered into my ear as we swayed together under the canopy of trees and twinkle lights.

On their wedding day, Maya's blonde hair fell in great waves down her back, she smelled of Dove soap and vanilla. Everyone smiled for hours, and the day felt perfect, almost complete.

21
May

Reese

I didn't want to talk to anyone in New York. After a lifetime of loud, I wanted to be alone. But on my first weekend in the city, as I was reading a book at the coffee shop three blocks east of my place, a girl wearing a dinosaur shirt said hello and asked me to join her book club. I thanked her and took her number. I never did call her, but after that I made a point of saying hello to more strangers.

When Jaylene, a frequenter at the flower shop, invited me to join a cooking club she was starting in the spring, I told myself it would be the distraction I needed. The club, my only social time, met the first Tuesday night of every month. The cooking aspect was a challenge for me—I may have inherited Bernice's Masterpieces, but I did not inherit her culinary skills.

There were five of us in total, the perfect number for a road trip someone said, and everyone except me laughed. At every gathering, wine and more wine led to story after story. Brittany and Monisa had kids; the former was happily married to her high school sweetheart, the latter was a single mom. Jaylene and Juanita were living the single life and constantly invited me out into the dating world. I learned about their past relationships, their jobs and drama. Still I stayed silent, at least at first.

After a month, we transitioned to meeting weekly, finding more excuses to come earlier and stay later. We rotated apartments, and I had to buy more plates for my company. After a lifetime of primarily male companionship, I found myself surrounded by a band of strong females, and I liked it. I craved it.

By the second month, I was meeting Jaylene for coffee almost weekly and Brittany for yoga every weekend. We still all gathered for cooking and dinner on Tuesdays, but I was growing close to the girls individually too.

We were all so different. Jaylene was quiet; Monisa was loud. Brittany was artistic; Juanita was an accountant. Monisa was from Germany, and Jaylene was from Canada. We all loved different things and hated different things. The biggest similarity we had was a growing appreciation for cooking, wine, and time together. When I stopped to dissect what drew us so fiercely to one another, I could only conclude it was our diversity. "We're our own eclectic family," Brittany said and the girls cheered.

"What about you, Reese?" Monisa demanded at the end of our salmon and summer salad dinner in late June. She was two glasses of wine in and had spent most of our evening telling us about her first love, Jared.

"Yeah, you're always so quiet," Brittany said and reached to pour me more wine. "Tell us your story. Start from the beginning."

I trusted them, but I made them wait. "Next week," I promised and the following Tuesday they insisted on making a casserole so the cooking part could be shorter and the talking time longer. Only Rocky and I knew the irony.

They gathered in my living room, hugging pillows and goblets of wine, and I told them my tale. I started from the beginning, or the middle, however you want to look at it—for aren't we all jumping into the center of a story that's already been started, already fraught with broken edges and someone else's history?

For some reason everyone was interested in my narrative. Maybe because the last year of my life had been filled with drama. Drama with Charlie. Drama with my dad. Drama with my crazy mother. Drama with my crazy mother dying. Even Blake made it into my stories. When I didn't give the girls enough details, they went nutty, asked for more. At some point, I started reading to them straight from my journal. I didn't want to think about how many times Jaylene filled my glass of wine.

They wanted to know why I walked away from Charlie and *oohed* and *ahhed* over his photos, which they finally made me pull out, and when I came back from the bathroom, I was pretty sure they'd been making bets about how soon we would get back together. (A week later, Juanita would confirm there was indeed a running wager, but it also included Blake. "But I'm Team Charlie all the way. Clearly," she said in a rush. "Well, Team Charleese.")

When I finished my telling, I leaned back and pulled Rocky close. "So, now you know."

Brittany reached to give me a hug.

"You're in a liminal state right now," Monisa said, and I squinted in response. She was a doctor of anthropology at Columbia, and I only ever understood half of what she said. "Liminality. It means you're in a transition, in a suspended state of being. You live on the threshold between your former reality and your next. It's most generally associated with a rite of passage, but I'm going to use it here."

I couldn't reply or the threatening tears would come forth. But I nodded, *yes*. Liminal. *I am in a liminal state of being. I am a liminal being.* It was the first idea in as long as I could remember that made sense.

"Come on, Reese, show us some more photos. Not the ones of Charlie, the ones you took of your family," Brittany interrupted. When Brittany insisted I could get a showing of my work in her uptown art gallery, I nodded sagely and then rolled my eyes. Rocky rolled his too.

"Just pass the wine."

After they left, I sat reading through old journals, making lists, throwing out half my closet. Over the next week, I processed film late into the night, listening to Mom's old "Full Circle" record on repeat, and I tried to forget.

I printed an assortment of photos I'd taken over the last year to give Brittany, but didn't hold my breath. I had no plan for them, no inspiration. I just knew they were special to me.

"It's pretty competitive to get a showing here," Brittany said with a worried look when I dropped them off at her work the following week. She flipped through them quickly, and I realized her wine-fueled optimism had dissipated.

"I know," I said and left. I still needed to try. I didn't know what waited on the other side of my liminal space, only that I needed to take the next step. I was ready, finally ready, to move forward, even if it was only by an inch.

October

Reese

When the doors opened at seven o'clock sharp, the gallery filled and the line outside wrapped around the building. My stomach took turns clenching and expanding as I went between people, shaking hands and answering questions. By eight, I'd dashed off to the bathroom to relieve my bowels twice. My hands stopped shaking by my second drink, and the mixing of colors and patterns, the sparkle of champagne, and the glow of bodies lingered the whole of the night. The evening itself was seeped in surreal, but I found a growing excitement at what I'd done. It meant nothing to anyone, really, but it represented everything to me.

After Brittany's gallery turned me down, something inside me had shifted, and I decided to give my photos another chance. Before and after work, I travelled between art venues with samples of my photos, collecting dismissals. The idea of having a show, of putting my family's story on display grew inside of me so fiercely that even as the rejections piled, I kept going. When I finally got a yes, from a cramped, dingy gallery so far east in Queens I wasn't sure we were technically still in the city, I didn't believe the owner.

"But why?" I asked before I could stop myself. "I mean, thanks." I backed out of the door. "You won't regret this. Not even for a minute." I was halfway down the street before I questioned whether or not I'd even introduced myself in the first place. I ran back. "My name is Reese, I'll call you tomorrow." I left before he could change his mind.

Ben, Maya, and Dad had wanted to fly out for the grand opening, but I'd asked them to come later—"Maybe the second week when it's quieter"—and they'd obliged. I couldn't put it into words, but I didn't want them seeing the photos for the first time in a sea of strangers.

My girls, as I called them—Juanita and Brittany, Jaylene and Monisa—told me they were coming the first night too. "With roses and new dresses," Monisa said, and I asked them to arrive early.

They came and toasted me, hugged me and covered me with kisses and praise. They told me they were proud of me until I blushed, and then I asked them for some space. We shouldn't do life alone—we all need community—but I wanted a few moments to myself. I didn't want to talk or laugh or answer questions or celebrate. I wanted to remember. We hadn't held a public funeral for my mom, and as far as I was concerned, this was it for me.

Long after the noise died down, and the champagne-filled crowds dissipated, Rocky and I walked alone between my images. My family seemed more real to me than ever before. "I guess larger-than-life-sized images will do that to you." I rubbed Rocky's head, and he wagged his tail.

My photos covered all four walls, twenty-eight of them in total. They were 40 x 60 inches in size and had cost a small fortune to print. "I'll be paying myself back for years," I muttered into Rocky's fur. "Don't think you'll be getting any of that fancy food you like for a while."

He barked, and I ran my hand over the brick wall. Next to each photo were excerpts from my road trip notebook. The exhibit, titled *Remember Us*, was a series of photos including Dad sick, others of Bernice, Carl, and Ben at home, yet others from our time with Guru Carl and on the road. Blake was in the background of two photos, small and with his back to the camera. It appeared allegorical, symbolic, and I lightly tapped the glass on his image. "Hi you." I'd printed a few small photos for Blake too, had been carrying them around for months, telling myself I'd know when it was time to write him, but the right moment had yet to appear.

I sighed and moved away.

Toward the end of the wall was the photo of Mom and me laughing, the moment I couldn't remember. I'd stared at it so often, willing myself to bring those seconds into some coherent memory, but it never worked. Next to the photo, a small plate read, *Forgiveness is never easy, but it is a road worth travelling.*

The air was chilly, and I pulled Rocky closer. He always barked at the next photo, a snap of my mother holding him and laughing with her head thrown back, mouth wide open, as if all the joy in the world over could fit inside her smile.

He barked and barked, and I sobbed and sobbed. I hated her for leaving me. I hated her for leaving me again. I hated myself for not driving that day, for not giving her one chance to explain, for not taking even one step closer to her world.

I hated myself for not knowing how to grieve, how to go back, how to make it right.

I hated myself for hating myself, and then, I was done.

When I gathered myself enough to see straight, I left the gallery and walked into the nighttide. The city beyond was ablaze with colors and sounds, and I ran into the flurry.

I worked late the next evening and contemplated going straight home. But I was still too excited about my showing and decided to hop on the F line out to Queens to make sure my photos were still there. When I showed up at the gallery, the curator handed me the note with a smirk. "You picked a bad night to be late. He dropped this off for you a few hours ago. He waited around a long time, but I told him you must not be coming."

"Who?"

"There's a red balloon for you too." He motioned to the desk.

"What?" But the curator had already walked away. I opened the folded paper distractedly, and it took me a minute to focus on the words in front of me.

Reese,

I happened to be in the city for a book deal and came across a poster for an exhibit by one Reese Hamilton. You really should go see the show—it's fantastic. And, yes, you read that right—my friend Reese is a famous artist and your old friend B is a signed author. I wrote a book about a girl who finds her way in this insane life. She has brown eyes, a heart of gold, and enough sass to fill the Atlantic. She is witty and she is fierce, most of all she is kind—an oft forgotten trait these days. Of course, "Names, characters, places, and incidents are a product of the author's imagination... Any resemblance to actual people, is completely coincidental." Completely, Reese. And fiction—who knew? Now they want a second book, about anything I want. So far I've only written the dedication. You'll have to come see me to find out more. I waited around for you all afternoon, but I suppose famous artists have more to do than stand around, talking to their patrons. If you want to meet up for drinks for old times' sake, leave a message at my hotel. I'm staying at the Roosevelt for one more night. I can't believe I'm so close and almost missed you.

P.S. This is even better than I imagined—I'm proud of you. I'm astounded at you.

I folded it with a snap, heart pounding.

It wasn't until I was in the taxi that I realized I'd moved. "I need to go to the Roosevelt," I said and slanted into the seat.

At the hotel, I headed to the bar and settled into the teal seat at the end, ordered a gin and tonic and shoved shaking hands into my lap. Even then I wasn't sure what I was going to do. I looked around the bar, half expecting Blake to appear, the last scene in a Hollywood movie. There were enough silver heads in the room to fill a soccer team, but no Irish-American with hair that curled around his ear and a smile that made my stomach hurt.

I'm not going to see him, I decided one sip in to the silvery gin and citrus. I pulled my notebook out of my satchel and started writing, hardly comprehending the words.

I'm not going to see him, I reminded my reflection in the bathroom mirror when I took a pee break.

I'm not going to see him, I told myself as I finished my drink, exhaled, and stood. I paid and headed to the check-in desk.

"Is Blake Kelly in?" I leaned against the counter. *Because it doesn't hurt to ask.*

"I can't tell you that." The clerk didn't even attempt a smile.

I have to see him, one last time, like he said for old times' sake. One drink won't hurt. "Please, it's important. He's an old friend, and he doesn't live here, but he's here for one more night. I'd like to see him."

"Privacy laws and blah, blah, blah."

"I don't think that's true. Can you call him for me and say Reese—"

As the clerk opened his mouth to respond, a large, loud group of tourists swarmed en masse around me.

"We need to check in."

"We booked ten rooms, but I think we need twelve. Isn't that right, Murphy?"

"Because Beth and Jerry wanted to share a room, but now they want their own," a lady with red lips agreed. "A little drama, if you know what I mean."

"No, Jerry is sharing with Sherry now—"

"I want some sherry, I'll be at the bar. Someone bring my key to the bar."

"Me too!" And two of the ladies shuffled away.

"I'm sorry. I'm flying solo here—my co-worker went home sick an hour ago," the clerk murmured apologetically to me. "If you can wait, I'll try to help you sort something out."

Half an hour later the group was still at the desk, arguing over who would get the room with the hot tub and who would get the room with two doubles. I looked between the clerk and the clock, then wrote *Blake Kelly* in large print across my folded letter. As I slid the pages over the hotel desk, the frazzled clerk glanced up, and I waved at him as I left. I went over the letter in my head the whole ride home.

Dearest Blake,

You are in New York, my city! Since I got your note, I've imagined I've seen you on half a dozen corners already. You are quite the distraction, my friend.

But I don't like to think of you in New York. I like to remember you in Ireland on a rainy day, in our pub, tucked away in the back booth where you think no one can see you, wearing your Cubs hat and drinking a pint.

I envision you wandering with the sheep, reading too much Tennyson, and writing your next bestseller.

Blake, you must keep writing.

You have a gift and the world needs to hear your stories. I would offer to mail you all the letters you've written me through the years—they'd make a lovely story indeed. But I shall selfishly keep them, the meager piece of your inherent wonderfulness I have left, tucked away from the curiosity of the world. For now, they are for my eyes alone.

Shall they be found posthumously and published? Shall our history be told long after we are gone?

I will wonder this always.

And what is our story, Blake?

I wonder this too.

I'll always be sorry I yelled at you that faraway night under the stars. I did follow Charlie around, letting his story, his victories swallow my own, pretending being with him was enough for me.

Yet you insisted I was worth more.

If I knew it once, I'd forgotten it. Thank you for never forgetting. For this, and for many things, you will have my undying gratitude.

Maybe in another lifetime, the first time I see love in your eyes will be the beginning of our perfect forever. In another lifetime, when I don't have the weight of unseen things on my shoulders and my own imperfections so clearly laid before me, I will fall into your arms to stay. In another lifetime, I hope it seems more simple, that we waste no time, that I am yours—and you are mine—for all our days.

Until that other lifetime, know someone very far away will be thinking about you, remembering you, believing in you always.

I will remember your kisses each time I see the stars.

I'll wonder how you are each time I drink a Guinness.

My heart will shatter into endless unseen pieces when word comes over the ocean you're dating some fabulous girl. When I hear you're engaged, I'll find photos online, see her red lipstick and smile as big as Pluto, and I'll be furious at you, melt to nothing inside.

But I'll be happy for you too, because, really, truly, I love you. And you taught me love is selfless, wanting the best for the other person.

Blake.

I'll love reading the books you write, the short stories, and essays too.

I'll love knowing you are writing, pairing words like no one else I've known.

I'll love knowing you exist somewhere else in this jumbled world and that knowledge will make each day somehow better.

I won't stop loving you, even when you don't see me, even when I can't say it, even when you forget me. Know that.

I can't help but hope that you, and my other lifetime, are waiting right around the next bend.

Besides, you still owe me that date.

x

Reese

I imagined the three photos I'd tucked inside, the photos I'd been carrying with me for months, hoping I'd gather the courage to write him, falling into his lap. They were the size of my hand, with rough edges and every shade of gray. One was a photo of Ben and Blake sitting on the edge of the Grand Canyon, the second was one of him running toward the camera. The third was a photo of Blake sitting by the window, notebook in hand, with a shadow of me on the wall in front of him. I wondered if he'd see that shadow too, think like I did every time, *Remember what it was like to be in each other's lives? So seamless, so natural.* Perhaps that shadow was all I was to him now—an idea, a glimpse of something almost, yet not quite. I wanted to ask but instead I scribbled on the back, *This is how I'll imagine you writing.*

Epilogue
November

Reese

    The only photo I displayed on my wall was of the four of us, a sort of self-portrait. We stood on the side of the road, with the Grand Canyon in the background, each of us in our Superman T-shirts. Even Mom, with her repealed embargo on T-shirts and soft cotton, had allowed us to purchase her a matching superhero tee in Arizona.

    I'd propped the camera on top of Ernie because Blake had gone off to explore. It was the first picture we took together as a family since my parents split all those years ago. And it was the last picture we took together before Mom died.

    The photo holds more hope than regret between the muted silver tones, and it feels like family.

    Under the photo was an excerpt from my journal post her death. It read:

I am too tired to hope.
But without it, I will fall apart.
So where do I go from here?
Where indeed.

    I long to say it ended like it began—with an interruption, a surprise, a journey. But when it came down to it, it wasn't so straightforward.

    My life, as it turns out, has been aberrant and complex, beautiful and raw, confusing and wonderful. I've grown brittle in bitterness, finally found the sweet grace of forgiveness. My life has been filled with simple adventures, unexpected twists, sharp regrets, more heartache than I ever imagined but more beauty too.

If I'd known two years ago what I know now, I wouldn't have had the strength to put one foot in front of the other, to get out of bed each day, to go on. So I'm glad I didn't know.

Time keeps going. Until it doesn't. I grew up and chased through my days as if I had somewhere to go, until I looked around and realized there was a difference between being busy and truly living. I slowed down and discovered that even living looks stale without the people who have brought us this far.

Ready to get on with the business of living, I turn and face the sun.

About the Authors

Lindsay Blake's dream list is one hundred deep. She has traveled to over thirty-two countries, caring for others and exploring our beautiful planet. She's jumped out of a plane, lived in a mud hut in South Sudan, nearly died from a tapeworm in Pakistan, and dreams of flying to outer space. She's shaved her head twice "just because." Lindsay lives the good life in Omaha with her son, Carsen Warner.

Layne James is from Kentucky and has been writing since she could hold a pen. She loves her sister and living near water. Layne spends her free time gardening, writing, reading, travelling, and keeping life as simple as possible. She lives with her husband in Southern Ontario.

Lindsay and Layne met in 2009 when they were on a volunteer team with nine other girls. Together they travelled to ten countries, advocated for social justice issues, and told stories with their cameras. This journey is the inspiration for their second book (title forthcoming).

They started *Remember Us* as an experiment.

You can follow their adventures here:

www.blakeandbeckner.com

Instagram: @blakeandbeckner

Twitter: @blakeandbeckner

Facebook: www.facebook.com/BlakeandBeckner/

If you'd like updates about *Remember Us* and future books, you can sign up with your email address at www.blakeandbeckner.com

Acknowledgements

We would like to THANK ...

Bryony Sutherland, our rockstar editor and BFF. You keep us sane and we can't wait to work with you for years to come. You are insanely talented at what you do and have been the best part of this entire process. (https://bryonysutherland.com, @bryonysutherlnd)

Our first round of beta readers, Anne and Catherine. Thank you for being the first eyes to see the (very terrible "first" edition of our) book. Catherine, you broke our hearts when you told us you hated our characters and that you were bored by our story...but you were right and we are forever grateful for your candor. Our lovable characters thank you too. Anne, your friendship and cheering has kept us going through many a long day and every long edit. Your loving yet truthful feedback challenged us to dig deeper and pull more out of our characters. Bernice thanks you.

Our second round of beta reads, Nicki and Sarah. You intimidate us, but you have made us better writers. Thank you for being trustworthy with our baby. Sarah, thanks for teaching us to kill our darlings. Our writing will never be the same!

Courtney, for sharing your professional editing skills with our author bios and the first few chapters of an early draft. Your confidence in our writing ability kept us going. Grateful we are.

Our dear launch team (Suzanne, Savannah, Karyn, Hannah, Anne, Esther, Shellie, Michelle, Katy, Kimberly, Christi). Thank you for jumping on board, reading online (ewwww!), catching our typos, and giving your feedback. You're incredible! Most of all **thank you** for helping us get *Remember Us* into the hands of readers everywhere. We are forever indebted to you and can't wait to champion your dreams.

Kim and Rachel. Thank you for hosting giveaways when you hadn't even read our book!

Megn who graciously read our book on a tight deadline and told us she believed in us. Your insights and love were both so helpful!

Everyone who responded to our cry for help with our company name. And especially Paul, who came up with the best name ever! #blakeandbeckner

Our team at MJ Publishing—thank you for the hours of work you've put into getting our book out into the world, for answering our dozens of questions, and for believing in us.

Victoria, who told us our book was well-wrought and well-written. You gave us the courage to keep going.

Jenny, who told us we had too many POVs. You were right and we're still embarrassed by the version of our book you read.

Marcy, who gave us advice on the first chapter. You were right.

Our dear friend, Cambria, who shared her twin birth experience with us.

Lee, who helped us with our Publishizer campaign and talked us through the details.

Kevin Grimes for communicating Blake & Beckner to the world with great design. You made us look good.

Abby who has never met us but gave feedback on our book anyway. We're humbled and grateful!

Those who pre-bought *Remember Us*, shared our Publishizer campaign link, emailed their mom, and sent word out to the masses via carrier pigeon. You believed we were brilliant enough writers to spend money before anyone else. We do not take that for granted.

It takes a village, people.

Finally, and not at all least, THANKS to our amazing family of future readers—we stayed the course for you.

Lindsay would like to THANK...

Mom and Dad, thank you for your unending support in this process and my life. For believing in Layne and me, for taking Carsen while we wrote, for celebrating every copy sold, and for being our biggest cheerleaders. It's time to open another bottle of champagne.

Emily, Sarah, Penny, and Jessica for taking Carsen multiple times so I could write and edit. Without your generosity this book would not have been completed.

Layne would like to THANK…

Mama, the original Bernice—you are everything and nothing like your namesake. Thanks for letting us use your name, reading an early draft of the book, and for commenting on and liking every single post we do!

Daddy, thanks for always believing I could write.

M, thanks for reading an earlier draft of our book and helping make it more realistic. I love you for so much you've given me—including a love for books. And you're right—Uncle Jessie did hang the moon.

Jonathan James, thanks for patiently supporting all my hours of writing. I know I've neglected you too long when I find you in our pear tree. Thanks for buying ten copies of our book and for believing in my dreams.

Review Request

"If our masses leave reviews on Goodreads and Amazon, *Remember Us* will be an international bestseller for sure," Reese announced from the porch.

Ben rubbed his hands together. "We could be the next Jodi Picoult."

"Or Danielle Steele." Bernice fluffed her blonde curls and Reese rolled her eyes as Rocky barked in agreement.

"Ernie and I could do a bus tour all over the country," Carl called as he wiped the wheels. "I'll throw a speaker on the roof and read out loud as I drive."

"But sugar, what about my cookbook?" Bernice demanded, braceleted hands high on her hips. "The one where I'm the star?"

"Mom, I've told you before—there are already too many writers in this book. Dad wrote in a notebook, I kept a journal, Blake became a published author." Reese patted her on the head. "Besides, if we want *Remember Us* to make it, we can't divide our energy, and we need our people to rate us on every possible platform."

"'Even the smallest person can change the course of the future.'" Ben sipped his beer with a nod.

"Well, then." Bernice spritzed wisteria in Reese's face and huffed away. "Take us to the top, baby—this is our time to shine."

Dear reader, there are millions of books in the world and we are so honored you picked up ours. We'd love your help in getting the word out about *Remember Us* to every corner. Please rate and review us on Goodreads, Barnes & Noble, and Amazon today. Then tell your mailman, your book club, and the stranger beside you in the Target checkout line—no need to be shy. Please post photos of yourself reading our book and tag us: @blakeandbeckner and #rememberusbook and we'll repost our faves!

Obi Wan Kenobi, you're our only hope.

Book Club Discussion Questions

1. What did you see as the themes of *Remember Us*?
2. Who was your favorite character and why?
3. To whom's story did you relate to the most and why?
4. Why do you think it was easier for Ben to forgive Bernice than it was for Reese to forgive her?
5. What do you think was the turning point for Carl and Bernice's relationship?
6. Do you think Reese needed to turn down Charlie and Blake to "find" herself?
7. Why was it easier for Reese to forgive Carl than Bernice?
8. Bernice never asked Reese for forgiveness. Do you think forgiveness should ever be granted even when it's not asked for? If so, when?
9. Did the Hamiltons' story remind you of your family in any way? If so, how?

Morgan James makes all of our titles available
through the Library for All Charity Organization.

www.LibraryForAll.org

CPSIA information can be obtained
at www.ICGtesting.com
Printed in the USA
LVHW04s0116220918
590842LV00004B/5/P